Being Emelle by E. M. Stoops

SMALL
TOMATOES
PRESS

For Nathan, as promised.

We're all weird little kids ...
well, the best of us anyway.

Prologue

When I was four, my father reappeared into my life for about two weeks. I found him utterly fascinating even though he scared me. He was entirely different than my good-humored if exceptionally loud grandfather and my various adopted uncles, all of whom appeared to follow the eat-everything-in-sight-and-then-chat pattern I had elevated to normal parlance. My father was a finicky eater and made my mother upset when he spoke. And she did the dishes for this man while I wrapped myself around the leg of the table and concentrated on his knees. She never did dishes for anyone but me or my Aunt Sprite. Explaining, as she was wont to do, that I was much too small yet and my aunt was another woman and I'd understand this later in life.

However, she offered no explanations about my father. He alone was allowed to sit at the table there after dinner, offer no help, and even berate her at her own table.

Although the memory of a toddler is probably fairly inaccurate, it seemed to me that he came rather less often than anyone else save for my aunt, who only came in the winter. So, perhaps once a season.

He had a unique voice, among the men I knew. In fact, he was quite an enigma to me. Verily, I decided that he was too special to do dishes or behave normally. And so in my mind, he became extraordinary in our ordinary world, and that is why, when I was five, I ventured out from underneath the table to twine around my mother's legs and grin at him.

He wrinkled his nose at me.

I was delighted, and squealed.

For some reason this memory is most clear; he did not smile back. So I squealed again as I peered out from between my mothers knees.

"He wants you to smile at him."

"Huh?" My father asked as he craned his neck up to look at her.

"Make him happy." She sighed.

"Why?"

"Because he's five years old and he should be happy." She insisted. "Besides, he really is cute, and he is your son."

And so he peered back at me. I grinned as infectiously as I knew how.

And he broke into such a beautiful and light-breaking smile that I fell deeply infatuated and instantly confirmed my theorem that this was a creature set apart from the others.

And most amazingly, he moved from his seat, not to make headway to the front door, but to crouch down and place his hands on his knees in a position I took to be an invitation to bridge the gap between us and get a much better look at him. Much to my surprise, he picked me up, instead of continuing to crouch, and placed me in his lap like my mother would have.

His nose hovered just at my reach, and in my endless drive to explore anything put before me, I reached up and touched it ever so carefully with one finger. There was no protest, and so I removed his glasses like my mother would sometimes let me do to her, and I placed my hands at either side of his face and traced the contours of this new landscape. I was completely oblivious to the conversation they were having, and must have for quite some time just watched and traced with my fingers this face that had finally come into focus with its multitude of expressions.

I realised they were talking about me some of the time, and I almost felt inclined to speak when my father asked my mother if I did.

"Oh goodness, all the time! And he picks up every new word he hears. At this rate he'll understand Shakespeare at eight." She replied and ruffled my hair. This explained, I didn't see reason to offer more evidence and went back to playing with his eyebrows.

Later, when the dishes were done, and he was set to leave, he leaned down and scratched my head ever so lightly, and it sent a shiver of what I thought was magic through me. He was certainly extraordinary.

Chapter One

My given name is Merryweather Lewis. I do not connect these words to myself. I know that my real name is Emelle. In fact, it won't occur to me until my early teens that this is a soft rendition of my initials. I love the sound of it as it rolls off my mother's tongue every morning as she wakes me and I love the way my uncles stumble over the vaguely French sound of it. I don't know any other people with my name and it is that thought that makes me begin to doubt the specialness of my father.

I have begun to suspect somehow that the rarity of a name distinguishes how or how not extraordinary someone is. And yet, my father has a most ordinary name, even if my mother somehow makes it sparkle when she says it. My uncles and my family seems to be of the rare-named and so I begin to suspect that my father is actually quite ordinary, but because he is in the company of extraordinary people the tables change because he is now the rare one.

I'm not satisfied with my answer.

So on his next visit, I brazenly clamber onto his lap and ask him why he has such a common name.[1]

He grins and lets out a little laugh. "I have a very ordinary name because my parents aren't imaginative."

I am dumbfounded. I have only ever had one set of grandparents. But, if his parents are alive then I must have another set. "Where are they?" I ask, jubilant.

---

1 His name is Ted.

"What?"

"Where are your parents? My grandparents?"

"Uhm." He responds and looks hopelessly at my mother.

"Emelle," she says, "they live a far way away. And they are much older than Gramma and Grampa. Traveling to see us is very difficult. You know your red blanket? Your other grandma made that for you. And she made your snow-cap."

I am not satisfied. "Can I see them?"

My mother shakes her head. "Not soon, sweetheart."

I begin to become sad, but then those magic fingers come up and scratch my head, and I remember my original line of interrogation.

"How can you be extraordinary if you have a normal name? How does that work? Isn't the name important?"

My mother starts laughing, but my father just stares down as though I am not speaking English. He appears to give me great thought.

"Am I supposed to think that you are attaching importance on people's names and the more important the person, the less likely it is that you have heard their name?"

"No."

"Then how does this work, kiddo?"

I suddenly feel very stupid.

I glare at him for having made me feel stupid, I don't like it.

"Emelle has decided that rare names also make for rare people. Apparently he has decided that you are a rare person but lacking the proper marker." My mother says.

"This environment is hazardous to logical deductions, isn't it?" My father says in an ugly tone of voice.

"Children are very different from adults. You and I have had several decades to discover that a rose by any other name smells just as sweet; he hasn't." My mother replies.

"Still, it's ridiculous."

"No it really isn't. It's just his philosophy so far..."

I sense something underfoot and so climb down and wander back to my room.

Chapter Two

When I am six my mother sits me down and tells me that she is sick and has to go to the hospital so that the doctors can remove what is making her sick. She makes it sound like a grand adventure, and I am temporarily disappointed that my father is moving in so that I don't have to go, too. Supposedly he is going to keep an eye on me and to help my mother. I am pleased to realise that this means much more time to explore him and discover the truth as to whether he is extraordinary or not.

Delightedly, I plan to join my father in his daily routine —I wander into the master bedroom where he is staying when his alarm clock goes off, and when he doesn't emerge shortly I crawl right in next to him. He pats my head and mutters about sleep being precious rare. Then he finally answers my anxious wiggling and gets up and sweeps me into the bathroom. He pulls the shower on and before I can leave he grabs me and tugs on my clothes.

I squawk.

"No? You don't shower?" He asks.

I have no idea how to explain that I don't shower, and anyway I never share my bath with anyone. It is as foreign a concept to me as eating with chopsticks. Which makes me both curious and scared.

"I could." I say, supposing that it couldn't be difficult.

"Well come on then." He says, almost irritably.

I turn away and undress and start to fold my clothes into a neat pile like I usually do, but then rather suddenly an arm comes around me and I am plucked from my clothes and held lightly against my father's bare chest as he steps into the shower. I squirm and he sets me down. The spray hits me, and I don't much care for showers right away, but my attention is taken away immediately by the body next to me.

I suppose I'm startled by the significant differences between my body and the body of my father who is supposed to be just like me. His chest is caved in, and his stomach is round, though he himself is skinny. Hair creeps up his lower legs but then stops only to reappear as a wooly overgrowth in his nether regions and beneath his arms.

I back into the cold wall and he notices my strange behavior.

He crouches down in the water and asks me what is wrong.

"Are you normal?" I blurt.

"Hmmmmm?" He asks, and my staring probably brings him to realize what I mean. "Oh, mostly." He finally answers.

He stands back up and I watch his entire showering routine. First he washes his hair and then his face, and then he picks up the soap and washes his entire body. He then hands me the soap, and I just hold it as I watch him rinse off. He takes it back from me and stretches his feet up to his stomach to wash them.

Having observed how one showers, I begin my mimicry of his routine and I realize that I am watched the entire time, and then, when I finish, he shuts the water off and brings the towels down from over the door where he has left them. I burrow into mine before he opens the door and lets in the evil cold air, but then I follow him out to watch the next part of the routine.

Just as I suspect, it is quite different from my mother's. He pulls a small case from a larger bag and opens it to reveal what I come to understand is a shaving kit.

I am instantly and utterly enamored with shaving cream.

He sees this and grins, and leaves a swish of white puff on my nose with his index finger. Adorned, I watch him smooth a cloud over his lower face and swipe a razor cleanly over his chin and cheeks.

"What is this?" I ask.

"Shaving cream." He replies.

"Mmm...."

"And what I'm doing is shaving."

"Yes." I say.

"And then I'll brush my teeth and my hair and then I'll get dressed for work. Then your grandmother will come and play with you today while I'm gone."

"What about the office?" I ask.

My father looks at me with an expression of shock. "What do you mean?"

"Mom says it needs attention every day." I offer.

I can tell he's very confused.

"She gives me things to do, and then she goes in there and sits at the computer or talks on the phone to people. She says she has to take care of the office or it gets nasty." My childish mind takes this to mean that the office will produce a monster if she doesn't go and visit it every day.

"Oh, her business. It'll be just fine. Brian is going to watch over it like he always does when she's not able to."

"Will he come and make the office happy? It won't get....nasty?"

"Nothing will get nasty, Emelle. Brian's a good friend of ours, and he knows what he's doing."

I like Brian, and so I accept that he can keep the office happy.

I like the smell of shaving cream and aftershave mixed with the sweet scent of his shampoo. It is very different from my mother's and I am ever the explorer in my world. It hovers on his work clothes, so when he takes them off I like to blanket myself with them and suck in the smell. His clothes are very different to me, they aren't like his normal clothes at all, and they don't look like anything my uncles wear.

"What do you do?"

"For work?" He asks while he fixes dinner.

"Yes."

"I'm a security officer."

This doesn't explain the funny clothes. I prop my head to one side and stare at him.

"I keep bad people from hurting good people."

"Oh," and then I add, "How?"

"Mostly by scaring them into compliance. I can be very intimidating."

"Why?"

"Emelle, there are a lot of people that would be happy to take advantage of trusting and good people if people like me didn't make them feel watched. If their own conscience won't rein them in, there are things that I represent that will."

I nod as if this makes sense.

"I'm a little like the police," he explains further.

"Are you like a shoulder angel?" I ask.

He laughs. "Somewhat...."

"You tell people that are being encouraged to do something bad that there will be consequences. That's like a shoulder angel."

"Okay." He says in a less agreeable tone than he had been using. "Why don't you eat your dinner?"

I am quiet while I chase peas around my plate. Too quiet.

"Can I see Mom?"

"No."

"Why not?" I ask.

"She's sick, in the hospital. She isn't strong right now."

"But I want to see her."

He looks at me. "I'll call her after dinner and if she says yes, than you can go."

On her affirmative, we go out to the car and he takes me to the hospital. As we are driving, he calmly tells me that my mother looks much scarier than is real, and that I shouldn't be scared. It was not quite an emphatic enough warning for what I do see.

Here and there are tubes and beeping monitors, and although my mother is awake and she smiles at me, she seems unlike herself because she doesn't scoop me up and throw me under the covers and tickle me until I shriek. She does, however, pat the side of the bed and encourages us both to join her there. I sit for a bit, and then grow bored at the sight of the machines and the quiet of the room.

I wander into the bathroom which looks strange to my eyes, with its gleaming metal bars and overly high toilet and enormous walk in shower. When I return my mother is sitting up, and my father is whispering to her as he holds her in a loose hug.

I'll forget all about how she looked when she comes home a week later looking fine, but still sick and very tired.

Meanwhile, I miss being hugged, tickled, and shown affection. Perhaps if my mother wasn't as exhausted, I wouldn't, but then again, I've begin to particularly want my father's affection as well as just wanting any at all.

"Mom hugs me in the morning." I say when I crawl halfway onto the bed the next morning.

He rolls his eyes. "Yes, she does."

"She tickles my feet."

He shuts his eyes. "I'm sure she does."

"Mom likes me."

One spidery hand comes up from beneath the covers and covers his eyes loosely in a classic for-gods-sakes image.

"Emelle...." he sighs, "What do you want?"

I wrinkle up my face because I have no idea how to explain what is going through my head. None whatsoever.

I sit down on the floor in utter frustration.

Staring at the carpet pattern, unbidden tears spring to my eyes and I bury my face into my hands.

It is far too long before an arm comes around me and I am rocked to the sound of a heartbeat. And it is not as reassuring as it should be. I suspect that it is not genuine.

His motions toward me become achingly robotic after that, much to my dismay.

He stays two more weeks and in that time, I try to recapture something that I felt early in the visit when he swiped shaving cream across my nose and smiled at me in the morning. But no normal actions seem to work, so on the day he tells me he is going home, I try and tell him what I have, in anger, determined.

"You aren't like us." I say.

"No, I'm not." He replies.

"That doesn't make you extraordinary, I think. It just makes you different."

"Okay."

"You are ordinary, just like your name."

"Sure." He says.

"I'm special, just like my name. It doesn't make sense that you make me feel things I don't like; because if I'm special and you aren't, then people like you shouldn't bother me."

He puts down his coffee at this. And I think he is angry.

But he gets up and sets his cup in the sink and leaves with out saying goodbye to my mother.

Chapter Three

My mother reminds me that I really ought not to say everything that comes to mind and I probably ought not to enlighten everyone to my way of thinking all the time either.

I never do actually learn the precise method of doing this.

Mostly because I lack any kind of good example.

"Emelle. I'd like to apologize for how I acted towards you while your mother was in the hospital," He says, when he is done being angry and has come back to spend time with us. He gives me a wrapped box.

"Okay." I say as I shake the box.

"I'm not a usual caretaker for you and I wasn't familiar with your routine. I was also very worried about your mother, and I snapped at you when I got tired. I shouldn't have. I forget that you are only six and that sometimes I have to adjust for that. And I'm sorry I didn't understand what you needed soon enough."

"Okay." I say, and dig into the box to reveal the first of many blacksmith puzzles that he will give me in my life. It is a miraculous thing and ingenious to no end. I am fascinated, and it makes me reconsider my thoughts about my father not being extraordinary.

But, the truth is that no gift will make up for the unloved feeling I had when he did not understand me, and the feeling he created in me will become something that I internalize in relation to him for almost a decade. My lack of words turns into a constant and I deliberately avoid, and not talk, to my father for a whole year. Unless I must. I am not encouraged to change my mode of operation, even after I run into some particularly jolting facts via eavesdropping.

"Why isn't he talking to me?" My father whines to my mother.

"I'm not sure."

"He talks to you; before he stopped talking, he never shut up. He practically talks to himself...." He says.

"He does talk to himself." My mother corrects.

"Maybe it's a phase..."

"Keep telling yourself that." She snaps.

"What?"

"He did this with Dad a while back. It turns out that he felt that Dad had insulted him. He's very touchy about feeling stupid. I think it's something you did."

"Well, exactly how am I supposed to know these things without him, you know, saying something?" He says exasperatedly.

"The way things are going, you aren't. You don't pay enough attention to him to know him very well. Frankly, I know you say you love him, but I don't see any genuine interplay that indicates that. I mean, you do come around. But do you hug him when you come in? No. Do you bring him things or candy? Little kids like that."

"I don't want him thinking, 'oooh! Dad is here. Presents!' and never connecting me to something other than material goods."

"Well, then you need to be worth something to him just as yourself."

"And how do I do that?"

"I'd start with involving him in your interests."

"How do I do that, the smithy isn't a safe place for a kid. He'd get burned by the forge or something."

"Don't give me that. You haven't been in the smithy for months. I'd know if you had been, seeing as the shed is in my backyard. You bugger around doing whatever and nothing that really has a long term payout. When are you going to invest some time in the long-term?"

There is a pause in the conversation.

"How come you always tell me that I'm not investing in my life when I'm not doing what you want? I'm not your husband. I'm not required to invest in you and the kid. You want me to and so you say that I'm buggering around doing nothing important. No, what I'm doing isn't important to you. I'm not investing time in your long term, that's not to say I'm not investing in my long term."

"You tell yourself that, and then you come and visit us every other weekend?" She sounds incredulous.

"I'm here because of guilt and obligation, not out of real desire."

I am not stupid enough to believe that, his voice is drenched in a tone that reeks of dishonesty.

I agree with my mother when she sucks in an exasperated snort and says "Keep telling yourself that. The rest of your mind knows what you refuse to believe, which is that you belong here."

"And you keep telling yourself that. The only reason I even partially belong here is because my forge is here. I'm leaving."

"You'll be back." My mother says.

I hear the clunk of a tea-mug hitting the steel of the sink. "I like knowing where most of my money goes." He says dryly.

"I'd sooner not have the money and have a father for my son."

"Do you remember your life before I started paying for things?"

"Yeah, I lived in a dumpy apartment over the bookstore because that was the apartment that I had the least success renting. Emelle was itty-bitty, but I thought you were gone and I could get around to healing the wounds you left in me."

"You weren't really upset to see me when I came back with a wad of fifties."

"Do you recall pleading with me? You said you had nowhere to stay. That you'd driven just to see us. You stayed two weeks, they were wonderful by the way, and then vanished. A real warm body was worth a lot more than the wad of money. Money is the weakest form of real support."

"At least you get it." He puts emphasis on the last word.

"Money for being your fuckpuppet[2]. Charming. I don't want anything if that's what it really is."

"You aren't that." It comes out low and snarly.

"Then what are you suggesting?"

"I wish you'd just take all the money I try to give you and leave me out of the picture."

"Pick up the smithy and move it, don't drive by after work and shine your brights into my room just to remind that you are alive and thinking of me. Send a check, be impersonal then."

"I don't have anywhere else to stick the

---

2   Yes, I really did pick up on every word said around me. Usually I was smart enough to not repeat the ones said in anger.

smithy[3]."

"Of course you don't. You've arranged it that way."

"Damn you." He hisses and leaves the kitchen and runs smack into me. "You and your kid both." He slams the front door on his way out.

Three or four weeks later he comes back.

He sits down on his feet and reaches out to me. I don't take his hand. I feel bad because I'm fairly certain it doesn't make him feel any better.

On one hand, extraordinary people shouldn't be made to feel bad about themselves by ordinary people, but assuming extraordinary ability, we should weather it better than ordinary people should weather the reverse. If Kings are extraordinary, and they are benevolent, then all extraordinary people, in my juvenile philosophy anyway, should maintain benevolence.

On the other hand, after nearly a year of silence, I've no idea what to say to him.

My mother comes in. "You?"

"Yes me." He replies and reaches out to scratch my head.

She raises an eyebrow.

He smiles, that deep, genuine and infectious smile of his.

More proof that my mother is a goddess; she doesn't crack.

"I'm moving in."

"No you aren't," she replies.

"Why not? I thought you wanted it?"

---

3   Overgrown garden-shed. It overlaps onto Brian's lot (which we own) rather illegally.

"Not if we are going to fight like the last time. I don't want to deal with it anymore. You have issues up to your eyeballs. You refuse to acknowledge them, and you refuse to get help."

"I'm sorry."

"You're always sorry when you get lonely."

"I'm not lonely." He refutes.

"Uh huh."

"My stuff is in the car."

"It can stay there. You'll be driving it back to your rock."

"It's coming in." He says and walks back to the door.

"No, really it isn't. I don't want you here right now."

"I thought you wanted me to invest—"

"— I did, but it won't solve much at all. There is a much bigger situation here that I don't fathom yet."

He looks completely dejected.

"I don't even get to try?"

"Try for what?" She asks.

"I do want a family. You are right, this is my family. Then maybe I should be here. I should try to be here."

My mother considers this. "I don't trust you."

He stands up, fingernails lingering on my scalp for just a second, sending shivers across my neck. He completely engulfs my mother in a hug, and kisses her head, and whispers something I can't hear.

"Can I make dinner?" He asks in a much less serious tone, light-hearted as if he had not just barely avoided an argument with my mother.

"What are you going to make?"

"Tacos."

"Yum!" I reply involuntarily.

"Yum?" He asks.

I nod.

"What do you think?" He asks my mother.

"Tacos are fine. No beans." She sounds angry.

"Blech." I agree.

We sit through an utterly silent dinner, until my father turns to my mother and says sweetly "So, can I stay?"

She sighs, hangs her head, "No. You can't."

He stares at her with his face tense. "Why not?"

"Because you will leave again. And that will cause me to fall apart, and it's not okay to fall apart when you have a kid." Her words are careful. I excuse myself, ostensibly to my room, but really to just behind the kitchen door.

"Is that how you look at me? A human weapon?"

"Yes, I do." She says. "Every time you walk about my front door, it hurts. Every time you hug me or say nice things; it hurts. I keep thinking that if I give you a few months that you'll get it, but I don't trust you enough to take you on full time. You can't even manage to set a stable time to come visit. Maybe if you could, maybe if I could see you as reliable, I could let you live here. But I can't take another three or four weeks followed by months of absence when your randomized internal clock and bomb detonation device decide to blow you up. I can't, and I don't want to. All I feel when I'm around you is a sense of estrangement anymore. I've come to expect a dose of pain when you come by."

"What? Why?" He sounds confused.

"You pick me up and drop me down. Your son loves you and gets ignored. He needs stable influences. He's a kid and you hurt him by not being a dependable person."

"I can be a stable influence."

"For how long? He's only six. He needs a stable influence for the rest of his life, that's.... right, the rest of yours."

"And if I don't do something now, how long do you think I'll be kicking myself for?"

"A week or two." My mother says with a dose of grouchy in her tone.

"I'm serious."

"Prove it."

"I brought something for Emelle, may I go get it?"

I bolt to my room, but listen very carefully to the sounds of the front door, a car door, and then the front door again. And then there is a sound I don't know... like metallic beads in a tube. I contemplate the noise, and have come up with some fantastic reasoning but nothing comes close to the truth.

I am presented with a tightly knitted chainmaille shirt that fits just a bit baggy. It is green.

I like it.

Much later, when I wake up, I hear them still talking.

"We can't be bought." My mother says.

"Not bought... bribed!"

"I'm still thinking about this."

I poke my head in the door of their room. My mother is resting her head on his chest and he is carefully petting her hair. He looks more comfortable than she does.

"Little boys love armor."

I agree.

"I'm sure they do." My mother offers.

"And little women love jewelry." He says after fishing something out of a pocket.

She picks it up and puts it on her bedside.

"What?" He asks when she says nothing.

"It's very lovely. Are you really serious about this?"

"Yes."

"Okay then." She kisses his head.

Chapter Four

Life with my father in the house is more chaotic. His schedule is a flexible, brutal thing. Many mornings start with him rubbing my head and then proceeding to be horizontal for the next eight hours. I'm not sure what his idea of stable influence is, but it's obvious to me he's trying because on a very regular basis he takes me for a romp in the park after dinner, and then for ice-cream.

But some days, he never leaves the smithy.

Then, a few days after the first snow has arrived and a few days before my seventh birthday, something terrible happens.

"Puppe[4]," He says, calling my mother by her long standing nickname, "I can't comprehend this." He turns and looks down at the phone he still holds in his hand. "He died."

My mother shoos me out of the room.

This event is the beginning, really, of the Great Animosity that develops over the next few years between my father and me. Previously, I disliked him, now he'll dislike me.

My mother understands grief and attempts to explain to me that my other grandfather has died and my father feels there were a great many things between the two of them that should not have been, but never were cleared up. I have no concept of the man, and I simply can't find a connection to him in myself. I try to imagine an emptier world, and I try to imagine a world without my other grandfather, but he is so vibrant and lively it is impossible to think he won't live forever.

---

4 German for *doll*.

I don't have an adequate understanding of a father either, and so while I can imagine a world without one quite easily, it doesn't seem very detrimental to the state of a person.

The unfortunate thing about this thought is that I tell him about it when he is particularly depressed.

"Emelle, go away and stay gone." He says and makes motions with his hands to emphasize the point.

And so I do. I decide, viciously, that if fathers can cause a person so much pain that they throw people away then I have no need for one. I can mostly pretend he isn't home anyway because he's taken every possible shift to stay busy and away from his own grief.

What I didn't know then was that his grief was a compounded, complex thing that was the result of years of unresolved conflicts attributable to both parties and years of abuse alternated with neglect contributed by his father. Decades of water under the bridge were not flowing by but rather, damming up. When his father died, the water no longer had a dam, and no longer had a place to go. My father chose to hide from the flood in projects, chores, and a general state of disconnectedness.

I tell myself that I don't care that he is absent. Over the years I'll come to expect the little things that he always does, but I keep myself emotionally uninvolved after that point. My green maille shirt will grow every year to fit nearly perfectly and every so often a blacksmith's puzzle will be lain out on my bed when I least expect it. I hand him the brass rings when I finish them. I don't connect them to his love or affection, and though I break once in a great while none of my affectionate actions connect within him either.

My mother notices and comments one day to my vaguely distraught father that this too will pass.

Chapter Five

I hate school. I do not willingly leave the house without clinging to sheets, my bed frame, dresser drawers, and doorknobs. I even occasionally clutch ruthlessly at the front porch. Alas, I am always thwarted. I always end up sitting in my desk reading dumb booklets and flying through my work and endlessly waiting for recess. It is never long enough.

Three months of my howling, whining, screeching, squawking, and general discontent, and my mother gives up and decides to home-school me. I like it because I don't think I am in school. My winter is filled with learning how to ski and how to play chess. I already know how to read. I don't realize it then, but my mother carefully chooses books so that I read historically accurate books, or books with good science. I am never not learning something from them. Or I read classics, but I don't know that.

In the spring, 'school' consists of a garden and I learn mathematics from measuring the plants and their output and still, I don't realize the nature of my daily routine as being a learning environment. Chess and cribbage are first and foremost games, not math exercises. Surely not. I am free and uneducated like my hero Tom Sawyer. Whereas everyone else has their tyrannical classroom, I have skills. I can grow potatoes, radishes, cucumbers, tomatoes and ground cover. I can read recipes and I love putting all the ingredients for cookies out on the counter so that my mother might see and then make me cookies in the afternoon. I can soon work all the appliances in the house, including the sewing machine[5] and the washer down in the basement.

The only missing piece is that I learn nothing about the trade that flows in and out of the smithy on weekends. It's not a lack of interest that keeps me out, but the growing effects of the Great Animosity.

Though I would like to know how to make swords, and though he would also like to teach me, we remain separate. The family trade isn't getting passed on.

As usual, my parents toss me from the kitchen one night to talk about it after a year of it going unsaid and slide the pocket door shut. And, as usual, I sit down right outside it, without pretense of doing anything but eavesdropping.

"Do you think Dad would be disappointed, in regards to the blacksmithing?"

"Well, I don't know." My mother replies. "He certainly didn't make huge effort to pass on the knowledge to you until he was diagnosed with cancer and thought he'd be dead in a year. You were twenty-four, then. Emelle is eight."

"But it was hard to learn then, he was lame in one leg, half-dead from chemo therapy.... I would have had a much easier time learning the skill if he had been younger and healthier. I mean, I learned a lot on my own before he decided that I was a good enough son to teach, but if he had decided I was worthy back when I wanted him to, I would have liked being his apprentice more."

"You chose smithing for yourself, though. He didn't shove the family business down your throat, like what happened to me. You aren't withholding

---

5   I mostly mend things. But I do make a potholder as my first project.

the knowledge, if it isn't something he's asking for. Give me a minute, I'll be right back." I hear a chair scrape and my mother steps out of the kitchen. She looks down at me. "Would you like to eavesdrop a little more comfortably Emelle? Why don't you drag a chair over here...?" She comments sarcastically dryly going back into the kitchen and closing the door again.

"Small ears?" My father asks.

"Yes, of the eight year-old variety."

I loudly scrape an armchair across the room and make sure the springs grind and make noise when I sit down.

"Oh well...it's what I said he could do." My mother comments quietly. "He is very literal."

"When it suits him."

She probably nods assent, and then continues, "Well, do you think it could be a good addition to his curriculum? We can try and see if he has an interest or talent for it."

So I start sitting in the smithy for a few hours most weekends while my father makes wrought iron fences for rich people. He explains that isn't his favorite kind of project but it is what Foster Iron and Steel Works is particularly known for since swords are not precisely stylish or common anymore.

Wrought iron fences are boring.

Working the bellows is boring.

Watching my father work is anything but boring.

He really likes smithing, when he finds himself in the mood. A bar of iron can become almost anything in his hands. The outline of a leaping tiger for a downtown restaurant, music scrolls for an outdoor artwork, breast-plate for a strange little man that doesn't explain what it's for, a sword for a man whose son has just finished a black-belt in Kendo. Anything that can be made out of iron or steel that fits within the confines of a converted carriage house flows from hands that are wasted at a day job.

We sit down for dinner one night after the man who is renovating his south hill home to southern antebellum splendor took delivery of untold feet of wrought iron pieces for his home. Nothing less than an impressive collection, and the kind of money spoken of when it came time to pay was jaw dropping.

"Why do you work at the mall still?" I ask him.

"Because it's stable, Emelle."

I look out the window at the most recent delivery of iron and steel bars, still on the front porch covered by a tarp. Pointedly.

"Smithing isn't stable. I don't know if I'll ever get a project the same size as the one I just finished again in my life."

"But a lot of little ones add up the same, don't they? Mom doesn't just rent one huge house... she has a lot of little units that add up into a big pile of money." I say.

My father looks at my mother over his dinner with an expression that reads something like he thinks she put me up to this.

"Don't look at me like that. He gets ideas all on his own!" She says.

"Big pile of money?" He asks with an upturned lip.

"It's a matter of perspective." She replies.

"He gets these ideas on his own, you say?" He

says, still amused.

"I do." I claim quietly.

Both my parents look at me.

"I can think, all on my own and everything." I redundantly grouch.

"Why in the world have you decided I ought to do smithing as my only job?"

I look at him. "Because you like it."

"Yes, and if I did it full time, I think that would change in short order."

"Why?"

"Oh, how wonderful it must be to ne'er bored be." He says sarcastically.

Dinner gets quiet.

Unintentionally, he's hammering shut my mouth, at least when I am around him. Unable to connect on any emotional level, I'm slowly disconnecting from other levels of interaction... processes he will alternately impede or accelerate but not reverse until I am seventeen.

Chapter Six

My mother makes my clothes in between fixing leaky plumbing, painting, and cleaning the chaos that occasionally get left behind in her Cheney apartments by hordes of college students. She also makes much of her own clothing and even some of my father's. She makes more or less whatever I want at a given time. One week I am in flowing artisan smocks, and the next in militaristic shirts with excessive pockets or proper pirate splendor.

From this spawns my favorite game of pretend after a particularly materialistic ninth birthday. My father has made me a slightly miniaturized Colt 45 revolver that cannot fire anything, but certainly look convincing, right down to the scrolled etching on the barrel. Tiny works of art that come encased in equally enchanting holsters that hang from a heavily stamped belt. My mother had previously made me a small leather jacket.

Prone to flights of fancy, I am already in the world of imagination:

Dangerous Dick, I decide, is older than my parents, but younger than Grimsy or Grampa. He is bitter at his day job and smokes too much. Desperate to stop the crime in his neighborhood after the death of his beloved dog, he turns to vigilante justice.

Like all super heroes, for Dick was certainly supposed to be a superhero in my head, he had a costume. A fantastic cross between Indiana Jones, a G.I., and St. George, he morphed into his present day form after a gift of a safari hat from my grandfather.

Digging through some of my early art proves

that the hat only sometimes appeared, particularly when the rain would drip theatrically from the brim. Mostly, Dick wore a chainmaille shirt, combat boots, jeans, a leather belt with double revolver holsters and a leather motorcycle jacket (despite riding public transportation like normal citizenry.) His hair is pulled back slickly, revealing a face mostly obscured by owlish glasses but craggy, with prominent chops seemingly permanently fused to a wad of gum or a cigarette. Eventually, I added fingerless gloves and the armored bracers, but that was only after Dick got himself fired from his job for keeping a bowie knife crammed down a boot.[6]

Although I act out no small number of escapades on rainy days, I actually enjoy telling my mother his story as she cleans more and even, in spite of the Great Animosity, try out a few of the tales on my father when he sets to dismantling the smithy to enlarge it into the new shed.

"And then—"

"Emelle?" My father asks from beneath the forge where he is unbolting it from the floor.

"Yes?" I reply.

"While Dangerous Dick sounds very interesting, and I'm sure his life is exponentially more exciting than the smithy at the moment, please tell me you know he isn't real, but a mere imaginary figment for distraction?"

I crawl back under the forge. "What do you mean?"

---

6   My earliest art is admittedly terrible, but there is a distinct change when I start drawing Dangerous Dick. In about two years it becomes a clear effort at cartooning, and by the time I'm in my first real art class, it looks professional. I credit my mother, because she kept me in supplies despite the expense.

"He's a character in your mind, you came up with him."

"Well, of course!" Did my father think I would pilfer someone else's ideas when I had so many of my own?

He twists his body and looks at me. "That's good. Sometimes I worry that the edge between reality and your imagination is no more visible to you than quarks are."

I go back to work, since there are nearly ten years of iron dust caked in grooves in the floor and walls. My mother wants to use the shed as storage for yard equipment and as a starter room for plants and thinks a going over is appropriate. I don't continue the story, which was just now interesting, because I suspect he neither cares what I think nor wants to visit my imaginary city that houses Dick. Though I have felt for years emotionally disconnected and inept, I'm now swiftly losing all contact with my father.

That night, I talk to my longtime favorite stuffed animal (The long suffering fuzzy green *thing* named Mosser that my mother made in college for my father) when I think my parents are asleep, having remembered when I opened my mouth to speak earlier that my father finds it disturbing when I talk to Mosser in front of people.

"He used to say I was whiny and bratty. Flighty and simple nowadays. I don't think he's ever going to think I'm anything but a nuisance."

Mosser looks comfortingly back at me. And so I continue. Unlike other people, Mosser fails to make me feel stupid even when I tell him wild stories or my philosophies. I wish there was a human Mosser, and

I tell him so. I suspect he wishes he could be real for me in ways that he wasn't already.

A few days later I eavesdrop on another conversation their bedroom.

"I'm not getting any better, Puppe." My father mutters.

"What do you mean?"

"I think our kid hates me. Or at least wants me gone. And your sister calls me 'the sperm donor,' sometimes to my face. I'm not adding anything here like I wanted to."

"Well, what do you want to do about it?" My mother asks him.

"Maybe I should go."

"Oh, I don't think so. Running away isn't going to work. I think it's time you faced things head on."

"How?'

"Talking about what's holding you back from the things you want."

"We talk about that all the time." He replies.

"Maybe you should talk to someone qualified?"

There is some silence and I slip out of bed to investigate. I sneak from my room to hers and peer in. She is sitting in bed against her reading pillow and my father is propped up on his elbows next to her. A book sits in her lap, face down, and she is gently scratching his head.

He moves in and rests his head against her stomach and wraps arms around her torso....."Mmmmm."   He mutters.

She smiles broadly and continues to rub his head.

"Come on, stop reading and join me."

"What?"

He flicks her book off the bed and pulls the chain that turns off her reading lamp. I can still see, however. She snuggles down into her pillow and kisses his forehead.

"You feel lovely."

"Yes, yes I do. But you feel nicer still." He responds.

"Oh stop."

"Why?"

"We might wake Emelle."

"God forbid?"

She whaps him on the head.

He grabs her hands.

She shakes loose and laughs. "Really!"

So he tickles her.

She squeals, "Mercy!" and he stops. "See, we really might wake him up....."

"Oh alright....we will be quiet then." He says, and kisses her.

Ew. Mushy stuff. I go back to bed.

The phone book is open to 'counseling' the next day when I pass by it.

Chapter Seven

I am blissfully free of public school until sixth grade. That is when middle school starts and my mother is decided on me going. Because I have to learn to make friends and socialize, she says. But, next year. Not yet.

There is a girl who rides her bicycle past the house everyday, beginning just before my 11th birthday. It is cold, but one day I make cider before school lets out and take the jug out to the porch and wait for her to ride by. I wave to her when I see her, and she waves back, and so I call out to see if she'd like a cup. She dismounts.

"Sure..." She seems hesitant.

"I'm home-schooled." I say, anticipating her question.

"Oh. I go to Roosevelt." She says.

"What grade?" I ask, because I think she must be my age.

"Fifth. I just had my birthday, so I'm one of the oldest." She says.

"I'm about to be eleven too."

"I'm Annalynn Spencer."

"I'm Emelle Foster."

We shake hands. I hand her the cup I'd brought out for the purpose.

"So, are you new?" I ask her, as I've never seen her.

"Yes. I'm from Montana[7]....I was home schooled there, like you. But that's because school was a two hour bus ride either way. Why are you

---

7   It's been my experience that a great number of very grand things come from Montana, Annalynn for one exceptional example of this being the case.

home schooled when the school is walking distance?"

"I just am. Mom says I have to go to public school next year, though."

"Oh."

"Yep."

"Thanks for the cider." She says.

"Would you come by tomorrow?" I ask.

"Sure."

And she does. Every day. After two weeks I offer to ride the rest of the way with her.

Then, it snows. So I start walking her.

"You know," she says one day, "I like this about my day. I like coming by your house and you are there and I get to talk to you. It makes school bearable."

"Really?"

"Yeah."

"Would you like to come over sometime and have tea?"

"Have tea?" She asks with a laugh.

"Or something." I say.

"Okay."

She comes by everyday of her winter break, save Christmas. I like it. We play chess and gin and watch Star-Trek reruns because she likes it too. My mother drives us to the park with sleds and we have a huge time.

"Emelle? What do you think of Annalynn?" My mother asks me one night over dinner.

I think. Annalynn is obviously different from other people, I picked her out of the hordes of people that trucked past the house on their way to school.

She has a lovely and rare name. Which

means, by my own standards, she's extraordinary.

"I like her. She's fun." I say. "Maybe school won't be so bad with her."

Famous last words, I suspect. I staunchly refuse to believe that I am going even as my mother takes me back-to-school shopping and buys me a back pack and supplies. The middle school is eight blocks away and she walks me down there to register for classes. Still I don't believe. It is a supremely cruel joke that she is taking me away from my garden and my chessboard and my beloved books. Summer seems an excruciating tumbrel ride to the execution of my education. The time stretches out to be teasingly endless, but in truth it is very finite. In early August, Annalynn is playing with my hair. It is not nearly as nice as hers so I don't see why she bothers. She says it's easier to braid mine than hers. She spends far too much time just brushing it to convince me this is the gods'-honest truth.

"Are you going to cut it when school starts?"

"Why would I do that?" I ask, horrified at the idea.

"I, uh, just figured you would. So, you know, you'd look like other people."

"Do you want me to cut it?" I ask suspiciously.

"No. But I was worried that you would."

"Never. I am never cutting my hair. Not for a million dollars."

"Not even a million? I'd cut my hair for a million."

"It would be too much like changing my personality for money. That's evil."

"I don't think I like my hair that much." She

says.

"But I do!" I chirp.

"My hair or your hair you like that much?"

"Both? Can I like both?"

"I think so." She says. "But aren't you worried about it?"

When I go home, my mother is in her office. I risk the demons that may appear should it not get enough attention and interrupt her:

"Annalynn doesn't think I look like other people, Mom."

"Oh sure you do." She says absently.

"I think she meant fashion-wise."

"Well, are you worried about that?" She asks.

I'm surprised to find that I am both very worried, and also, very opposed to the idea of changing.

"Well, I don't know what other people wear really." I say, fingering my handmade shirt. "I thought that everyone just sorta wore clothes... apparently there is such a thing as popular fashion." I say, using Annalynn's unfamiliar words. 'And.... Short hair."

She looks up at me. "Well, do you want me to stop making your clothes?"

"I don't know." I say, hesitantly. I don't think I've ever had more than two or three store-bought shirts at a time, and I've never had store-bought pants. The only things I own now from a store are screen-printed fantasy shirts with wizards, dragons, and fairies. I know, on some level, that as much as I like them, they aren't what other people my age wear all the time.

"Maybe you and your father can go shopping tonight at the mall, and you can see about it?" She offers.

"Uhm, maybe." I reply.

I hate Northtown Mall, it's busy and big and glitzy and I'm convinced that something evil goes on in dressing-rooms. (Well, naughty things certainly go on in there, but I don't know that yet.)

My father pulls me along, telling me to try and look less like I'd just fallen off the turnip-truck. Right. And he looks so natural himself with my same long hair and handmade clothes.... Hypocrite.

But then, I may have just as well fallen off the turnip truck; a decade of carefully avoiding the outside world and I don't get it. Northtown might as well be the Las Vegas strip instead of a semi-urban shopping center.

We start with jeans.

A life of wearing pre-washed, custom fit jeans has in no way prepared me for the heavily starched, square-cut, cardboard-like denim jeans that the stores sell. I hate them, and I get the impression from my father that he does too.

An hour of jean-shopping and he tells me, "Your mother can, I think, make jeans to fit and look enough like everyone else, why don't we just worry about shirts?"

I hate those too. The only comfortable things are the pre-washed, custom dyed and screened fantasy tees, of which I already have three. He buys three more with reluctance and we get in the car to go home.

My mother is waiting for us when we get back.

"What did you find?' She twitters.

"The usual." My father replies.

"Oh, nothing? That bag doesn't look like nothing."

He raises an eyebrow and shows her the contents of the bag.

"Well, Emelle, I give you points for knowing what you want, but none for variety. Off you go, time for a shower." She says.

I go up the stairs, but pause half-way up the spiral to listen.

"... where are you going?"

'Fabric store, they are open late tonight." She replies softly.

"Why?"

"He needs more than just that to wear." She says.

"We don't really have a lot left to spend on clothes. Those shirts he likes so much aren't cheap. I thought we'd agreed to not spend too much on school clothes until he'd seen the other kids."

"I know we did, but, Ted, he's not going to change his mind on what he wants to wear. He's happy wearing what he always has and he'll be stubborn about it. Besides, I won't buy anything expensive, just some cotton."

"Paul, don't shoe-horn him into being an outsider."

"Ted, listen for just a second, okay?' She pauses. "He doesn't have a snowball's chance in hell. You didn't, I didn't, and he doesn't now. Weird is never a good way to be in school and he comes by it honestly. I talked to Annalynn's mother the other day, because she was worried about them being friends. Annalynn isn't a popular girl. Mrs. Spencer said she didn't want me wondering why Emelle was struggling from day one, but she didn't want to take away her daughter's one friend either so she just thought she'd tell me a few things and let me make whatever decision I wanted to regarding it.

"We've wondered for awhile why such a conservative catholic family would let their one daughter play with the son of the heathen slut down the street— don't look at me that way, that's what that slag across the street calls me— Anyway, this is why. She doesn't have friends at school. I didn't want to say any of this really, if I could avoid it, because it just takes me back to that time in my own life, but no matter what he looks like, he's not going to be 'lucky'. He might as well be himself and in his own clothes."

She leaves.

My father comes up the stairs before I can effectively pretend I've been in the bathroom.

"You heard that, didn't you?"

"Yes, I did."

"And..." He falters.

"Annalynn is amazing."

"She must be," he replies, maybe he intends otherwise, but it sounds like sarcasm and I regret having said anything about her.

Later that night, I hear the distorted voices of my parents talking.

"Maybe they shouldn't be friends." My father says, the inflection and tone lost in the duct-work.

"Why, so he can have a chance at popularity?"

"He doesn't need to go in with a ready-made

liability, you know."

"We did, we survived."

"Maybe, but at what cost?"

"It's his life...." She replies.

"You say that, but honestly, you let him live a daydream. It can't be good for him."

"What do you mean?"

"He's not like other kids because you never made it necessary for him to be like them. He didn't like school, well, you didn't make him go. He didn't like modern clothes, well, you didn't make him wear them. He wanted to learn to garden and sew and cook. He came up with wild ideas and started making them real, at least to himself. He's a self-made weirdo, honey. And he lives in fantasy land."

"We all live in fantasy land." She retorts. "This isn't about Annalynn, or really Emelle's childhood, is it?"

"No, I guess not. But I do want him to be happier at school than we were."

"He will be if his parents aren't expecting popularity and princedom." She says. "Which I'm not."

Chapter Eight

Because of this, because of who I am and how I grew up, it is an utter shock that she really does expect me to go that evil Wednesday morning. But she does, and so I do. Annalynn walks with me rather bravely. The other students all look at her strangely as though they perhaps couldn't fathom her having friends.

Only one person behaves differently; he comes right up to us and says as loudly as possible without yelling, "Annalynn, you found someone as dorky as you. I was almost convinced there wasn't anyone quite as nerdy as you, but well.... Like attracts like, eh?"

"Shut up, Les." She says quietly and moves closer to me.

"It'll be unfortunate when you two bitches breed, maybe you'll share a dork king?"

What? Wait...

"I agree with Annalynn —you should shut up." I say to this diminutive bully.

He looks at me, registering surprise and satisfaction at the same time. "Oh..... this is your neighborhood friend that we all thought wasn't real. How did you bring your imaginary friend to life, Annalynn? Naughty things in the middle of the night? Did he enjoy them? Why'd you make him look like such a girl?"

She shies away from him, grabs my hand and drags me towards her locker.

We vanish into a crowd of upperclassmen and the little goblinoid doesn't find us again.

"Who was that?" I ask her.

"Les Schopenhauer." She says, obviously

upset.

"What a simian creep." I say.

"Simian?"

"Knuckle-dragging ape." I explain.

"Yeah. I hate him. He singled me out every single day last year."

"He did?" I can't believe it.

She nods, and looks terribly vulnerable at the moment, like the world had crushed in. "I thought he'd grow up and stop, especially after I had my mom call his mom."

I don't think of his insults as terribly inventive, or even believable, but I can imagine a year of them got wearing, and to be looking forward to another year might very well be crushing. I do the only thing I can think of and hug her awkwardly. "You don't have to put up with anything alone this year."

"....Gawd, they're getting younger every freakin' year....I wish they would just like.... Ewww, find somewhere else...." Someone in the crowd says loud enough so that we should hear it. I shoot them a dirty look and let go of Annalynn but grab her hand and grip it tightly all the way to class. I realise I am more reassured that I don't have to face anything alone this year than Annalynn most likely is.

Yesterday, eleven felt so old. Today, I feel like a little kid.

School is slightly less hostile than open-warfare trenches. There are no machine-guns. This isn't to say that some wouldn't mind changing that. Annalynn dumps me at my homeroom and vanishes into a crowd.

I debate going in.

I could still run.

Fast.

Les Schopenhauer is sitting smack dab in the middle of the room.

Yup, shoulda run for it.

I sit as far from him as is conceivable. This places me next to a wilting corn plant, musty magazines, and no one else in the classroom. Cost of caution, I tell myself and prop my feet up on the desk in front of me. It's a small class, there are plenty of empty desks, even after the bell has rung to indicate class has started.

Well, ours hasn't. No teacher in sight. Les looks at me and smiles the same way I imagine zombies smile... only in malice.

"So.... Fag.... How is it that you know everyone's unfavorite boobless broomstick?"

Boobless broomstick. Whaddya know, alliteration. How clever. I cough. Not clever.

The whole class, dead silent is now looking at the two of us. I suspect I'm supposed to say something. Anything....

"You aren't very perceptive, Les." I say quietly. "Why don't you stop sharing your obtuse observations with the world? It will make us all much happier."

"I like that you respond to your new name like an adopted dog, Fag." He says. The class sniggers.

A blonde obese woman in hot pink enters the classroom looking mighty sloshed. "Good morning class.

There was a mixup in the office and so I'm running just a smidgen behind!" Her voice is chirping, cheerful, and utterly false. She sounds peevish underneath.

"I'm going to call your names and you'll tell me if you go by that, alright?"

She runs down the list and gets to the inevitable "Merryweather Foster?"

"I'm afraid I've been re-christened this morning." I say, finding some intestinal fortitude to spare.

"This morning?" She says, disbelieving.

"Indeed. Les" I point to him nonchalantly "tells me my new name is Fag."

Her eyes narrow, she turns reddish and looks at Les, sticks an arm at to point at the door and says, "Office. Now."

He leaves.

"I assume you prefer Merryweather?"

"No I don't, I prefer Emelle."

"Very well." She makes some marks and continues on.

She pairs us up in a 'get to know each other' activity before letting a young man take over the class so she can go to the office. I end up making incredibly awkward small talk with a girl who is wearing the naughtiest shirt I've ever laid eyes on and the reddest lipstick commercially available. She tells me her name is Shelia and I can't help but think she's going to be the first person to get pregnant at this school that I know, and possibly soon.

Not only is the shirt naughty, it's incredibly cheap. I end up noticing that the elastic neckline is way out of whack while she is telling me about the 'hot guy' she met at the mall last week and how she and her friends are going to get together with him and his friends again this week. She plays with her gum while relating the tale.

"Uhm." I interrupt. "You should fix your shirt."

"Huh? What's wrong with it?"

"The neckline is messed up. Here, let me get it." I reach up to fix it and she slams herself backwards in her chair and shrieks.

I believe the teacher teleports to my side in order to loom over me.

"What is going on here?"

"He tried to cop a feel!" she says.

"I tried to fix her neckline." I say at the same time.

The teacher drags me outside the classroom. "Ms. Madison is nice looking, isn't she?" He asks in an easy, friendly tone.

I don't want to appear rude. "Sure."

"Maybe looks a little older than she really is?" Uh....

"She's trying to, yes." I say , completely mortified to be asked about the appearance of a student I can't help but judge.

He looks at me. "Oh." His tone is completely flat. "You really weren't trying to cop a feel." He pauses for a second as if thinking. "You were home-schooled, weren't you?" He no longer has the friendly tone, though it isn't unfriendly either.

"Yes, I was."

"Look, you can't touch other people or their stuff here. You can't flip their tag back into their shirt for them or fix a bunched-up neckline, and definitely not on the other gender."

"Oh." I'm glad no one important noticed my awkward hug with Annalynn this morning.

I am looking forward to my next class by the time the

bell rings. The silent staring is getting to be a wee much and I already have a feeling that my mouth and my actions will be around the school in no time.

Indeed, the first thing I notice is that people stop talking when I come in the classroom and a girl similarly dressed to Shelia is shooting daggers out of her eyes. I sit down, this time next to a dusty box full of mathematics books. I then proceed to put my head down and ignore them all.

I feel a tap on my head.

I look. Annalynn smiles down.

"That bad, eh?"

"I got Les sent to the office. That's going to come back and haunt me. I also got accused of trying to feel up some slutty-looking girl."

"Oi."

"You?" I ask.

"I have Josh 'the Rocket' Clevenger in my homeroom." She says cryptically.

"Who is Josh the Rocket?"

"Apparently, he was a sixth-grader last year, but he got held back. He's a year older than us, and he thinks he's just so awesome. I think I learned everything I never wanted to know about male anatomy."

She hides her face behind her hands.

"He talked about his penis?" I'm incredulous.

"Actually, his 'little man,' but I suspect it's one and the same." She replies from behind her fingers.

"Sounds like a gem."

"I'm sure there is no shortage of girls who think he's dreamy."

We share some pleasant snickering until Mr. Rocket himself walks in and sits down next to us.

"Great." Annalynn grumbles and faceplants into her desk.

A tiny little man with a big smile walks into the room.

"Hello, I'm Mr. Earl, welcome to World History."

"The Mr. Earl?" I say without thinking.

"Well, I'm the only Mr. Earl. Why do you ask?"

"My mother had you for World History." I say back.

"And who might she be?"

"Paul Deckman." I give her nickname.

He opens up his mouth and releases a gigantic laugh. "Does she have her little empire, yet?"

That's what my mother calls her collection of buildings. "Yes, she does."

"Tell her I look forward to seeing her at parent-teacher conferences." He makes a note in a little notepad, and then addresses the class. "Well, as you can see, I'm about as old as the dirt around here, this is my 34th year teaching. Why I'm practically a part of the history I teach!" He smiles at his joking, and then continues, "Now, I want you to know, I was never the best student, and I'm sure some of you aren't either, so there's a question you need to ask yourself today, the same question I asked myself on the second day of college: how well do I want to do? How much of this class will I invest in me?

"It's okay with me if you say that a C is the best you want, that this class isn't something you need to succeed in your chosen path. But remember that your grade is the one you choose. I know what it's like to be a bad student, but I also know that when you straighten out your priorities, you can succeed to whatever level you like. So before we go any further in this class, I'll ask you take a minute and decide what you need from this class and how much you need of it. Then, I'll pass out these contracts so you can sign up for your grade and I'll explain how that works.

"But you," he says, looking at me, "don't have a choice. You get to sign up for an A." He smiles again and I can see the glint of his gold teeth.

The contract does make sense. You can sign up for an A, a B, or a C. If you fall short of your desires, you get a D, or an F. Not quite all or nothing. Annalynn is about to sign up for a B, but then looks over at me dutifully signing up for an A, and signs the dotted line for an A..... It's not an insignificant amount of work to get the top grade.

I'm predisposed to like Mr. Earl, but his manner and laugh completely win me over. I'm quite sure I'd go to lengths to keep him happy. He probably knows it. I think he instills either a deep loyalty or a deep animosity in his students, and he likes it divided that way. His world has little in terms of grey, I'll discover.

The best thing that happens in that class, however, is that he moves Josh up to the front. I feel saved from certain torment, which seals my loyalty to the man. It has also given me a haven in this new place.

Chapter Nine

Despite the ever-present Les, life is going well until right after Christmas. My parents are again sailing bad waters. I have been using homework and trips to Annalynn's house as way to avoid it, but on a very cold January night, the usual indications start up: sighing and half-finished gestures until I'm tossed out of the kitchen and my parents hide there and start one of their quiet conversations. I am unable to hear them yet, but I know that sooner or later, my mother will raise her voice and so will he. So I settle in with an unfinished art project and wait.

It is not long.

"No Ted, I don't want a loving husband. That's an ideal, a concept we give to very small children to keep them innocent. I want a real person. In this case, you. With all your nasty little faults. The fact you pick your nose and examine it, the fact you never, ever bring me impromptu gifts; that you can never manage to be on your best behavior, and everything else. I want that in my life because it's offset with the good! You don't drink—"

"—anymore." He interjects.

"You don't smoke, you don't go out and cavort with strange women or cheat." She takes a breath as if to continue but he interjects.

"You did." He says calmly.

She what?

"No, no I didn't."

"How do you figure you didn't?"

"You asked me to start sleeping with other people!" She replies.

"Meanwhile you continued to try and remain with me in a half-hearted way and occasionally told me about the others, which you must have known I hated."

"How about we look at this in a different light?"

"How about we don't. I'm leaving." He says.

Clunk. Teacup in the sink. He throws open the door and runs smack into me.

"I think you should go back in there." I say.

"I don't care what you think." He snarls and tries to shove by.

I shove right back, dig a shoulder into his ribs, and push as hard as I can.

He lands in his usual chair.

"I care what I think. She does too, and you should." I roll the door back into place.

"Bloody Dudely Do-right." He snarks.

"You're only jealous." I yell through the door.

He changes the topic. "Well, about this other light?'

"I was pregnant, and later, I had a baby. Brian, being the best kind of friend anyone could hope for, came and helped. He thought you had no business leaving a baby behind. He left a stable life to come help me when my own parents wouldn't. You told me to start sleeping with other people... why wouldn't I choose him? He was our best friend; yes, your best friend first, but he was the best friend of both of us when we needed him to be. I don't know what I would have done if he hadn't been where I needed him. He saved me and in doing that, saved you from worse consequences from your mistake."

"What about...whatsits from Boston?" He says, sounding defeated.

"Malcolm?"

"Yeah, him... that one really hurt."

"Ted, you dumped me months before I saw Malcolm. He was cute, he went home to Boston, he didn't want to deal with 'someone else's kid and someone else's should-a-been wife.'"

"You shouldn't have been with him. You should have realized I was lost and still needed you."

"How was I supposed to know that?"

"I came around, didn't I? I promised to be there for the birth."

"And constantly told me to let you go in my heart and let you go on with your life."

"Well you didn't manage that either, did you? You've failed every test I've set before you."

My mother sounds upsets when she starts speaking after a lengthy pause. "I did my best during a very difficult time in my life. I reacted badly to you leaving, and made a series of extremely far-reaching missteps after that. You can only deal with what you have at the time, what you know at the time, and that's what I did."

"And you did a remarkably cocked-up job."

"And let's see, you did a great job with yourself after that point?"

"At least I didn't get entangled with new 'love.'" He comments sarcastically.

"No, you traveled light, tried to sleep with a couple of girls much younger than you and completely out of your league. Then you came home and held onto me until you decided it was time to be 'free' again. I guess. Oh, and you dated that other man's wife for a while[8]; the one who was sleeping

---

8   He later told me that he loved her a great deal and was strung along for

with everything else with a penis."

There is another long pause.

"It was all very messed up and stupid." She says. "What is stupider still is the fact that while I'm willing to forgive you, you won't forgive me and so this doesn't become water under the bridge like it should be after ten years. Like it should have been untold ages ago."

He makes a wordless, primal sound at her and stomps through the house, leaving with gusto. It has a feeling of permanence. That worries me. It worries me more that my mother runs off to her room and locks the door. She hasn't done that before.

I ride the bus out to his trailer the next day. Great Animosity and its requisite silence not withstanding, I'm going to have to speak to him about this. It's just not right. And the next best thing to silence is hostility, as far as I can tell, anyway. I knock loudly on the door. I know he's home, and I know he's most likely sleeping.

"Does your mother know you are here?" He croaks at me when he opens the door.

"No."

He lets me in, hands me a soda.

"You have to come home."

He looks at me in a patronizing fashion.

Good enough, I think. "She misses you."

"Uh huh." He says with no shortage of sarcasm.

"She's never as happy when you aren't

---

months on promises that she was going to leave her husband to be with him. Apparently, finding out that he might have AIDS because she was a sex-addict ended things very brutally.

around." I say. "Also, among your lack of vices, which she went over yesterday, you actually have some virtues." I say diplomatically.

"I'm well aware of this."

"Oh, you are?" I say.

"Yes I am. Remarkable, but I know my own good points well; and I can tell you this much, they go unappreciated!"

"No, no they don't." I argue back.

"Look kiddo, you've nicely interrupted my sleeping, which is important for my job, to argue something you know nothing about. I'm very sure your mother didn't send you, but I'm going to have to ask you not to do this ever again, even if she does. I want to live in peace much more than I want the rare comforts of another human."

"This," I say, stretching my arms out to signify the trailer and the plot of land on which it lives, "is not peace. It's defeat."

"Why would you say that?"

"If love conquers all, then the only way to not be defeated is to be an ally. And alliance, in this case, must be acceptance."

He looks at me in a new and different way. It could be extreme anger or thoughtfulness. I choose the reaction that pleases me and run with it. "It isn't like there is anyone else, for either of you. You asked her to try, she failed. You went out and tried on your own and found no one who would accept you would also please you. If you truly desired peace, as you call this, you would have left us both a long time ago and not continued your returns. If you keep coming after something, even if you won't really let yourself have it, you want it nonetheless."

"Hmmm."

"Actions still speak louder than words." I say.

"Indeed, they do, but that doesn't make words less powerful, it just makes them less powerful than actions." He pauses for a good while. "What is in this for you?"

"What is in what?" I ask.

"If I come home, what is in it for you?"

"Honestly, not much." I say, though the reality does sadden me.

He looks at me, and he looks disappointed.

"You didn't choose acceptance with me. Don't be so surprised that you were defeated." I say. "You didn't really choose acceptance with yourself either. Probably the main part of the problem."

I toss the empty soda can in the overfilled trash-bin.

"Come home soon." I say, and try to leave.

"You know," He says, "Brian came by and said mostly the same things, but he wasn't near as diplomatic. And also, he's been in this from the very start, but I didn't believe him. Thought he was a puppet to your mother."

"Oh?"

"You saying this means something more."

"Oh."

"I'll think about it all."

I almost leave. Curiosity wins instead.

"Who is Brian exactly?" I ask. Brian's been a friend of the family for years. He's lived in the building next door for as long as I can remember and comes over for dinner all the time. But he's sort of a non-entity to me. He and my mother have always spoken on topics well over my head. But he does give me the best gifts when he thinks of doing so.

"Brian's my best friend from high-school. Probably your mother's best friend too since after Michael died. He's important to us, immeasurably so." My father says. He sounds wistful. "Through bad times mostly. I owe him an apology if I end up doing what you ask...."

He pauses. "No, I'll do it. Two minds were better than this one, at least this time around." I look hopeful at this. "Not anytime soon. I need things I don't have yet."

I want to hug him, but I go and catch the next bus home instead. He did leave again, after all.

Chapter Ten

I didn't know Michael was dead. I always thought he was off in lands afar. Maybe that was how my mother viewed it or she simply let herself think that to get through having a baby at twenty-one nearly on the tails of the funeral of her best friend.

I ask her.

"Michael didn't want to live, Em." She says. "He wanted to die young and beautiful from something exotic, or at least exciting. Which, is I guess how things turned out."

I look at her expectantly while I chase the broccoli around my plate.

"They estimated he was going 124 miles an hour in that damn car of mine. I know better, never told them, but we were going over that. Out on the Palouse highway at four AM in the morning. We didn't think we'd run into a soul, and certainly not something as stupid as a blown tire on the road. I don't know really what happened, it's blurry. I think we hit the tire—he was already braking— we went airborne. When you are going too fast, a car becomes just like a balsa airplane. We flipped end over end. He wasn't wearing his seat-belt because he never did. He was dead before we slammed into the guardrail. I wasn't though."

She pauses and wipes a few tears from her face. Then, she gets up and grabs one of her photo boxes and pulls a few out. She hands the first one to me. My very young mother stands in front of an immaculate tricked-out 1970's muscle car. The next picture is most likely the same car. But I only come to that through conjecture; it could just as easily be a ball of crumpled foil.

"I don't know how you walked away."

She looks down. "I think if anyone was going to be an angel, it was Michael. I called him that, my cocaine angel." She pauses.

"Cocaine?" I ask.

"He wasn't high that night. I let him drive that night because he'd always wanted to and it was the first time he'd been sober in awhile."

"Angel?" I ask then instead.

"He was, he really was. No matter how messed up he got, I loved him all the same and so did everyone else. When he started doing drugs, I told him he needed an angel to watch over him, and he said he had one in himself. So I called him the cocaine angel. Maybe he really is one. I think so. If he wasn't, how did I survive that?" She says as she jabs the picture.

"Fate train." I say, her words for destiny.

"Even fate doesn't perform that kind of miraculous."

"No," I agree. "She finds others for the purpose of miracles. I suppose you did have a cocaine angel."

"I like to think I still do." She replies. "I'd better have an angel if life has deprived me of the best friend I've ever known." She pauses. "I think Michael hand-picked Brian for us." She amends.

"What about my father?"

"Michael always had a sense of humor."

Michael must be an angel. Or Brian and I are persuasive. Or both.

My father really does comes back home like he said he would. And sits down in our living room after I reluctantly let him in.

"She's not here." I say.

"I know. I wanted to talk to you." He replies.

"Why?"

"You probably deserve better parents."

"No, I deserve a better dad." I say sharply, still angry that he had left again.

"I'm not going to disagree."

"Then why don't you change?" I say.

He says something in German.

"Sprech englisch." I reply, rudely.

"Sprechen sie." He corrects half-heartedly.

"No." I have never understood his penchant to turn to German when he was upset with me, so I don't play to it.

"Maybe because you never give me a chance." He says, answering my earlier question.

"You never give me a reason." I say.

He is silent until my mother comes home.

She has a bundle of books in her arms and her face falls as she puts it aside and sits down. I know she wanted have an evening to herself, which was why I was so reluctant to let him in.

"Hello Ted." She says, instead of whatever else might have come to her mind.

He reaches out to her, and she shakes her head. "Not right now. I've been thinking about everything. And—"

"— me too."

"You interrupted me." She says quietly.

"I'm sorry." He mutters back without looking at her.

"I can't do it anymore. Not at all. I've lost a lot of my life in loving you if you never truly come back. This torment has to end. I'll let you chose how to do that, but it has to be done now."

She looks terribly fragile when she finishes saying this, as though she might burst into tears again, and it makes me deeply, deeply dislike him.

"I cleaned out the trailer and got rid of everything— pretty much. I had a fellow come and haul the trailer itself away too. There is nowhere for me to go now. I have no escape route, Puppe. I've finally decided that I can't really travel light anymore."

"Go on...." She says.

"I don't plan to live here, at first." He stares at his feet. "I don't deserve to. I rented a place down the street." He traces a circle in the carpet. "Can I take you out on Friday night?"

"What?"

"I don't trust me either. We should start somewhere basic, that's what all the books say." He attempts to explain.

"Books?"

"I read a few books on relationships when I realized that I wasn't going to do much more with therapy." He says sheepishly. "They seemed like a good start to fixing things for good. Please come with me?"

"Yes, I'll come." She says. She forgives him more easily than I do.

Friday, my mother sits at her sewing machine and very calmly makes herself a wraparound dress and shawl. Usually, I offer to help with sewing, but this time I just watch as the fabric moves from one side to the other and miraculously comes out as a dress instead of jeans, like normal.

She looks lovely.

He manages to look less mangy than usual.

I have to give him points, though. He brought her starter tomato plants and carefully wrought copper bangles as gifts. He made the jewelry, obviously, but the plants seem to have come from the expensive local organic greenhouse.

For all the distance that there is between them, my father does seem to understand that my mother was never really a woman of the modern world. She is content to run the family business, sew her own clothes, and grow vegetables in the backyard. Although she is competent, perhaps even talented with the electronics that exist in modern times, she always seems out of sync with her peers. Most women want flowers, chocolates, expensive jewelry—not my mother. She looks at the tomatoes with a gleam in her eye and puts the copper bracelets on as though they are fine gold.

After they leave I run my hands over the machine she was using to make her dress. It is still warm to the touch. She calls it the beastie, and indeed, it's a beast of a machine when compared to the streamlined, high-tech machines that sit haughtily at the dealers' stores where we buy needles and belts. It is more solid, if more basic than they are. She has another machine, not quite as old, that she uses for synthetic fabrics because it has the stitches for that. I use it sometimes myself, but this one has always been more familiar somehow with its chrome, bakelite and brightly painted steel. Perhaps because it fits with the house.

The house, built sometime in the turn of the century, has grown and changed with times. There is still the original claw-foot tub in the upstairs bathroom which my mother paired with an elegant mission-style lowboy-cum-vanity and white porcelain sink. It feels only vaguely modern. The master bedroom has giant 1970's mirrors on the closet doors, but the shag carpet is long gone. Modern windows clash completely with 1920's woodwork in the living room and the kitchen is a bizarre time capsule, partway between the 1950's remodel of the original and 1960's remodel. Some parts are original still, too.

And the sewing machine, from somewhen last century, makes sense with the house as a whole, as does my mother. Though I would not call her a bumpkin, she is not a sophisticate. Like the house, she is a mishmash of bygone ideas, not stuck in the past, but not fully in contemporary times either. Partially too, from some future not yet realized. I suspect I'm no different. I'm the only kid in my junior high that knows what a vinyl record is, the only kid with much knowledge at all regarding the recent past. And the only person who knows how to read Tarot cards.

I pick up the bright orange rotary phone in the kitchen and call Annalynn.

"Can you come over?'

"Sure." She says, knowing all about the date and also knowing that I hate the house being empty. It's a leftover sentiment from my childhood, the dislike of the big empty house.

"Annalynn," I say when she gets here, "do you

think... you know, that they will work things out?"

"It's been ten years of up and down, hasn't it?"

"Yeah."

"Well, you know how my mom constantly yo-yo diets?" Her mom doesn't really yo-yo diet, that's just a polite way to describe Mrs. Spencer's battle with some indeterminate eating disorder or mental hijink.

"Yes." I reply anyway.

"I think your mom has yo-yo dating. It's good, it's bad, it's good, it's bad. I think she's as likely as not to get stable, same as my mom."

We are twelve. Annalynn and I are just like the house. Our true age is obscured. The house is unique, peerless you might say, and so are we. We sit at the table in the kitchen and sip hot chocolate and talk about our parents, not in terms of hatred or from disconnected vantages like our classmates, but in terms of concern for the next thirty minutes.

"I wish Mom would realise how pretty she is, and how this dieting is making her a mess. Perfection is neurosis," Annalynn says. "And I wish my Dad wouldn't pretend like it's not going on." She says this often enough, but tonight it makes my head connect a few dots and before I can stop it, I find myself saying something that is both very true and incredibly difficult to admit.

"I want the Great Animosity to stop. I don't want us to constantly fall into the patterns when it's obvious we both have so much to say and no avenue to speak, and it just gets deeper and wider and angrier between us. I don't know how though, and I'm also afraid that the Great Animosity is just a nice way of keeping myself delusional to the fact he might really be an asshole."

"Emelle, your dad makes you stuff, he takes us around to places. I mean, he isn't great, but I don't think he's an asshole. Besides, you shouldn't call people that." She says without realizing I've just said something very important.

"But, then he goes and does stupid things that hurt everybody's feelings and doesn't have enough conscience to be guilty or empathic about it. Sometimes it seems like he's just covering up the rot with temporary prettiness. Maybe he is just buying time with imitation goodness and generosity." I worry to her.

"He's not, Emelle, trust me. I can smell a bad person. He's not that way. He just has his own issues to get past before he can stop his own yo-yo living. He loves you guys, he hates his emotional baggage, and you are part of the emotional baggage sometimes."

Chapter Eleven

Later in the spring, Mr. Earl tags me before I leave for my next class.

"Wouldn't you like to be on the track team?"

I look at myself, I'm all legs and arms. I'd probably be a good runner. "Never thought about it before." I say truthfully.

He looks me up and down.

"You should come and turn out for me."

"You are the coach?"

"Yep."

Well, in that case it's not even a question, and he knows it. "Sure. I can do that."

"Bring Annalynn. You guys can be our first cross-country team in four years." He says.

"Uh. Sure." I say, confused as to why he didn't think we'd both turn out.

"You won't always be each other's shadows, Em."

I look at him. He wiggles his bushy eyebrows. "I see two people, even though," he points to the noisy hall, "they don't."

"Oh." I say.

"Next week, Saturday—dress in layers, there may be snow on the ground." He says with a wicked, yet inviting smile.

Saturday is not only freezing, but there is an incredible drizzle coming down when my mother drops me and Annalynn off at the school. We are dressed in two layers of long underwear each, and my mother made us both some sort of warm but breathable tracksuit. It is still cold. We are two of the few that have shown up.

Mr. Earl walks out in a nice sheepskin coat, a steaming mug of something jammed firmly in his fist.

I recognize a few people, Travis from my math class, he's mousey and studious. Jordan, who plays piano at lunchtime in the band room by himself. Meikalia who is another honor roll student. And Sean, a friend of Jordan's who is also a fairly good artist like me. I get the idea that Mr. Earl might have handpicked us.

"Well." He says. "This is track, isn't it?"

We look at him.

"Start running."

Some of us take off like rockets, some people take off at a low, confused pace. Annalynn and I take off at an easy lope and keep pace with each other. I am not surprised when Mr. Earl tells us that we are his new cross-country team.

"Both of us?"

"It's coed teams now that track doesn't have the funding it used to," he explains.

Several practices in, I realise I like track.

I like stretching, I like running. I feel powerful and graceful instead of gawky and clumsy. When I run around the track with Annalynn at lunchtime, sometimes other teammates joins us, and I feel like I'm someone as apposed to an afterthought. We aren't all the best of friends, but there is a wonderful sense of camaraderie and common intention.

And, when Annalynn and I win a cross-country event, I like it even better.

The acceptance means more to Annalynn, and I see that it makes a big difference in how she carries herself in the halls, and how she interacts with our peers.

But, we still retreat to each other. The track team is a very eclectic pile of people, and though we get along fine, we don't have overlapping interests particularly.

Months later, summer comes around and my parents finish their round through couples' counseling. My father finally quits his job at the mall, but takes up a Friday night shift privately to help out a business associate. He enlarges his business in terms of time and contracts and grows happier, not sadder.

Annalynn learns how to knit, and spends hours sitting on my bed while I draw the world around us. My mom takes this in a stride and starts making lunch for four, not three. Annalynn catches on to this regularity and convinces her father to bring over several boxes of canned sodas, popsicles, and other things that tend to vanish when Annalynn and I are a-lurking.

Things are going remarkably well for the Deckman-Foster residence, so long as my father and I don't attempt to talk.

Chapter Twelve

Yo-yo living. I think Annalynn has coined the term that will define middle school. It is certainly a yo-yo of states, fortunes, and moods. And, I've discovered, it is only going to become more interesting. I'm becoming, I think, almost unlike myself. I'm stumbling into my own body perhaps in the strangest way possible. I haven't yet come across pornography or even sexually explicit books, and my mother is waiting for some obvious cue to have the talk with me. Having explained that I wanted to fall straight through the floor and never look at my classmates again after being tortured by sex-ed in sixth grade (an experience she'd already been through herself), I haven't yet been subjected to some uncomfortable chit-chat about it all.

I realize that there are changes occurring in my body and someday I'll eventually be an adult, but it doesn't precisely hit home until I realize that face in the mirror is changing, and perhaps not for the better. My hair has gotten shaggier and coarser and I have a terrible suspicion my nose is actually growing larger than it already was. I've gotten all gaunt and gangly. And bushy in unfortunate places. Secondary sex characteristics are god's way of reminding humans that yep, we're just the top dog in the animal kingdom, but still animals.

I touch my fingers to my face. Even my skin has changed into a weird texture. I tap my own lips, and the oddest thing to date happens— my body responds with a twitch from down-bellows and my nipples perk up.

"Oh, this isn't happening." I mutter to the mirror and will it all away.

I curl up around Mosser and think about this after dinner.

I have long enjoyed my childhood, my refusal to become the falsely sophisticated poser that my peers so often aim to be. I've reveled in my lack of sexuality so far, thrown it in their faces that I wasn't going to be corrupted early by a world that had minimalized childhood for material gains and created a weird intrastate of tweenhood. They couldn't make me a horndog or anything else they wanted. I'd be as dowdy and as unsophisticated as I pleased.

My father's head pokes around the doorframe. "Are you okay?" He asks when he realizes that it is early evening and I'm curled up around Mosser like he's going to save my life.

"When did you go through puberty?" I ask without preamble.

"A long time ago."

"I meant how old were you." I say flatly.

"Uhm, 13 to 17, I think."

"Did you hate it?"

"Not really. One day I realized I was probably stronger than my dad and found out I could protect the pets from his rage with that strength. But I suppose honestly, I could have done without a lot of the strangeness of it all." He sits down on my giant leather bean-bag. "Well, actually, I think other than finally getting big enough to protect the pooches from Dad, I really hated it."

I'm still holding Mosser, albeit loosely. "Your dad did what?"

"A lot of bad things that I still hold against him, though I shouldn't."

"He beat up dogs?" I'm aghast.

"He tried. As soon as he discovered if he went for them, he could have a real human instead, he just started going for me all the time. In fact, to exclusion of his usual favorite punching bags."

My jaw pops open.

"I thought you knew all of this?"

"No... I didn't." I say.

"Well, I suppose you are old enough to know. Dad beat up Mom all the time. When she put an end to her own abuse, it just fell on us kids and the family animals more heavily than it had. He really preferred to slam my sister into the wall and watch her cry until he discovered I would fight back. He liked that even more." He says it so nonchalantly.

I'm completely gobsmacked. I was expecting 'the talk' and am getting a frightening load of family history.

I've never been hit in anger, I've never impacted walls propelled by anything different than my own stupidity, and I've never had reason to wonder about abuse. And here it was all along.

I swear both my parents have more than a dose of telepathy because his next words are: "When you arrived, I decided nothing of the sort was ever going to happen again in my family, to hell with tradition. It probably helped that you were an easy baby. You grinned, you gurgled, you slept a lot, and you were so happy and cute. Well, when I was around."

I nod. I have no idea what to say.

"Having you was, I think, then end of puberty, because I finally grew up mentally though my body had been long since finished. 'Hmm. I appear to be twenty-three and have a son.' Before that, I was an eternal seventeen-year old."

He is quiet for the next eon.

So it seems.

"But you were asking about puberty." He says in an apologetic tone.

"It's probably hateful. But not as hateful as... uhm"

"Well, you don't seem to have noticed until today." He laughs a bit.

"Huh?"

"You've been an adolescent for a while now."

"I don't want to be." I say.

"Why not? It's the natural state of things."

"I don't want a sex drive. I think it sounds dangerous."

He looks at me, uncomfortable, head tilted to the side. "Oh. It's not so bad as some would have you think." He looks up and motions and my mother comes in with a basket of laundry which he takes from her after standing up.

They both leave.

My mother comes back in with a sheath of paper and pencils— the usual prerequisites for any lengthy or detailed explanation. Not that she necessarily draws things related to the explanation, sometimes she just doodles until she comes up with the right words.

She doodles.

"Emelle... do you really not want to grow up?"

I resign myself to where she is going. I'm apparently getting 'the talk' no matter how much I'd rather fall through floorboards.

Annalynn and I are walking to school the next

day.

"Annalynn? Have you ever, like, played with your own lips?"

She looks at me. "You mean like twisting them up into goofy shapes or something?"

"No, just brushing them with your finger tips lightly." I clarify.

She attacks her lips as though she has smeared ketchup on them.

"Not like that!" I say. "Let me."

She stops and faces me and I brush my fingers very gently across her lips.

She looks at me expectantly as though I'm supposed to have caused her to burst into flame.

She doesn't.

Burst into flame, that is.

"Is that all?" She says.

"Well, what does it feel like to you?" I ask, suddenly feeling alone with my weird sensations that I can't relate to.

"Like your fingers touching my lips, Emelle, what were you expecting?" she says.

"I dunno, maybe you'd feel something sort of... tingly?"

She races me to school instead of continuing the conversation and while we sit in American History I wonder how she can't feel something with her plump, pink lips. I certainly feel something looking at them, though I don't know precisely what it is.

I can hazard a guess.

But I don't want to.

Les obviously saw this exchange on the way to

school, and by lunch-time everyone knows that "Oh. My. God. The dorks are getting ready to breed because Emelle touched Annalynn's lips." People are even avoiding us.

More so than they usually do.

Les saunters over to us in the cafeteria. "So." He opens.

Annalynn stands up. "Shut up, you second-rate Napoleon."

I'm stunned, he's stunned, she's stunned. Annalynn couldn't stand up for herself if the world depended on it, and yet she just has.

"I'm not a *little* man." He says.

"Yes you are. You are a cold, nasty and small goblinoid." She says back.

"Want me to prove that I'm not a little man, Spencer?"

"Reality doesn't matter, Les... your attitude tells me everything I need to know." She smiles and indicates about three inches between her thumb and index finger.

His face twists up as though he might start screaming and he stomps away.

"Got some anatomical processes going on downstairs I should know about?" I ask after he's left.

"You asking if I grew some balls?"

"Yeah."

"No, I grew something better."

"What's that?"

"Working ovaries. They cause PMS."

Fist-pound. "Awesome."

Chapter Thirteen

The summer between seventh and eighth grade there are bus passes and Les Schopenhauer.

The first item because my mother buys them for us because we are old enough to want to be out and about, but young enough to be limited to bicycles or the bus. In this case, both.

The second because our inescapable, smart-mouthed, unfortunately-lives-in-the-neighborhood school yutz can't leave us alone. A jerk of epic proportions, and it seems he shows up everywhere— the bus terminal, the mall, Dick's hamburger stand downtown. I'd almost say he's following us, but Annalynn says I'm too much of a conspiracy theorist already.

When Schopenhauer doesn't show up conveniently, Annalynn and I have a wonderful time. We are giddy with the bus passes, there is barely a place in Spokane that we cannot invade. Mostly though, we go downtown and ride the carousel and watch matinee movies, because after the third week of us watching movies at home my mother handed me a wad of twenties and told me to get out of the house. Naturally, I drag Annalynn along with.

Because an old mystic tells us it would be good for our health, we buy cheap jade rings from a spiritual supply store one day before wandering up to the top stories of the Parkade to catch the breeze coming off the river. Standing out, our heads thrust out over the edge, our hair is blown back by the wind.

And then along comes Schopenhauer with his usual vocal rubbish.

"Awwwww. How sweet. You know if you moved

to Alabama you could already be married and pregnant. You should do that."

"And if you moved thirty feet to your right, you could be just as screwed." I say, motioning to the long drop down to the sidewalk.

"You think you are so smart, Foster. Truth is you're just a guy with a gay name that's got to defend himself too often and tries to do it like some wimp, with words." He sneers.

I nod to Annalynn and we both attempt to leave. Good ol' Les tries to block the stairs.

"Oh for god sakes, Les.... Stop it for the day." Annalynn gripes and waves a hand at him.

He notices the jade ring and instantly searches my hands.

"Oh, so you are married? The whole school has a betting pool, you know, on whether you've done it yet. How is she, Foster, warm and wet, or does she just lie there and take it?"

"I know living under a rock has mental repercussions, but cut it out."

He follows us with the same line of jeers and even continues on the bus while we ride home. I'd love to interrupt a few of his more requisite bodily functions with a well engineered kick, but I think better of it.

As if she has something to prove, Annalynn makes us go to the Parkade every night for a week. Schopenhauer figures out what we are up to and harasses us for three nights and then is mysteriously missing on the fourth.

"I don't exactly think we got the better of him here." I say.

"Verbal repartee isn't, I think, his benchmark

for whether he's gotten bested, but maybe he took a night off to think of responses." Annalynn says to indicate agreement.

She leans out into the wind.

She's beautiful.

I'm gawky.

And awkward.

So I nod my head and pause for something else to come to mind.

"Em? What are you thinking?"

Oh damn. "Oh, bugger..... I dunno, it's a nice night, you're beautiful, and I'm awkward. My, my, the wind is cool!"

Annalynn cranes her head around to look at me looking anywhere but at her and raises an eyebrow.

"What?" I snap.

"I'm beautiful?"

"From time to time." I say and smile.

"Oh, so sometimes I'm....?"

"Sometimes I'm not thinking about it."

"Okay."

I'm surprised that the world does not implode after this exchange. I anticipate the mighty smite-y hand of the powers-that-be will come howling down out of the sky to whack me with the idiot stick any moment, but it doesn't. And so, it seems that this is only a ripple, not a wave within our friendship. The proverbial cat is in the bag, and is not yet itching to get out.

So I tell myself.

But I sweat bullets that night anyway.

I get up at two when hope of sleep is

impossible and sit in the kitchen with a glass of milk and a nice book about... something or other. My mind is far from reading. It's doing circles about the idiocy of telling your best friend how lovely she is.

I don't hear my father come home from work or drag a chair out to sit down so he can stare at me. Finally, he gives me a little prod to see if I'm awake or not.

"Mmmph." I say.

"I know you like to get up early, but three in the morning is something else. Something on your mind?"

"Nope." I say.

"And our porcine friends are sprouting aviarian tendencies?"

"No, pigs aren't flying." I reply absently. "But there is probably a pachyderm in the living-room."

"Hmm, no shit." He says as he unlaces his boots.

I glare.

"Oh, you meant one other than the usual elephant between us?" he says, and he sounds a bit disappointed.

"Mmm." I reply.

"So, you've noticed Annalynn is female?" He guesses close to home, as usual.

I glare harder.

"I assure you, she hasn't noticed that you have. Everyone else probably has though."

"Annalynn is my friend. Not my girlfriend, not my crush. My best friend."

"What? And I thought you guys were enemies." He says.

"Ha ha."

He finishes wiggling his feet out of the boots and thinks for a few minutes. 'I know you guys are friends. You are also each other's only friends. It's a nasty world out there; maybe you don't want to lose your best ally. How best to do that, I don't know. It might not matter that she's a she and you a he. Then again, it might matter a whole lot."

He rubs his hands and then looks up to smile at me. It's the same infectious grin from when I was young, but with more lines radiating out. I almost break and smile back but years of ingrained behavior and a residual distrust squelches me.

"I trust you to do the right thing. I'm going to bed." He finishes flatly.

If I knew what the right thing was, I'd be doing it, and fast. But I don't, and so I just drop it before it begins, and finish the rest of the summer without another dangerous exchange. If Annalynn notices, or cares much, she doesn't say so.

Chapter Fourteen

Annalynn asks me to be a hooker on Halloween because her mother is only going to let her out the door with someone similarly dressed. Translation: Her mother doesn't think I have the wherewithal to both convince my parents to let me *and* show up to school dressed in stockings and heels. I don't think the thought that Annalynn might have tried to convince someone else crossed anyone's mind.

This intrigue doesn't concern me; I was with her from the word please, and now, I'm hunting for shoes.   I have tiny feet as growing boys go. Just a smidgen too big to be a seven like my mother. I attempt to steal her stilettos for the purposes of Halloween but she stops me with a glare that tells me that I'll be buying shoes with my own money.

Annalynn, on the other hand, has "monster" feet. A "walloping" size nine she says. Fortunately, due to the drag scene in Spokane we find her shoes right away. Six inch platform heels in patent pink leather. Mine take longer, because apparently only drag queens get to wear really spectacular heels. We finally find them in a consignment store: glittery blue spikes.

The local thrift stores offer up layers of blue lingerie for me and a tartan skirt in pink for her that she pairs with a very sheer fishnet black shirt and a lacy, ruffly pink bra that isn't of the push up variety. Neither of us have adequate chests. I point this out rather insensitively. "Annalynn, don't hookers have ...." I gesture rudely, "big kahunas?"

Her eyes narrow. "What are you suggesting?"

"I need boobs. You need boobs, or a better bra."

"You don't just need boobs.... You need hips and an ass too... although you've kinda supplied the latter."

"I have a perfectly.... Huh... WHAT?"

She glares me as she digs through a box of costume hosiery.

"Annalynn if you are trying to convince people of something with this costume... I dunno why. It's really a pretty silly costume, especially when your street sister is me. I'm not even a girl."

"I'm not!" She insists. "I'm trying to find something to go with that...." She stops and grins.

"Something to go with what?"

"You'll see."

It takes us forever to find the hosiery she wants. She even forces me to buy satin and lace garters to wear. "Why?" I ask, since the hose stay up on their own.

"It's the look, dork."

We get back to her house and she spreads our finds out on the floor and motions for me to wait and guard them. I squat down and look at them under adequate lighting. The fabric is incredibly cheap on some of it and the pinks don't quite match. It's just a costume but if Annalynn is trying to convince her tormentors that she's just as hot as—

"Look!" She dumps a pile of pink hair on the floor.

She has a dyed pink mink coat.

With a gold lining.

It's horrific.

"Oh my god, Annalynn."

"Is it not the screaming piece de resistance for this costume?'

"Only if you have the gaudy costume jewelry to go with. Where did you get Mangy here?" I ask. It smells of mothballs and, more recently, cedar.

"Remember my Grand-aunt who died last year, the one from the east coast I didn't know very well?"

"Yeah."

"She left a bunch of awesome costume stuff." She has her hands behind her back.

"Please tell me I'm not wearing dead animals?"

I'm not, but it comes to be that I will be wearing some black corduroy coat with fake fur at the collar and cuffs that may have never been haute couture or even in style.

My mother watches me haul the bag of stuff into the house and taps her nose.

"Yes, Mom?"

"I'm going to call your grandmother and ask her to come over and show you how to cover up that nose some."

"Spike heels are lethal weapons Mom."

"You need the help."

She's right, and my grandmother could make Tammy Faye Baker look positively hot.

Grimsy shows up with a makeup purse better described as a transcontinental suitcase that she flops open seconds before she comes at my face with tweezers, makeup brushes and sponges at the same time as she is grinning like a maniacal circus clown.

I have no idea what happens to my face. She tells me everything she's doing but it sounds like Greek spoken by a hyper gerbil. When I look in the mirror afterward, she's shrunk my nose and made my eyes huge. This in no way makes me comely or enticing.

"Thanks Grim." I say anyway.

"Go put on the costume! I want to see it." She demands.

I pull on the hose, the shoes the layers of slips and the gawdawful coat.

She looks me over appreciatively and calls my mother up the stairs. "Doesn't he look fab?" Grim squeals.

My mother barely glances at me. 'Mom!" she gurgles.

"What?" Grim replies.

"He looks like a waif. Haven't I been feeding you?" She asks me.

I do look like a waif. I do not, however, like her pointing it out.

"Hey! It's not like I could have pulled this off if I was heavy!"

"No, that's true. Your face looks good." She says.

Three days later I'm sitting in the bathroom, unbraiding all the tiny braids I put in my hair to make it 'big hair'. I'm all dressed and trying to hussy it up through some choice makeup; i.e., blue eye shadow and glitter lipstick. My mother left early to take care of a sudden plumbing emergency in one of the older buildings, or she would have been helping.

Though I am only marginally successful at recreating what Grim did, I think I look pretty good. For a guy.

I shrug into the coat and transfer my backpack

to a faux-leather hobo bag with plastic jewels decorating the side. Grim had dropped it off yesterday, telling me I'd mess myself up if I tromped around with a backpack. She had then insisted that I learn how to walk like a lady, too.

I wiggle into the shoes and clatter down the stairs to the kitchen where I intend to get my lunch before I walk out the door. I should have just left and paid for lunch at school. But here I am in the kitchen and my father is still up, reading the paper and drinking tea. I hope he's too tired from work to think about what he's seeing, so I begin to sneak—

"What the hell are you wearing?"

"A mangy coat, glitter heels and stockings."

The paper floats to the table top. The teacup is set down with a meaningful thud. "No, you aren't."

"I am." I shrug the coat down over my shoulders and push out my chest with my arms akimbo in my best petulant Peter Pan stance. "See?"

"Go upstairs and change. Now."

"No. It's Halloween and I promised Annalynn I'd go as a hooker with her."

"How can you make a promise without permission?"

"Why do you even care what I'm dressed up as, Mom certainly doesn't care." I snarl.

He looks disgusted, probably at the both of us.

"I'm late, and I'm leaving." I say, grab my lunch and launch out the front door.

I don't expect him to come barreling out after me and drag me back in, but he does.

It's an odd reversal of years ago, me clinging to doorframes and porch posts to avoid being forced to attend school. Now it's me clawing to get out.

Literally.

The phone rings.

My father answers it while gripping my wrist. I think about sinking one nasty spike heel into his bare toes.

"murrmmmrurrmmmmmrmrmr?" says the phone.

"What?"

"mmrmrmrmrmaummmrmrmurmmur, murm!"

"Yes, Annalynn. He was just on his way out."

He lets me go. 'Fine! Look ridiculous and get yourself into trouble." He sits down at the paper and his tea, nigh on visible cranial smoke rising from his head.

I meet Annalynn at her house where she's being followed around by her mother who has a twenty in her hand trying to convince her to just wear normal pantyhose.

"It doesn't go with the coat, Ma....."

"You sure?" Her mother's voice is shrill and her face contorted.

"Yes, Mom!' Annalynn nearly shouts.

"Well, then.... Just be safe and don't let anyone think you are a whore for real." Mrs. Spencer says, defeated.

We finally spill onto the street, wobbling down the sidewalk and wiggling our way to school. Before long, I am wishing for the comfort of my track shoes.

I am very thankful to collapse into a desk in my first class. My feet are... howling. Like a thousand denizens of hell, whipped by a thousand lashes, my nerves plead for mercy. I wiggle my feet out of the shoes and audibly sigh.

I get back into them to leave for my next class

and walk right into a circle of people in the middle of the hall. My gut instincts say that something isn't right.

And something really isn't.

Annalynn and Les are surrounded by a group of people who are gently goading a fight just by being there. Les likes an audience. Annalynn doesn't and she's trying to back away, but keeps knocking into people that are slowly pushing in. I shove my way through to her.

"Oh, so there's two bitches for me in this school. And here I was happy to just have one." Les says.

"Neither of us a count as such." I say and grab Annalynn by the elbow and start pulling her towards the edge of the crowd. It parts to reveal, to my dismay, lockers.

Annalynn has always made be braver (or stupider, pick one) than I would be on my own and so I turn, flip my hair at Les and saunter over to him making sure that my hips sway.

"On second thought...so, you want a bitch at this school?" I attempt to purr.

"Kiss him, Foster!" Someone shouts and the crowd picks it up like chant. They may not like me or Annalynn but they despise Les. Everyone does.

I wrap a hand harshly around his wrist and pull him around by his waist up against the lockers and zero in, as if fascinated by the idea the crowd is so eagerly singing.

And then I ferociously bash his head with my own right into the lockers.

He reels, and attempts to deliver a knee to my crotch, but only succeeds in smashing my thigh so hard that I land ungracefully and my cotton boxer-briefs are revealed to all the world.

"You're sick and gay, Foster." He wipes his lips as though I had kissed him, and since the crowd didn't see much behind my puffy hair, they probably think that I did.

People disperse, and the rest of the day is uneventful, if I discount the stares and whispering. Which I do, it's only par for the course. I think maybe it will end next semester.

Chapter Fifteen

Nope. It doesn't stop, it only gets more disgusting.

Attending public school, it's impossible not to have some knowledge of sex, pornography, and masturbation by eighth grade. And also, attending gym class with Josh 'the Rocket' Clevenger, it's impossible to escape a working knowledge of these things either.

I know, I've tried.

Vacuums and cantaloupes will never seem the innocent objects they really are again.

With Josh, everything somehow is girls, how to get them, how to lay them, and when they aren't around, how to simulate them... or just get off. And with Josh, every class that I share with him is somehow about girls, pornography and masturbation. Which is every class except for Advanced English. But gym, in the locker room, is where his incredible 'knowledge' truly shines.

This is the only class that Les Shopenhauer and I have shared a willing (if silent) alliance. We hide from Josh, and he in turn, torments us. Later today, Les will make Annalynn and I a paired target in English, but right now, he and I both hiding in the shower stalls where we change.

"Hey Rocket, did your brother drop off the new titties last night?" Someone asks.

"Oh yeah! This week's centerfold is so awesome, she has nice jugs, really nice jugs. Not so big they look stupid, but still, you can imagine how soft they are. She totally makes up for every frigid spike that goes through my dick when I see that Spencer girl."

Cranial smoke escapes my head. I think about bounding out there, but the last time I defended Annalynn, I ended up making things worse when they decided to speculate on what goods she must have in order to command my loyalty.

Josh continues his showboating with; "Anyway.... So I get the magazine yeah? And I think, 'it's time to pump it up 'cause this girl is worth more than a usual game of choke the chicken'. Anyway, what I did is..."[9] and he begins a loud conspiratorial whisper that I don't quite make out as my shirt goes over my head.

I try to leave last, or nearly last, but today Mr. Rocket is behind and when I shimmy out from behind the curtains, he instantly latches onto a dirty thought. "You hiding in the bathroom, Mary?" He asks.... "Got some troubles to wank out?"

I look at him with an expression that clearly explains my positioning of him on the human totem pole —he's underneath the dirt in which the wood is buried.

"Hey! I bet just the mere thought of the Spencer bitch's boobs had you raging for a couple up and downs..." He taunts. "Course, you know, most people use her image to wilt a hard-on instead of pumping it up." He pauses. When I don't rise to it he comes up with the next gem. "She looks just like a faggot boy... like you. Guess you imagine shoving it up her boy—"

"Foster, Clevenger! You are late. Get your butts out here and give me twenty." Our ex-marine

---

9   Annalynn told me that this ongoing obsession positively identifies him as a minute man with an angry two-incher.

basketball coach turned P.E. teacher screams at us.[10]

Twenty push ups is an unusually welcome distraction from the anger. But it gives me time to think.

While I don't know what it is I feel in my mind and body when I really pause to think about or look at Annalynn, I do have a growing feeling that my penis's morning desire for *something*— Annalynn related or not— isn't going to go away nor will the results of it getting what it wants without my permission be pleasing.

But the alternative just sounds so exceptionally gross.

I put it out of mind momentarily like I've been doing for a few years.
My parents leave for a night out and I decide that it's high time for me to get over things.

"It's supposed to be healthy." I comment to myself as I draw a nice hot bath.

I slide into the bath and sort of wait for inspiration. Or an erection; either would make this whole process a lot easier.

Ten minutes later I discover that simply wanting either doesn't make assured their arrival. Perhaps just laying here is not the path to nirvana. I try and remember what seems to usually trigger things and I pull a blank until I remember the incident with my own lips.

Yep, that seems to be a step in the right direction. As I trace them, my body begins to change into a different state. All of my hair stands up and

---

10 Are all gym teachers ex-marines with a beer gut?

my nipples perk up as does the object of my
attention.

It all seems frightening for a second. And
sitting in the hot bath, I suddenly feel a little chilly.

Maybe I won't just zero in on the target.

And then I give up about twenty minutes later
when I've accomplished nothing.

I get out of the bath and do something I rather
suspect I ought not do.

My father thinks he's hidden his smallish
collection of not-quite pornographic materials well,
but he honestly underestimated my curiosity. I know
he no longer looks at them, as the pages are yellowed
and they are dusty, but they are his, and there is
just something about this which makes me giggle
nervously when I dig them up.

To my dismay it's mostly blond women with
unrealistic bodies I can't relate to, too much makeup
doing things to themselves that seem unappealing. I
was hoping for a flirty pin up, maybe. I flip a few
more pages and view a few more blondes and
suspect that if it weren't for my mother, my father's
taste would suck completely. Then I stumble upon
an artfully done spread of a flirtatious brunette
wearing period lingerie and playing around with
antique sexual devices.

I pick up another magazine and sure enough,
among the blonds doing typically trashy things, there
is another artfully done spread, this time a redhead
in increasingly less of her latex gothic outfit, playing
in a jungle gym of wrought iron and chains
decorated heavily with candles of all sizes. I dog ear
the page of the layout. Something about it makes me
feel the same way running my hands over my lips

does.

I pick up another one.

The magazine practically falls open to a two page spread of a man in the most gorgeous metal work I have seen.[11] I find the picture very appealing. To his expression of pure bliss and happy contentment I connect completely. I can imagine the feel of the chains, the feel of the cold metal and the warm metal. I can imagine the bars of the rack digging into my back, spine... all over my body. I want whatever he's having, and soon if possible.

I suddenly understand what it is to be turned on.

The sensation is too much.

I slam the magazines closed and shove them back where they belong.

Then I call Annalynn.

We go to the park and drift on the swings.

"How are your parents doing?" She asks me, probably guessing at what is bugging me, and it's not a bad guess.

"They're okay. I think the couples' counseling thing is actually accomplishing something. It's been a while and he hasn't left or done anything unforgivable. That's not really to say that he's more connected to us, though. Sometimes I feel like the house is just another stopover for the Ted train. I think it's better for Mom, but I still feel stupid talking to him."

"Why bother then?"

---

11 When I think about it later, I tell myself that my father was merely admiring the metal work, or possibly copying some of it for one reason or another. Bisexuality and other answers didn't occur to me until after I knew the truth.

I want to say that she's got a point. But the truth is a lot different. "Not like there's anything wrong with talking with you or my Mom on account of your plumbing, but there are a lot of things I could talk to him about and it would be a whole lot less embarrassing. And it would be nice to talk to someone who isn't working on theoretical knowledge."

"Or lying."

"Hmm?"

"Josh the Rocket comes to mind. I'm pretty sure things don't work the way he says they do."

"If only it were that easy." I grouch.

Annalynn looks at me and stares. "What?" She asks sharply.

I just realise how this might have been taken. "No, I don't want girls to be easy. That has nothing to do with it."

"Good!"

I flounder for a few more minutes.

She hangs her head upside down and stares at me. "So... what you want to be easy is dealing with puberty and weird urges and sensations? Like it seems for him."

"Precisely."

"It's not easy. Haven't you noticed that he's only acting?"

"How can you say all that teasing he dishes out is only acting?" I ask.

"I didn't say that the teasing was any less obnoxious because it's all an act." She corrects and then rights herself. "He's acting, if he was really comfortable with his body and his size and performance and everything, he wouldn't try so hard to convince everyone."

She's right.

"Okay, that's great and all, but it doesn't really fix that I'd like to talk to someone who doesn't only have a theoretical knowledge of what I'm experiencing."

"Look, you and me share like 99.8% of our genes or something like that, we've got to be more similar than different. We're also about the same age, so whatever you're experiencing can't be that different." She says.

I blush horribly.

She looks at me thoughtfully.

Tomatoes are pale in comparison.

"This is about sex, isn't it?" She says, and it sounds accusing.

"Not exactly." I love the way my voice cracks at odd times. I curl up in the swing, sideways. Quite the trick at my size.

She laughs.

"It's not funny, Annalynn."

"You calling me up to come talk to you about something I can't possibly help with because you want to talk to a guy is hilarious, Em."

"That's not what I said." I argue. "I said it would be nice to be able to talk to my father, and that while my mother seems to be able to do that more easily these days, counseling doesn't seem to be doing much good between him and me."

"And the reason you care is because talking to women about your body isn't something you are up for."

"Right, uhm, something like that."

"I'm on the rag." She says.

"I beg your pardon?" I say.

"I'm on the rag, my breasts hurt like I caught them in a bear trap. Between the cramps and the gas, I don't feel like eating. Not exactly a vixen here. Two weeks from now, I'll get gooey just thinking about the way you smell because my body is convinced there is value in producing a baby as soon as biologically possible."

Annalynn has just sprouted horns, wings and a tail.

"Seriously, hormones are a cosmic joke, and our bodies don't handle them all that well. And society, well, society tells us everything we feel is either imaginary or immoral."

I'm not having this conversation with Annalynn.

"Men get the worst end of the stick I think.... Half-naked women all over town on billboards, in the advertisements, and the real thing downtown because it's hotter than 55 degrees and the fashionables must show their fake-baked bodies to everyone. All I have to contend with is you."

I guess I *am* having this conversation with Annalynn.

She looks at me pointedly.

"I've honestly never given much thought to the billboards or the advertisements and I think the fake-bake look is bad." I say.

Another lengthy pause passes by.

"And what do you mean you have me to contend with?"

She looks at her fingers. "I was nice and honest, your turn!"

"Oh. Well, I'm not on the rag. I don't have gas,

and I don't have bear traps on my chest." I stop and stare at the wood chips of the playground. "See.... I don't think you can really identify to me, and I can't really identify to you."

We swing in silence for a while.

"Actually, Anna.... It's not what I'm experiencing biologically so much." I say. "It's this new set of desires that itch and I don't know how to scratch them, or even if it's a good idea."

She looks perplexed and continues swinging for a bit.

"Sometimes, I wonder what your skin feels like, and what you look like underneath it all." She says. "It took me forever to put that together from the sensations and thoughts. I don't know much beyond that I think it's worth finding out what itches and how to scratch it. I haven't even considered the moral merits of scratching yet." She says and I think it took some effort.

I try to be equally brave. "I know what is itching, I think I know how to scratch it. I'm worried about the moral merits now."

Good silence, thinking silence, sits between us.

"Probably, if no one else is impacted in the scratching, it's okay to scratch." She finally says.

"You mean negatively impacted, or just impacted?"

"Just impacted. People our age don't need to be doing stupid things that lead to other stupid things. We don't know where the line is."

"Are you sure?"

"You know how you said I was beautiful last summer?" She asks, as she settles herself upside down again.

"Yes."

"Do you still think so?"

"Yes. I do." I reply.

"It tugs at some place inside me I don't understand yet. But, I know a lot of things are yours for the asking since you think so." She says. "If I think on it. It's not quite right for it to be that way. Because not everything is in place, and so the line isn't there. So it isn't there to cross in our minds. You see the problem?"

"I think so. If we can't see it, that doesn't mean it isn't there. Which means we can cross it too easily and up in some place we weren't intending or wanting to go."

"Yep."

I walk her back home. For the longest time I've been giving her these awkward little hugs when we part, though not often at school. I almost give her one, and then instead I sit down on their porch swing and pat the cushion next to me.

"What I don't get is, some things that do impact others carry no social stigma, but other things that don't impact others have a great deal." I say.

"Arbitrary ethics." She replies. "Just arbitrary rules and regulations. They don't apply if you are trying to be logical."

"My hormones are not trying to be logical. In fact, I think their job is defined by irrationality."

"Amen." She says.

"What if, logically, I know where my own line is, and I'm fairly certain it's more conservative than society's line?"

"I still don't think it's a great idea." She shakes

her head. "We can too easily walk a straight and uninhibited path to hell as teenagers. The only way is to avoid taking even one wrong step."

"Hell is kind of arbitrary, isn't it?"

"Hell is just a place holder to indicate a place you don't want to be." She says.

"Ah, all right then."

She looks at me, and I look at her.

I do not give her an awkward hug. That might just be a step towards hell given the things we've just spoken about.

"Good night. I'll see you tomorrow."

I go home and have a nice scratch that doesn't impact anyone else.

Chapter Sixteen

Mom decided that this summer since I'm going to be a freshman in high school I need to work.

Sooooo.... she puts me in charge of the most problematic building she owns and tells me to keep an eye on it.

In between keeping the plumbing working, I slowly make repairs and try to keep ahead of the usual perils of sketchy renters. Most of them tend to fly by night and, true to form, in July some of 'my' renters leave without paying their rent or cleaning the apartment. It isn't trashed per se, but it is a pretty big job. Annalynn graciously offers to help me on Saturday.

I feel like a vulture as we go through the things they left behind. Some of it must be fairly intimate, and some of it worth money. We sort it out. I can probably get a couple hundred from the sale of the television, stereo and bike. Maybe another hundred for the CD's. I'm not sure what I do about the pile of jewelry, some of which must be stolen.

"Hey Emelle... what do you think this is?" Annalynn shoves a locked box towards me as we clean out the bedroom closet.

The lock is a cheapo combination lock which we pry off pretty quickly.

Inexpensive leather goods spill out. It dawns on us separately, but mostly at the same time that these are *sex toys*.

"ACK!' We both say at precisely the same minute.

The stuff gets shoved back in the box and we throw it back in the closet.

"Uh, what are we going to do with that?" She

asks.

"Well, I promise we can't donate it to goodwill or sell it." I say.

She drags it back into the middle of the room. "I dunno, there might be something worth some money in there." She says as she pops it open with her shoe.

It's all cheap leather or inexpensive plastics. Nothing worth saving for anything but a few pieces that might make good costumes. That being what Annalynn likes and takes with her, since Halloween will come around again and she is intent on topping last year's whore costumes (I don't know how.)

"What do you think this is for?" I jest as I pick up an obviously phallic object.

"Oh, I dunno," she replies as she rolls her eyes. 'What do you think this was for?" She holds up a pair of leopard-print fuzzy handcuffs.

"Child discipline device, like, duh." I affect valley-girl speech for the delivery.

"Gee I hope this wasn't." She says as she throws a cheap wooden paddle into the trash.

A rubber duck that vibrates, seven leather handcuffs (but only two matching pairs), a pony bridle and some dog collars go in the trash too, and then I give Annalynn the box to put the leather corset, harness-like thing and lace-up vambraces in so she take them home without stares.

"Dog toys?" I ask when we dig those out of the same closet.

"Woof." Annalynn replies while batting her eyelashes and then deepens her voice "let me be your puppy tonight, dear."

We laugh about the box over the Chinese food

we have delivered for lunch and then get back to work. The sooner we can clean the apartment, the sooner I can rent it again, and the sooner I make money.

That night, before we go home, I give Annalynn a quarter the pawn value for her help and give the rest of it to my mother later. It totals well over three-hundred dollars after I get rid of the jewelry.

"I wonder why they didn't take it with them." My mother says as I hand her the check.

"I'm thinking it wasn't exactly theirs to begin with and they might have forgotten that they had stashed it in the closet." I reply.

"Well, whatever, that pays about half the bill they still owe." She writes me a check for one-hundred dollars. "Look, good work, here's some of the share. You deserve it." She goes back to work.

I go into the kitchen and start a salad for dinner. My father joins me as I'm almost done tossing greens. He starts some burgers.

"So, how was it? Your Mom said the pawn value nearly covered the bill they left behind."

"Yeah, I wasn't expecting a pile of real gold."

"You'll find the strangest things in apartments. When you were little, I helped your mom take out over 200 pairs of shoes from one apartment. Most of them hadn't even been worn. This other apartment was a taxidermists nightmare, I think there were over fifty species represented in the collection and every last one of them was moth-eaten."

He pauses.

"Uhm, we found a box of sex toys." I say.

"What?" He says.

"Well, I should say we found some booty in a

pirate chest, actually." I say, remembering the way the box was made to resemble an old-fashioned sea-chest.

He laughs. "You win. Not even the fridge with one hundred pounds of mostly rotten Chinese takeout can top that."

"One hundred pounds of rotten Chinese takeout?" I ask.

"Yeah, a twenty-something had rented the apartment and he died really suddenly. He ate nothing but Chinese takeout as far as I could tell. He smoked like a fiend, too, I think we found four unopened cartons, not packs, of cigarettes. His neighbors said he suffered from a case of very fast living."

"How did he die?"

"An accident involving a retro Vespa scooter with bad brakes."

"Wow."

"His brother wasn't very upset. I remember that now. Said these sort of things happened all the time. Weirdest thing I've ever heard— how many times can you die?"

"Maybe all the artificial preservatives in the takeout were keeping him alive?"

"Maybe." He replies as he puts the burgers out on the table and gestures for me to sit down.

"Isn't Mom going to eat with us?"

"No, she's busy."

"Oh."

The conversation stops cold and I suddenly have no appetite after I think about what I ate for lunch.

"You going to eat that?"

"I don't think so...."

"Why not?"

"I had a Chinese food for lunch. Now I'm thinking about a hundred pounds of rotten stuff churning around in there." I say. "And sex toys. Ugh."

"Hmm. More for me!" He says happily and takes the burger off my plate and plops it on his own.

"Why is it all about sex?" I grumble.

"At your age? Because it is."

"Ragingly brilliant philosophy."

"No, just the truth." He says and then takes a big bite out of my burger.

Chapter Seventeen

I am immediately suspicious when I come down Christmas morning and the house is bulging with gifts. Santa packed heavy this year and so did Mr. Tree. Well, for me. There is only one, small package under the tree for my mother from my father. It is professionally wrapped.

This is foreboding.

She opens it and squeals.

I wonder if the sound will somehow cause a massive coronary in the sperm donor.

It doesn't.

He grins stupidly and so does she.

"Well, don't you want to see it, Emelle?" Mom asks.

Not really. "Sure." I say.

It's big. It's sparkly. It's a ring.

"This is just what I wanted. This is the best Christmas ever." My mother says sweetly and pecks my father on the lips.

"This is just what I wanted." I mimic. "Actually, Annalynn, this is the worst Christmas ever." I say when she comes over.

"Haul, buddy, haul." She says and gestures to my stuff.

Under any other circumstances, I'd be insanely happy. The handmade leather dragon is awesome and carefully designed to perch realistically on a number of things. I needed new running shoes for track team tryouts in the spring, and the stereo headphones are frankly, top notch.

"But.... I don't want to be bought off!"

"I wish my parents liked bribery." She snarks.

My indignation deflates. Her parents have been in a state of flux for the last six months, and they aren't really paying much attention to Annalynn. They spend money but it's not thoughtfully spent at all. I sigh and get her gift.

It isn't a brilliant leather dragon, or a devious iron puzzle. It was a silly idea that was not superseded by anything better.

She rips off the paper with zest and pulls out five Bristol boards of full-color comic action scenes featuring herself as various Amazon Queen type action heroes. "Uhm, it's dumb." I say.

She stares down at them. "No, I like them. A lot."

"Really?"

"I like my hair like that." She says and uses her fingers to make a facsimile of the art. "I didn't know it, but it's just what I wanted."

Chapter Eighteen

"What the hell?!" I squawk at Annalynn. "My parents got married and they didn't invite me? My mother's excuse was, "but sweetie, no one was there but us, the judge and the county witnesses.' They eloped!"

"It was over in eight minutes. What was there to see?" Annalynn asks me.

"My parents got married.... Hitched....tied the knot.... Sealed the deal! It's sort of important, you know?"

"They got married in jeans, for Christ-sake. Don't hemorrhage over it."

"But they got married without me there." I whine.

"Look, if it had been a church wedding with the whole shebang and best man and dresses and crap, sure: I think you'd have room to bitch. But honestly, shut up. It was jeans and nice sweaters and over in no time flat. There is nothing you missed."

"Well it's very nice that you can be pragmatic about this, but I think I should have been there."

"Honestly, Em, I wouldn't have let you be there if I were your parents either. You know that part in the middle about how anyone that wants to contest the marriage may do so then or hold his peace?"

"Yeah?"

"That ceremony would have taken six hours if you were allowed to testify against it. You never hold your peace."

I have just been owned.

"I don't think you get it." I counter.

"Well, probably not, but I mean, calling me on

the phone while I'm vegging in front of the television and doing my toenails so you can spit nails about your parents doesn't really incline me towards 'getting it' either." She says.

"I still think I ought to have been there."

"You'll be around for the marriage itself. That should be the higher of the two compliments anyway."

"You mean worse of two tortures."

"Oh now, come on." She says.

"Now we're stuck with him."

"Oh, like that wasn't obvious ages ago."

"I could at least pretend!"

"We're teenagers. Make-believing things away has therefore been passé for a while."

Touché.

I groan into the phone.

"Don't give me that. Or..." Her voice peters off.

"Or what?"

"I'll hang up, and I won't answer again, and you'll have to go back downstairs and deal with the newlyweds."

"I'd stay in my room. Really I would."

"Given that it's steak dinner tonight? Ha ha, I don't believe you. You'd hold out for three seconds past your Mom calling dinner."

She's right, and I know she's right.

"Do you have any sympathy?" I ask.

"Not really."

"Fine. You win. I didn't need to be there, and I'll shut up about it."

"Cool. I thought you would. So, you are going to bring leftovers over here after dinner?"

"Are you home alone tonight too?" That's three

nights in a row... I don't know what has gotten into her mother....

"Yeah..."

"Well, why don't you come over and celebrate with us?"

"Cause it's your family and I'd feel weird."

"Oh. Okay."

"See you later."

"Yep, bye then."

Chapter Nineteen

It's spring again. I know this because I'm spending a lot of time dressed in skintight long-underwear, trainers, and short shorts. Track is so very stylish. Today I'm dressed in blue camouflage waffle-weave long underwear and orange running shorts and jacket. My hair is a very tight braid—the kind my mother calls a hairdresser's facelift.

"Did you get dressed in the dark, Foster?" Coach Joan asks, but in a friendly way.

Actually. Yes. "Yesum."

"Smashing ensemble."

"Thank you. I made the shorts and jacket."

"You picked that color?"

"It's visible at night." I say as I reach for my toes.

"So is gold lame." She replies.

"That's next week, Coach."

"Don't you dare, Foster. I will not have that coming up on my review."

"Don't put ideas in my head then." I reply.

Coach Joan is pretty good-natured about the mouthy sarcastic misfits she inherited from Coach Earl, which is good; none of us are keen to change.

Annalynn stretches next to me. I attempt to ignore the view.

Mmmmmm. Legs.

I yank my eyes away.

"So, how many miles do you think Coach will have us run today?"

"Dunno. The course is about seven, isn't it?"

"Is she going to make us run Bloomsday again?" Annalynn grumbles.

"Yes, you WILL be running Bloomsday again."

Our dear coach rests eyes on the team as she proclaims our fate.

"Do. Not. Want." Sean mutters next to me. He's our sprinter.

"All right. That's enough lollygagging." Coach Joan sucks in a breath and gives us a loud two-fingered whistle. "Ten laps—from everybody."

I lope. It's the running equivalent of ambling.

Coach Joan comes up to my side. "I know you can run faster."

I speed up a smidge.

"All right you. Hurdles." She points to them.

"But but but."

"No buts."

Annalynn snickers.

"Hush you." I say, before veering off to the hurdles.

Halfway through practice Annalynn and I are doing the bleachers. Which I hate.

"Annalynn. Where are your parents again?" Both our parents are out of town. Mine for a convention, and I'm not sure what's going on with hers. Besides, conversation is the perfect excuse to slow down some.

"Las Vegas." She puffs.

"Why?"

"Dunno...they want to be?"

"Why are they gone so much now?"

"I guess they think I'm old enough to watch after myself now and then."

Now and then? It seems like every other weekend to me. "It just seems uncareful."

"It's not so weird; it's just that your parents practically never leave the house. Mine only seem weird by comparison." She says in a sophisticated tone.

I am tempted to argue, but Annalynn's parents have become something of a touchy topic lately. Instead I ask her how long they are out of town.

"At least another three days." She says and smiles as she cuts me off on the next stair.

Something is bound to happen tonight, because it's too good an opportunity to miss.

"You want to watch movies and eat popcorn tonight?"

"Where?"

"My place." I say.

"That sounds good. But."

"But what?"

"I get the first bath in your Mom's claw foot tub. You keep telling me how amazing a soak is after practice, now I get to find out."

I make a show about whining about how it's my house and so I should get the bath first, but I don't mean it.

When she gets out of the tub, I take a really quick shower instead of my usual luxurious soak because I know that if I don't chime in on the movie, we will end up watching something like M. Night Shyamalan.

"Night Gallery, actually." Annalynn says. "It's on Sci-Fi."

"But it gives me nightmares."

"So draw stuff or ignore it like you always do."

I run grab my rickety easel and art supplies while she makes popcorn.

We settle into our comfortable, typical

positions. She loves horror films, suspense fiction, mysteries and knitting. After her grandmother taught her to knit and crochet, it became de rigueur to find Annalynn chowing down on popcorn, watching the most hair-raising film you can imagine while clicking needles together at the speed of light. Me, I hide behind the couch pillows with my eyes shut while thinking of happy places. Or, more likely, I draw her, occasionally in fantastic outfits which she certainly doesn't own.

Tonight, I draw her and she shovels popcorn in her mouth like it's coal into a steam engine while paying close attention to the television I'm so adamantly tuning out.

I start with her head and then try to draw her in a form-fitting super-suit. She pauses the movie and looks over. "I wish I looked like her, but seriously, I don't look a thing like that." She says.

"What should I change?"

"Uhm, everything. My legs are stickier, my arms are stickier, I have slightly more boob than that, and a lot smaller feet. And uh, my stomach pooches out." I dutifully erase the entirety of the body portion and attempt to redo her with the alterations as requested. I don't see it, at all, and finally just rip up the drawing when the erasure marks overwhelm the work.

"What was that for?" Annalynn asks.

"I'm not seeing it." I reply. "Maybe if you were in different clothes. But not while you are wearing something that leaves a lot to my imagination." I say, trying to take the edge off by being funny.

"You seriously can't imagine what I look like?"

"Not really, I guess. You look to me in my mind

118

like what I drew first."

She switches the television off.

"Bring your stuff." She says and then gallops up the stairs.

I come into my room and Annalynn is standing in the middle of the room stripping off her shirt. My eyes bug out.

She flashes me a smile.

Off comes the bra, the jeans, and the underwear. She stands in front of me and throws her arms out like da Vinci's Vitruvian Man. "This is what I look like."

I try to process. My brain fails me and I end up looking at the bones of her feet and ankles.

"You can look up, you know."

I drag my eyes up her legs, which are nicely toned from track, whiz by her nether regions and try to not spend over-long ogling her breasts. I finally look her in the face, and I think from her smirk I look dazed.

"Can I draw you, like this?"

"You mean, naked?"

"Well, artists call it 'in the nude.'" I reply.

I drag my leather bean bag over to her and set up my easel. "Just sit down as if you were wearing clothes." I say. She tries, but it takes on far too much a cheesecake feel. "Really! Relax." I say again.

"I don't think I can." She says, and rolls over on the beanbag, resting her chin on her overlapped hands.

"Funny, you just did. Hold that pose." I begin to sketch, and the blood flows out of my pants, and back to my brains. I fill in the sketch and ask her to move to the bed. "I want one of you stretched out like a cat."

She smiles obligingly and slithers over to the bed from the bean bag.

I sketch her twice more, and then begin to clean up my art supplies.

"You could get dressed, if you wanted." I say, feeling awkward as I do.

She looks up at me. "Am I still beautiful?"

"More so than I imagined." I say before I look.

There is a long pause and all the things I think to say get lost on the way to my mouth. When I draw, everything is lines, light, and shadow. Now I'm looking at her through my normal eyes and I'm having some decidedly lascivious thoughts.

"Are you?" She asks.

"Am I what?"

"Beautiful."

"I don't know, I don't think I can say." I reply.

"Let me, then?"

I peel my shirt up over my head. "I'm not so sure about this."

She just stares at me until I obligingly remove my jeans and with no small act of bravado struggle out of my underwear. Instead of offering myself up like the Vitruvian Man, I curl up on the stool in front of the easel uncomfortably. She gets up out of bed and goads me to stand up for her.
She looks over me for what seems an eternity. I focus on nothing over her shoulder.

"Can I touch you?"

I nod and a nervous sweat surfaces. I wonder how she managed to be so composed.

She's very tentative, a brush of fingertips over my shoulder and another across my chest. She runs a hand down my arm and I shiver.

"You can relax, you know."

"I'm trying!" I squeak.

She turns one hand over and rests her cheek against my palm. It's cool and soft. She then lets it go and grips my hand as she runs her other fingers over my abdomen. Suddenly, she drops down and snuffles my navel and I jump back.

"You're twitchy." She says.

"Annalynn, what are we doing?" I ask, saying the words too quickly to hide my fear.

"I'm not sure." She says.

I let go of her hand and perch like a gargoyle on my stool. "I'm in over my head."

Annalynn looks disappointed. "I didn't mean to do anything..."

"I'm terrified, that's a good indicator that we shouldn't be doing this." The nervous sweat rolls over my skin in a wave. "I'm sorry."

"No, no... it's okay. Should I go?" She asks.

"I don't know."

She dresses quickly and then hands me my clothes. I slide back into them, and feel terribly guilty for having disappointed her.

"I don't even really look at myself much in the mirror." I say. "I'm not comfortable in my own skin like you are."

She's busy wiggling back into her socks. "You really are beautiful though." I repeat.
"Emelle?"

"Yes?"

"It's okay. You don't have to be perfect."

"I don't?"

"No, you don't have to be perfect. I wasn't

really sure what was going on anyway, so it's probably best we stopped." She says, but she still sounds disappointed as she slides on her shoes. I know that I don't want her to leave, but I'm not really sure how to handle the awkwardness if she stayed. Everyone is an untalented beginner sometime in their life, I remind myself.

"I think of you that way, sometimes." I say, risking complete and utter humiliation. She looks up from her shoes. "I like the idea of it, when I imagine it. But it's always some time in the future. It's so much less scary at a distance. You're beautiful and I think of you from time to time— well, often really— as someone for...." The air goes out of my mental lifeboat.

"Someone for?" she prompts.

Words swirl through my head. They all sound crass suddenly.

"That kind of pleasure." I whisper.

Time slows to the pace of a dawdling snail.

"I feel less guilty then." She says. "For thinking of you the same way."

"Do you? Really?" I ask.

"Sometimes. But it is always the future, never now."

We consider each other as though in trances.

"Stay." I finally say.

"Where?" She lets out a nervous laugh.

"By me. Tonight."

"Why?"

"I'm not ready for so many things, but I'm ready for a taste."

We curl up facing each other in my double bed.

It seems huge, it seems tiny. Eons of time pass in between each tick of the second hand on my wall-clock. Darkness mixed with moonlight has enchanted us and the moment, and emboldened me. I reach up and run the back of my fingers down her face and neck.

She smiles, and it is deeply reassuring, so I slip my hands over her cotton-clad body. She's particularly cute in my pajamas. Affectionate strokes pass between us and we slide out of our shirts and press up against each other gently. Her fingers play down my back, and I return the gesture. Stomachs rub in slow circles. It's warm and comfortable, not stark and cold like being naked on my stool. Annalynn entangles our legs and begins to rock us back and forth a little bit and then a bit more firmly.

I relax into the motion and am rather startled when she gasps sharply.

Pinched skin, squwooshed finger? "Are you okay?"

Her face is flushed and I can feel her pulse against my own.

Oh.

Wow.

"I'm fine." She says in the time it takes me to figure out I'm being dumb.

"I just realized that." I whisper as I untangle our legs and roll onto my back.

She rests uneasily on her side. "Are you...?"

Oh goody! It's her turn to be at a loss for words.

"I'm fine, I'm satisfied." I say to answer her question.

We pull our shirts back on and curl up facing

each other again. I reach out for her hands and sandwich them between my own.

"Good night." We whisper.

Chapter Twenty

I wake up, as I often do, at five-thirty. The sun peeks at me from in-between the trees that shade the backyard and the breeze is chilly through my open windows. Annalynn is still in deep slumber beside me.

Today is the first day of the rest of my life, and things are looking perfect.

I am struck by sudden brilliance and slide out of bed to draw Annalynn as she sleeps. Wishing I could better capture the sense of what the picture feels like, I sketch the drape of the silk cotton voile from the shirt she borrowed from me and the washed-to-softness cotton of the heirloom quilt, but the picture hardly does the textures justice. But then, I think that it will be a long time before looking at this sketch doesn't remind me sharply of them.

She sighs and rolls over onto her back and flings an arm over her head. The shirt twists, becoming nearly skintight. I pick up a pen and draw the hollow of her throat, the line of jaw. One smooth foot peeking out from the covers. Perfect eyelashes that call attention to her cheek bones.
I stop drawing to watch her breathe, but then finish what I was working on and crawl back into bed. No point in starting the first day of the rest of my life too quickly.

We get up, we do normal things and with every hour that slips by after dinner, we both wonder silently if we should spend the night together again. Her parents will not be home for another five days, and mine will not be home for another three. That leaves tonight, tomorrow, and the night after for this

to be a live choice and legitimate question. Or we can slam the door shut right now.
Ten-thirty slides by on the clock.

"Not exactly keen on getting home, are you?" I say.

"Not exactly keen on getting me home, are you?" She replies without looking up from her book.

Uhm. Ack. She's got me. "Nope." I say.

"What are we up to?"

"Not quite four years of best-friendship." I say.

"Really, it seems longer. In a good way. But, seriously now..."

I consider the question carefully. "I don't know. Probably nothing our classmates haven't long since blown past and checked off their lists."

"Uhm, they've probably blown past *everything*."

"Tab E isn't going anywhere near slot A." I say.

She looks at me like she's about to ask me what I mean and then she gets it. "Uh, no, of course not. Not a good idea."

"You don't sound convinced." I say, because she doesn't.

"It's hard to explain. No, I don't think it's a good idea." She says more firmly.

"Curiosity, a good way to get into a lot of trouble very quickly?" I say.

"Something like that."

Laying in bed staring at the ceiling after we've crawled in, I think about both what I do want, and what I don't want, and try to temper the two with each other.

"What are you thinking?" she asks.

"Stuff. A lot of stuff. Trying to decide what, if anything, I want to do."

She nudges my foot with her foot.

I nudge her back.

She nudges me twice.

I nudge back three times.

A small foot war ensues.

"This isn't quite what I was thinking." I say as she grabs my ankle with both feet in something akin to a death grip.

"What were you thinking?"

I want to tell her that I love her but it gets lost in my throat.

"I'm not sure."

She slides an arm over my midsection and toys with the hem of my shirt.

I stay her hand by covering it with one of my own.

"I'm sorry," I whisper to her. "I'm not in the mood at the moment."

"That's okay… I'm feeling awkward anyway." Annalynn confesses.

We roll into an affectionate blob of bodies and fall asleep.

Thunder rolls across the house in the early morning.

A crack of lightening wakes Annalynn.

I don't know if it rains like this anywhere but in Spokane; lightening cracks and you hear the clouds open and you can see the rain coming down before it hits, like a thousand needles from heaven. The heat breaks and cold rolls over as though old man winter doesn't accept the sovereignty of summer.

I love it.

I see it as another proof of divinity.

Annalynn looks searchingly at me.

"Mana from heaven. Needles from heaven." I say to her.

"Hmmm?"

"In the winter time, when the hoar frost on the mountain shines in the coldest air and sunlight, it looks like mana from heaven. In the summertime, the clouds open up and the rain comes down like needles from heaven."

"And?"

"It makes me believe that there are divine things in the world."

There is a long pause.

"You make me think that." Annalynn says.

"Are you serious?" I ask.

"Yes." She says.

"Why?"

"After we moved here, I prayed every night for friends. To every saint I could think of. And then I gave up when I ran out of names. A few weeks later I simply prayed to the powers-that-be as opposed to the catholic god. The next day, you asked me to stop for cider."

"Really?" I say.

"Yep."

"I never knew that."

"That's because it sounds really strange and I've never had the guts to say anything about it before."

I want to say so much, but it gets lost in my throat just like it did before.

I get up and walk to one of my windows. "Mother certainly is good to us. I think that means that she doesn't mind."

"Mother?"

"The South Hill. She's a hill spirit, so says Mom. She feels happy." I open the screen and stick my hand out into the raindrops.

"You think the hill is a god?"

"No, I think there is something that inhabits the hill that is not like us, but has influence on us, and we influence her. Think of her as an avatar of Mother Nature, I suppose."

"And you think she sent you to me?"

"If she sends needles and mana from heaven, why not?"

Annalynn nods. "And you think that she's all right with us doing...." She looks perplexed.

"...being more than friends." I finish. "More than all right, I think she's happy."

Chapter Twenty-One

Two more nights pass in motivated snuggling, and then we hide the evidence, stashing the pictures behind a heap of things in my closet and changing and laundering the sheets lest somehow, parents are equipped with something worse than a 'guilty' or 'lying' detector.

Not that, precisely, I'm guilty of anything. They didn't specifically tell me I couldn't have Annalynn spend the night. They told me to be good, and not do anything stupid.

"Well, this certainly doesn't count as bad. I'm not sure what their take on stupid would be though." Annalynn offers.
"What about you?"

"I could walk in covered in bite marks and wearing nothing but lingerie and a satin robe – my parents wouldn't notice."

"Oh now come on, I know they ignore you enough, but it's not quite that bad."

"Yeah, it is."

"Really?"

"Yes, really."

"Annalynn.... Why? It seems all of a sudden that they've gotten so negligent. I mean, your mom chased you around the house for an hour trying to make you wear normal hose with that hooker costume, and then, bang, they start ignoring you."

"You know how my mom yo-yo diets?"

"Yeah." I say.

"She's basically overly concerned with appearances. She was concerned when I didn't have friends, she was concerned when I started hanging out with you because you aren't our class, I guess.

She was concerned that people would think I really was a hooker. Even if it was Halloween. Before it was apparent I could manage on my own, I was a handy way to give her the appearance of concerned Mom. It's all appearance, like dance..."

"I thought you liked dance?" I say.

"Until I realized that the only reason I was dancing was because her co-workers kid danced and the co-worker felt it was the only kind of refinement to be had in our town. When we moved, and she wasn't so concerned about appearing refined, that was the end of dance."

"That's nice and repugnant. But I don't think it's on par with letting your daughter walk around in a satin teddy with bite marks on her neck." I say.

"Oh well you know, I'm in a phase all the time these days. What can she do really?" Annalynn feigns helplessness in her tone.

"You mean she's appearing to be a concerned mother with a slightly rebellious daughter. Meanwhile, she's letting you do pretty much whatever?"

"Yep."

I roll my eyes. "That's dumb."

"Yes, it is."

I pause to think and cook lunch.

We sit down to ham sandwiches.

"But think about all the things we can completely get away with?"

We share a nice evil grin that would concern parents everywhere.

"'Course, we won't." She says.

I look at her, puzzled.

"Thank god your parents are watching out for

both of us."

"They are?"

"Yes, you idiot, they are."

"Right." I say, not entirely convinced.

Chapter Twenty-Two

"He's sixteen. He wants a car."

"Ted, when did *Easel* become *Car*?"

"Easels are boring. I want to get him a car."

"Yes, you want.... He wants something else..... like, not a car."

"Nah. He wants a car. Really."

"He wants art supplies." My mother says back.

"But, I found the best thing ever. As first cars go."

Usually I'm on my mother's side, but well.... A car would be great. For stuff. Maybe if I had one I could get a date. With Annalynn. And I did really well in driver's ed. I only ran over one cone.... And that was early on!

"Best thing ever?" My mother says skeptically.

"Nissan Sentra, manual transmission, crank windows, and a new paint job. The engine has been converted already." He says. He sounds wistful.

"Ted, why don't we look at something more affordable?"

He makes some non-committal noise.

"We can't afford it, end of the story."

I don't get my hopes up, especially since I don't see anything large being hidden; and a car, sub-compact or not, is still large. It sticks in my mind though.

Annalynn asks me what I think I'm getting for my birthday. "Art supplies." I reply. But honestly, I really wish I could say 'a car'.

"Boooooooring."

"Hey, better than clothes." I say, which is what she got for her last birthday.

"Everything is better than my parent's

thoughtless gifts." She says.

"I got you those Twilight Zone episodes." I say, regarding her last birthday.

"Yeah, I need to finish them too. After your parents are done having your party at home, we should watch a few." She says as she slurps up the rest of her milk

"We could do that." I reply.

I come home to the usual crepe-paper decorations. The smell of a cake is wafting out of the kitchen. Birthdays are pretty traditional around here, nothing really changes, except for the colors and the candles. And the gifts. My mother takes a picture of me with the cake each year and I'm surprised how little and also how much things change.

There are a couple of wrapped boxes in the living-room, and unusually, my father is nowhere to be seen. Generally, in the case of the presence of baked-goods in the house, he lurks within a few inches of the frosting bowl and attempts to clean it out using his fingers and tongue. My mother protects it violently with a spatula. He then spends two hours staring at the frosted cake and drooling.

I go upstairs, otherwise the aroma will overwhelm me and I'll take over his role as kitchen pest.

My mother appears a few minutes after I sit down to contemplate my homework.

"How was your day?"

"Pretty decent. Nothing interesting happened."

"Really? Well, I got a call from your school guidance counselor. They want you to join the running start program next quarter. You'd get to go to Eastern Washington University, for free."

"Wouldn't I be kind of young? I thought you only got to do that as a Junior or Senior." I ask.

"Well, you are allowed to start when you are sixteen, and they are willing to send you because of your grades and scholarship. You could still be on the track team." She says.
I think about it a second.

"Mom. I'm not well accepted at high school. Everyone tells me how young I seem, and how I'm not normal. I don't know if college would be a great idea. Wouldn't I just be more awkward and more lonely?" I ask honestly.

I know my mother wasn't happy at college. She was happiest, she has said, in her last year when she was taking care of me while finishing her education. I gave her purpose. Her exact words were "love gives you a V-8 engine."

She sits down on the bed. "You have a good point, but they have a good point too. High-school doesn't have much to offer you."

"It has Annalynn."

She looks at me. "Do you really think it's a good idea to let your life revolve around her as much as it does?"

I get offended, she notices. "I don't mean that the way it sounds. I adore Annalynn and I trust her. But I sometimes have a terrible fear that she'll go somewhere else and you'll be emotionally destitute."

"Or I go somewhere else, and she'll be emotionally destitute." I say sharply.

"You wouldn't be leaving town. You could still spend weekends together and you'd still be the cross-country team."

I think about it. Nope.

"Mom, I'm not ready for college. I'm not ready to be a complete fish out of water."

"I figured on that. Next year is soon enough."

Next year? Is she nuts? I'm sixteen years old, I'm not college material, I'm barely an acceptable high schooler.

"Sure, we can talk about it for next year." I say.

What? I didn't mean to say that.

My dad wanders in just in time to take a nice swipe of icing off the cake.

He looks at my mother with his finger shoved into his mouth up to the third knuckle and makes a deep rumble-y 'mmmmmmmm' noise. "I'm back, when do we get to eat cake?"

"It appears you've already started, where have you been?"

"Out."

"Doing?"

"Stuff."

She opens her moth to ask more questions so he loudly announces that it's time for a birthday party.

So it is. There is singing, which always embarrasses me. There is no dancing, but there is feasting, as there is every year. I eye his addition to the stack of gifts. It's a tiny box. I'm guessing he's made me one of his heavy Celtic-style rings. They've been selling well at the local jewelry shops and I've been fairly vocal about admiring them. I was kind of hoping for a new puzzle, but I guess I'm old enough for other things now.

The big box is the new easel I wanted so much and had been admiring for months. The other box from my mother (ostensibly it's from both of them, but I know better) contains new shirts. As usual I admire the fabric and try them on for her. They always fit, and I always like them. The next box is flat and rattles. I guess I'm getting a puzzle after all. Yup, Iron and brass with etching on the brass. Finally the last box, the little box. My father hands it to me with a gleam in his eye. I rip off the paper with my usual glee, but there isn't a wooden ring box in there at all. Instead it's just a flat cardboard box like you'd get with store-bought jewelry. I open it and look at the key-ring and attached key dumbly for a moment.

But we couldn't afford a car, Mom said so. And they'd already spent plenty of money on the Easel and the clothes.

"Ted!"

He ignores her. "Well, would you like to see it?"

"I.... uh.... Did you really get me a car?"

"Yes." He replies, making it sound like 'yesh' which means he's excited.

"TED!?" My mother says.

"Later!" He steers me out the door and smiles at her.

Chapter Twenty-Three

Christmastime is coming again, and so I take an old mirror out of the basement and hang it up in my room so I can draw self-portraits for the family like everyone seems to want. Most people want a nice, normal 'nice boy' sketch of me, but Mom wants a sketch that is more artistic. Annalynn hasn't asked for anything but I actually have a wonderful idea for her anyway.

I'm not sure if it's appropriate. Things have definitely taken a cooler turn since the beginning of school. Really, the extent of our explorations into the world of romance was limited to the four days our parents were out of town. There wasn't the time or freedom to do what we wanted, even if we had known what it was, after that. We are still whatever we are; comfortable to snuggle up into a ball while watching movies on the couch, equally at ease without contact. Unlike so many of our peers who have ossified together at the lips or hips.

Appropriate or not, it feels right, and so one night when the world is slumbering, I take off all of my clothing and sit in front of the mirror and sketch a rough outline of my body. I broadly fill it in and add hair. It's not quite right, and my room is cold. I hug myself, shiver for a minute and then absently tap the pencil across my lips, which has unintended but inspiring effect. I've never drawn male anatomy, ever, and this represents a good time take a stab at it. I move closer to the mirror and sketch the wrinkly, hairy scrotum and then the semi-floppy penis. I curl a foot in my lap when I shift positions and draw the contorted foot and then I draw one with the toes splayed, braced against the wall. The strange, lumpy male throat followed by hands. On paper, it looks like a feminist statement about men, but really it is just the beginning of a much bigger project, so I think. Drawing myself nude is going to be quite the challenge.

I crawl into pajamas and curl up in bed.

Sometime in the night the power goes out, and my father comes in to wake me so I won't be late for school.

"Emelle, what is this?" He says when he turns and finds the easel full of body parts. I'm sure he sees it as an example of my inner-psyche or possibly as a horrible acquiescence to feminazi theory.

I'm at a loss for words.

"This is indecent."

"It's just my body." I'm not indecent!

"It's pornographic!"

"It's just...." I give up.

"What is this for?" He demands.

"Art?"

"No, this is obscene." He says quietly, angrily. "We don't support your art so you can draw naughty pictures. Were you giving this to anyone?"

"What? No, not that one!"

"Oh, so this was practice?"

"Yes, it's just practice for nudes."

"Nudes are full bodies, not a super-sized penis surrounded by hands and feet. This is disgusting." He rips it down the middle and wads up the halves. Underneath peeps the rough sketch of me on my stool. He takes one look and rips that up too.

"Get ready for school, and don't draw these things again." He says angrily.

He leaves and I sit for a few minutes, staring at

the few flecks of paper on the floor and then go hide in the closet and cry. I have no idea why, precisely.

Annalynn comes in at a quarter to eight.

"Emelle?"

"I don't want to talk." I mutter.

"We need to go to school."

"Go, I'm staying in here."

"Why?"

"He ripped up my art from last night." No need to say who.

"He didn't?" She's aghast.

"Did too."

"Why?"

"Said it was pornographic." I reply. "I really don't want to talk, you can go to school...."

Minutes creep by. Maybe even half an hour. She doesn't go. Instead she sits down with me and puts an arm around my shoulder. I very gracelessly snivel.

"What the hell is going on here?" He says when he comes back up, realizing we haven't left.

Annalynn stands up. "Please, you aren't helping. Would you go, please?" She says.

"This is my house!" He responds.

"No, this is Paul's house, and it always will be." She replies very calmly.

"PAULA!"

My mother thunders up the stairs. "What is going on here?"

"They won't go to school." My father states like it's a felony at the same moment Annalynn explains that my art was ripped up.

"You did what?" My mother asks.

"It was pornographic!"

"Annalynn, if you'd excuse us?"

"Uhm, sure." She hauls me to my feet and pulls us downstairs and makes tea.

"You should go.... Eventually this is going to be loud."

"I've heard it before...." She says and sits determinedly.

We sit in silence. It will come.

"Ted, this is normal. This isn't an offense. The human body isn't any more evil than say, sketches of a horse or a hippo." My mother yells. "Get out of your overly-Christian homophobic hole in the ground and go apologize!"

"NO!"

Annalynn giggles.

"It's not funny, it's embarrassing." I grumble.

"Overly-Christian homophobic hole in the ground?!" She laughs.

"Right." I'm in no mood for humor.

The argument loses clarity and eventually my father goes storming out of the house. My mother comes downstairs with pieces of ripped up art under her arm.

"Emelle, Annalynn?" She says.

"Yes?" We both chirp.

"I'm going to call the office and explain your absence. You have tomorrow off, don't you?"

"Yes." Annalynn says.

"Why?" I ask.

"Why don't both of you mosey up to the cabin for the weekend and stay there?"

"Uh.... I don't know about what my parents would say." Annalynn says.

"Would they notice?" My mother and I ask at

the same time.

"Probably." She says.

"I can explain to your mother, if you like?" Mom offers.

"Don't worry about it. I'll just go home and get some things and explain it then."

Chapter Twenty-Four

We leave about half an hour later for the cabin. It's almost an hour long drive and I dread the conversation I figure I am about to have.

"So, when are you and your father going to get over your Great Animosity?" She says the last two words sarcastically.

"Uh." I say unhelpfully. "When he stops doing what he does." I say more firmly.

"Which is what, precisely?"

"Barricading every avenue of communication that is theoretically possible between us due to extremely rigid thinking," I explain.

"Em, he isn't a bad guy. He just isn't. I mean.... From my end it looks like raging incompetence."

"Raging incompetence?"

"Your father trips through life, one foot in the hole, and digging it deeper more than half the time. I've had a lot of time to think about this, since he got you the car for your birthday. He's got no clue. He's not trying to be a raging asshole. He just comes out that way."

"Anna, he's spent his entire life making people regularly feel like crap. He had a few years of counseling. He's got to know!"

"I didn't say he didn't get that. I said that he's clueless. By that I mean he doesn't really know how to stop with you. So he's had counseling to help him out with his adult relationships. Great. Maybe he even had some help with dealing with kids, but we aren't kids anymore, and we aren't really adults and besides, parents never see us as old enough to really be adults. If you look, there are signs he's trying."

"You've got a lot more imagination than I do if you think ripping up my artwork is somehow an effort to be a parent." I reply.

"Weren't his parents like, fundamental luthcrans?"

"Uh, I think so, that sounds right."

"I have a little bit of experience with religious fundamentalists. Trust me, his response was positively liberated."

"He doesn't even believe in God."

"You don't have to believe in God to have the rhetoric installed in your brain. I sure don't believe in their god, and yet... I think I'm most likely going to hell."

It's not a new revelation. "Okay, you have a point."

"Look, your father was raised in a very religious household; his morality, and mine too, it isn't connected to our rational mind; it's connected to our emotions. The religion is designed that way."

I can my Kant speech, even if it is begging to be let free.

She continues, oblivious to my supreme effort at good behavior. "He kind of wobbles, I guess, between his parents' rhetoric—which is what he falls back on when he's way out of his league—and what he thinks is better. But you change too fast for him to really keep up with you, so he falls back on his old thoughts and feelings more than he does with your mother."

"Let me get this straight. You think that he goes into irrational mind-like-a-rusted-bear-trap mode when he's overtaxed, and he acts like a normal person when he's been able to think through the situation for awhile and really decide on what's good?"

"YES!" She says, excited.

"So what you are also telling me, is that his natural inclination isn't good?"

"Well, when you put it that way, no wonder this still going on. Emelle, no. His inclination is good. It's just he's got two standards of good, and the one that doesn't serve him as well is still the first one to come to mind."

"Okay, that still isn't much better."

"It would help if you didn't expect his every action to be based on the worst ideas possible, because he does do good things when he's been given enough time to think."

"Annalynn. This man told me I was stupid when I was a kid, that I wasn't worth talking to. He told me I lived in la la land and that I should shut off my imagination. If I learned to treat his actions as suspect, I certainly had good reason."

"And he's learned that's how you respond... and so this is all going to go on and on."

"Maybe not... maybe he'll apologize." I say.

"Will you let him?"

"I'll try my best." She glares. "My real best, Annalynn."

Chapter Twenty-Five

The cabin is dusty, no one has been up in a while and so Annalynn and I give everything a wipe down while the stove[12] warms things up.

"So, how did you get your parents to let you come up here?"

Annalynn looks over at me. "I told them that your art had been ripped up, and you were stressed out. Your mother was sending you up here alone and I didn't think that was so great, so I thought I'd come with you so you wouldn't just sit around and simmer and stew."

"And they were like "okey dokey?""

"I dunno yet. I just left them a letter."

I blanch. "Really?" I have a terrible image of Mr. Spencer coming after us in the middle of the night.

"They don't know where this place is, and they aren't going to admit I left them a letter to your parents. It'll be fine."

"Won't they ground you into next year when you get back?"

"No." She scoffs.

"Uhm, why not?"

"It's you. They just don't argue with me when it's you."

"I thought your mother thought I was sort of a bad influence."

"That's complicated." She replies. "She wants

---

12 A unique thing; it runs on leftover oils of all kinds and is remarkably clean. Apparently, my father's father designed it, and my father adapted the design for the cabin. The cabin, I should mention, is completely off the grid. The whole place runs on a couple of inconspicuous solar panels and two of these stoves.

me to have good reliable friends. And no one can say you aren't good and reliable. She wants me to be dating a nice catholic boy, and you aren't nice and catholic, but on the other hand, you aren't exactly trying to get in my pants either. A lot of that back and forth kind of thing. I think it ultimately comes out that she doesn't like you or dislike you. She accepts you, and realizes that you are important to me, and it's not worth fighting a war to get rid of you, because she'd lose. She liked you a lot better before she got off on this most recent religious kick. Dad loves you to pieces, however. He thinks you and sliced bread have a lot in common."

"Oh?"

"Nutritious and good for snacking on. Yum, fresh baked Emelle."

"Seriously..."

"He wishes Mom would get off it... perfect weight, perfect looks, perfectly religious, perfect lawn....he thinks less than perfect would be... well... perfect! He's always been more reasonable and moderate than Mom, but he doesn't really stand up to her domineering when she gets on her soapbox."

"What happens if she did try to break things?"

"I'd become the kind of out-of-control daughter she likes to pretend she has." Annalynn grins sweetly.

Well that's a concerning prospect. Annalynn has every capacity, in my opinion, to become an utterly terrifying rebellious teenager. I don't think she really wants to be, though. We are fairly calm as our age-group goes.

I make some hot chocolate for us and we play one of the multitudes of board games collecting at the cabin. Annalynn wins the first two, and then I win the last game of Scrabble.

We finish our second cups.

"I'm tired." I share.

"I'm not."

"What do you want to do?"

"Move, or run or something."

"Something?" I say sweetly.

"What do you have in mind?" She asks, one eyebrow arched.

"Well, it's getting dark...." I note.

"Full moon though. We can go outside and transform. Bwhahahah."

"We could dance." I say suddenly thinking of the stereo in the closet.

"I don't know how to dance!" Annalynn protests.

"I don't think that matters." I say and snag a polka CD. "I think we just sort of make fools of ourselves until we get the hang of it."

Annalynn laughs. "Well this should be entertaining...."

When I come home, the house is immaculate, which is rare. Usually there is the smallest bit of clutter somewhere. No one is home, it seems. Also odd. Generally my parents can't be paid to leave the house.

I thunder up the stairs and drop my bags inside the door of my room and almost leave to commandeer the computer, but notice that my father is sitting quietly in my bean-bag chair and that my room is also immaculate. Though I generally keep it tidy, it never looks this nice.

"Where's Mom?"

"She decided she needed a short vacation. She went to Vegas, she'll be back on Wednesday."

Hrmmm. That can't be good. "Are you guys okay?" I ask, genuinely concerned.

"Probably not for awhile." He pops his eyes open and looks searchingly at me. "She's not going to be settled with the world until you and I get along."

I resist every urge to look at my easel.

"You can look." He says.

I do, and see at first a mess of scotch-tape and charcoal smudges, but then I make out that he's taped up what he's ripped apart and ironed it flat again. It's distorted, but it's recognizable again, now.

"I'm sorry," he murmurs.

I try to say something like it's okay, or that's fine then, but really a bit of tape and some careful ironing doesn't fix this.

"You need to go back to therapy, and hammer out whatever made you rip this up, or it will happen again, and we never will get along." It's the best I can do.

He makes to leave.

"Did she trash the house?" I ask. My mother doesn't exactly throw things when she gets angry, but she does shove things around, and upend bookshelves and pull things off the walls.

"Yes."

"And you cleaned it?" I hope not.

"Yes."

The color involuntarily runs out of my face.

"She didn't do much to your room, and I certainly didn't dig through your things." He says.

True to Annalynn's prediction, I don't quite

trust him and the first thing I do is check my private things. My art supplies are just as I left them, my sketches of Annalynn still collecting dust behind other dusty things in the closet. Good. Then I check the box, which due to the fact I use it from time to time, can't be hidden in the dust. It's safe.

I really shouldn't have it, but I've been trying to embrace my awkward sexuality that seems to be more connected to bondage than I'd like. I've known there was that element since I ran across the pictures of the bound man, but it really sprang to life when my father asked me if I had any use for fifty feet of silk rope he'd found in the smithy.[13] I figured I did, but didn't realise that the best idea would be to tie myself up. Nor did I think I'd really like it when I had done so. I had thought it would be a one-time curiosity satisfier and then I'd be done with my silly fantasies.

I have a lot more than fifty feet of silk rope now.

I sigh, mostly at myself, half-admonishment, half acceptance, put it back under the heap of laundry and then wander downstairs to put the leftover nibbles from the trip to the cabin in the pantry and make some inconsequential small talk with my father.

He's in the kitchen, drumming his fingers to unknown cadences.

"We have some errands."

"Oh?" I ask.

"I thought we could go get you a decent mirror for your room, so that you can draw the way you want to."

---

13 What was fifty feet of silk rope doing in the smithy? Someday, I'll ask.

"What happened to the one I dug out of storage?"

"Hurricane Paul." He says.

Oh, wow.

"And we need new dishes. And cups. And some lamp shades."

"What?" I ask.

"That was me after she left." He admits, sheepishly.

"Please tell me you guys didn't do anything really stupid?"

"Like take a sledgehammer to her sewing machines?" He asks, grinning.

"You didn't?" I say, sinking, knowing that I'm going to have a murderess for a mother.

"No, Emelle, I didn't. Only in my head, and so far, we don't have thought police."

"It's Mom..... we might as well."

"True. Why don't we find her some new dishes so she is distracted from needing to read our memories of this conversation?"

Chapter Twenty-Six

My father dutifully goes to his therapist twice a week. We all pretend like it's not going on because deep inside, we all like to think we can manage just fine on our own. It's the family short-coming.

One night at dinner, after he's gotten home a little late, my mother bravely brings it up.

"Hmm, so how's it going?"

He pushes his broccoli around on his plate to make it look like he's eaten it. Says nothing....

"Eat your broccoli." She suggests.

"Yes, Emelle, eat your broccoli, it's important."

"Ted....." He looks up and notices that our plates are cleaned of the vegetable.

"Oh.... Right." He takes a mouthful and chews it thoughtfully. "I don't like broccoli."

"You don't like vegetables." My mother corrects.

"Hey... I like corn!"

"Corn is a grain!" We both say impudently.

He sighs loudly. "It looks like and tastes like a vegetable to me!"

"Denial still a river in Egypt?" Mom asks.

"No, it's a town somewhere in the prairie, and it's pronounced Denali." He grumbles, but it's good-natured. "Seriously, it's going okay. I wish I had more promising progress to report. Most of the matter is aimed towards reintegrating parents into the lives of younger kids, you know, for after divorce and the war. Some of it is applicable, though." He turns to me. "Speaking of which, you and I are supposed to come up with some sort of weekly ritual —"

Snerk.

Giggle.

"What?" He asks us both.

I make some noises that I think of as being voodoo-esque. Mom stirs an imaginary cauldron.

His shoulders sag. We instantly shut it off. If anything, the last few weeks have pointed out that my father's progress is fragile and I can impede him too easily.

"Weekly ritual, I assume that means some regularly scheduled event that is of interest to the both of us?" I prompt.

"I'm taking all brilliant ideas under consideration." He says and moves his broccoli around some more.

"As in, we go with the first one?"

"Something like that."

I think. I don't really come up with ideas that don't sound like dates in a weird, very creepy way.

"Maybe we could come up with a project we work on at some set time instead of an outing." He suggests.

"Like what?" I ask.

"Uh...." He offers.

"I have a building in Cheney that needs lots and lots of help." My mother says.

"I don't think that was the sort of bonding, communicative experience that we are looking for."

"Dang... and here I thought I had some nice cheap labor."

"We'll think of it. Give it some thought?" He asks me hopefully.

"Yes, I will." I say, and then leave to finish drawing Annalynn's gift.

Mom gets her cheap labor.

While it probably isn't the bonding, communicative experience that we were looking for, it manages to team us against her because the work is dull, aggravating, and bitterly cold since the building is being gutted from the inside out. The work is honestly hateful.

Annalynn comes one Friday afternoon in my car to bring us both hot chocolate and try and wheedle my presence from my father.

"Tomorrow's Christmas Eve." She whines when he tells her no.

"And this needs to be done before the new quarter starts." He says. "Or no one is going to move in and we won't get money for the effort."

"I'll help the week after Christmas if you let me borrow him tonight." She counters.

"Now, that is a bargain I can like." He says, pats me on the back and sends me across the floor to her.

We escape to the cabin after I drop by the house to get her gift. She tells me she has a surprise planned which both intrigues me and worries me. Annalynn's ideas usually do.

She drags a box into the cabin with us and I realise that she's been here earlier. There is a heap of pillows on the bed and the stove was going at some point. She walks around lighting candles.

"Annalynn?"

"Yes?" she chirps innocently.

"What are you up to?"

"Atmosphere. I am setting the atmosphere."

"For what?" I squeak.

"You are going to give me a massage!"

"I am?"

"Yes. You did read the book I got you for your birthday right?"

Multiple times, and practiced on a stuffed animal too. "Yes."

"Good." She says, and then adds, "I also brought movies for us to watch."

"Really? What?"

She dumps the box on the floor and struggles with getting the television out.

"Annalynn, are all these movies cabin-in-the-middle-of-woods slasher flicks?" I ask as I flip through the pile of titles.

"Uhm, yeah."

"Annalynn do you think this might be a problem?" I say as I point to the walls around us.

"Uh no, wh..." She stops mid-questions and squinches up her face. "Oh, so stupid."

I flap my hand at her. "Don't worry about it, we can handle it." Famous last words, I might add. She's brought with her a good sized-selection of massage oils, all designed to be warming and relaxing, and a copy of the book she'd given me.

"You bought two?"

"They were a good price, I figured it wasn't a bad thing to know."

"Probably not, why don't we start a movie and I'll get to work." I say, and then contradict myself. "No, you should open your present first." I hand her the packing tube.

She takes the roll of heavy paper out of the tube and lays it flat on the table. I had done the drawing of myself on an oatmeal-colored cotton paper with a sienna colored crayon. In the candlelight, I'm surprised by how much the picture comes to life.

"It's beautiful, Emelle."

"Thanks, it was hard."

"Doesn't look that way." She says pointedly.

"Har Har." I reply.

She rolls it back up. "I want to get it professionally framed. Soon. Even if I can't show it to anyone."

I smile ecstatically at this. I'm such a dork.

"You know, though, this makes us even." She wags a finger at me.

"Yes, that had come to mind. But you could probably blackmail me worse than I could blackmail you."

She shifts through the pile of movies. "How about this?"

I read the back. "*Roxy (Samanatha Bolings) has just returned from rehab, and her parents send her to their lush condo in the Rocky Mountains so that she won't fall in again with her partying friends over the summer. What should be a pleasant vacation from L.A. heat turns into a terrifying ordeal when Roxy takes on her stalker and would-be murderer; the seemingly friendly Jeff Burtenshaw (Wayne Hogarth).*"

"Sounds good!"

"They all sound the same," I whine.

"Doesn't matter, you don't watch them anyway." She says.

True.... I pat the bed and gesture for her to lie down. I pop the book open to the page on back rubs, and when she returns from fiddling with the player, she shimmies out of her shirt and lays down for me.

"Nice purple bra." I say sarcastically. "It even has lace...."

"It was three bucks and it fit." She explains.

I'm a little disappointed. "You didn't buy it especially for me to see?"

"No, I didn't."

I theatrically sniff and whimper a bit.

"You'll survive." She says without much sympathy.

I reference the book on what oils I should use and carefully pour some out into my hand. It glows golden in the candlelight. I roll it around in my hands and then begin very light work on her lower back like the book suggests.

"Harder."

I push a little harder.

"I'm not porcelain." She says.

"I know. I'm following the book."

"We'll get the hang of it sooner or later."

"Generally." I say, and push a bit harder.

"Mmmmmm." She murmurs.

"Sooner, in this case." I tease.

I watch the movie out of the corner of my eye once I've found a good rhythm. Roxy is chasing Jeff around with a battery-powered drill and is mostly covered in blood as she ultimately nail-guns him to the floor of her now-trashed multi-million dollar condo.

"I don't think someone has that much blood." I say.

"It's b-grade Hollywood, of course it's got stupid amounts of blood." Annalynn bounces down from the bed and digs through the tapes. "This one sounds good: *Daniel Heathgarden flies to his friends' secluded mid-western lake-house to join them for the summer. The terror begins when he arrives to find his girlfriend dead and his best friend missing. Daniel races against the clock to save his own life after the killer sabotages his plane."*

"Define what is 'Good' here," I ask.

"Well, I'll like it." She says, and pops it in before returning.

I toy with her bra-strap. It's in the way, but it seems too forward to just get rid of it.

I wish I were braver.

"Is it in the way?" She asks.

"Not exactly."

"If it is, you can move it around or something."

That sounds like an invitation. I fiddle with the catch and finally figure it out. I am enlightened as to why my mother makes her own bras too. She lets me slide the whole thing off.

Padded cups?

"Annalynn! False advertising?" I tease as I dangle the plush foam cups in front of her.

"It's comfortable." She replies and swipes at the bra.

"Sure..." I say, feigning disbelief.

"It is."

"If you say so." I drop it over the side of the bed and finish her shoulders and back while Daniel carves up the killer with his newly-repaired airplane.

We watch another slasher flick, this time five friends in a beat up truck being hunted by a man and his overly-vicious German shepherd. Because of the dog, and its death at the end, this film actually rattles more of my nerves than the previous. All I really want to do is huddle in my sleeping bag and have the images go away.

Even Annalynn is wide-eyed. "That dog was so creepy and sad." She says as she pulls her shirt back on.

"Yeah." I agree.

I shove my sleeping bag closer to hers and slither in.

If I weren't so nervous, the heap of satin pillows surrounding us and the curtain of mosquito netting would seem quite romantic, but instead it seems like the backdrop of yet another slasher flick, and I keep seeing a knife come through the netting. I am not feeling the least bit romantic.

"I can't sleep now." I finally say after tossing around for almost half and hour.

"Neither can I." Annalynn sympathizes.

"This was supposed to be romantic, wasn't it?" I ask.

"Uhm, yeah sorta."

We fish around for each other's hands and grip tightly for awhile before attempting to sleep again.

We have the heebie-jeebies and needless to say, by midnight when the wind picks up there isn't a whole lot of sleeping going on. A great deal of cold sweating and modified prairie-dogging at every passing noise, however, is.

Then we both hear it clearly, the low hum of an engine. Crunch of tires on the crushed gravel of the drive up. Thunk of a rusting car door and the unmistakable grind of bloodstained boots on the concrete stepping stones.

Annalynn looks at me with wide eyes and I shimmy from bed and loose the shotgun from its leather holster that dangles from a rusted hook on the wall.

The shadow of a massive man falls across the window as he comes around from the carport. A pistol grip is clearly outlined on his hip and something slides across his shoulder. A dead body of the girl he just murdered?

Keys slide into the lock and slide the deadbolt to the side as Annalynn and I obviously deny it permission to do just that. A head sticks in and my hands are frozen though I have it perfectly sighted. The head rotates, a maniacal grin already beginning to play on its lips.

"Emelle! Put that down!"

Annalynn barks a relieved happy noise.

"What the hell is going on here?" My father says, taking on the mask of his security guard persona, an action that is vastly improved by his uniform that he is, strangely wearing.

"Uhm."

"We thought you were an axe-murderer, Mr. Foster." Annalynn offers up.

He looks confused.

"Never mind." I say.

"Your mother sent me up because the wind is picking up pretty badly, it took down quite a lot of Brian's big tree. She wanted me to make sure things were okay up here." He looks around. "Seems like it. Be careful with the stove, before you open it shut the flue almost all the way so you don't end up with a fire." He sets down a spare sleeping bag on the floor that he had been carrying over his shoulder and glances once more around the cabin. His eyes narrow to slits when he looks at the heap of massage oils and, right next to them, Annalynn's lacy purple push-up bra.

Whoops.

Despite knowing that I'm in for a bit of stormy weather, his visit breaks the fear, and we fall asleep a bit after he leaves.

Chapter Twenty-Seven

I come home to a brewing fight.

"So." He says to Mom after lunch. "Annalynn and Emelle are having sex up at the cabin."

"All righty." She replies.

"All righty? WHAT?!"

"Was this supposed to not happen?" She asks.

"Well, no. It wasn't. Teenagers absolutely shouldn't be having sex."

"Ted. Think about that for a second. They are all hormone boats, biologically designed for constant nookie."

"Paula, that isn't the point."

"What is the point?"

"We should have never let them go up to the cabin. I told you it was trouble. How long do you really think it's going to be before something goes wrong and Annalynn gets pregnant? Huh? They're sixteen years old! They don't need to be giving into carnal leanings and possibly suffering the consequences."

"How does the cabin have anything to do with this, dear?"

"It was a blank check to do whatever they wanted to do." He replies.

My parents are talking about my imagined sex life. Ew. And he is calling her Paula, not Paul, or Puppe. That means he's serious.

"It was supposed to be." She says.

"What do you mean it was supposed to be?"

"It's nice, it's safe, and it's private. The likelihood of birth control being used in those circumstances is significantly higher than say, the backseat of the Toyota[14]. Besides, they've been best friends for a long time. They've undoubtedly given thought to this, and they aren't going to mess up their shared life with an ill-fortuned baby. They wouldn't do that to each other."

"Well that's naïve." He snarls. "If I recall correctly, foresight is not something typically associated with teenagers."

"No, it's not, but Annalynn and Emelle aren't typical. Ted, they've been given a blank check because they have foresight and they use it. They very much deserve their privacy and that's why I've given it to them."

"If this is how they use your generosity, it should be taken away, it isn't right for them to be having sex, Paula."

"It's FINE if they have sex." She says. "I don't care if they go for it for hours up there, or if they *don't* have sex. I don't care, Ted, it's not important. What is important is that it's safe and sane, because I know it's consensual. I don't think it would be safe or sane in the other situations in which it might be had. Do I want them at some creepy hotel or parked out on some back road? No....would they necessarily do that? I don't know, but I sure don't want to find out from the police that they did and that another car hit them, or that there was drug-related violence and they got into the middle of it by accident. It's my cabin and I say they can have it."

My mother gets points for her nice and logical soliloquy.

"I don't want them up there, doing these things or even not doing these things!"

---

14 This will be an amusing fact later in my adult life.

"I know, you said all of this the first time around, when they went up. I told you then, and I'll tell you now. I'm not backing down on this."

"I disagree entirely. But you know, since the cat is already out of the bag, fine. Just fine."

The backdoor slams. Very shortly the smithy starts up in a bevy of clanks and clangs.

I creep down the stairs.

My mother looks at me.

"For the record... we aren't sleeping with each other." I say.

"I know." She says calmly. "I think he knows too, he's just... not paying attention to his intuition." She sits down and then turns to look at me again. "But sweetie, I really don't care if you are or aren't, just so long as you're careful."

Chapter Twenty- Eight

Intuition is not a trait I generally saddle my father with, but perhaps under layers of rigid judgmental thought patterns, it's there. From my perspective, however, it's not that which therapy has unearthed, but something a fair bit more frightening. I've begun to understand that there are many types of therapy—whatever counseling he had long ago and the pre-marital sessions before the wedding were an entirely different breed than this current round. Instead of lending him some much needed grounding and stability, he seems to be growing less and less able to handle the world.

When my mother reaches up to cradle his cheek before leaving for her semi-regular trip to visit her sister, he flinches as though she had gone to slap him, and hard at that. In her distraction she doesn't seem to notice, but it bothers me.

When we get back from the airport, he putters around the house like usual, as though he's not quite sure what to do without her there. But he looks tired and old and unusually upset by her absence.

"Uhm...." I finally ask when he paces past my reading chair in the living room for the fifth time, "is something wrong?"

"I don't know." He says very quietly.

"You and Mom didn't fight right before she left did you?"

"No." He replies.

"Would you like me to get out of the house for you?" I ask, fishing.

"Not really. I'm fine." He says and wanders back into the kitchen.

I shrug and call Annalynn to see if she wants

to go out for Chinese food.

"I'm kinda worried." I say to Annalynn.

"Why? He always gets weird when your mom is out."

I shrug again, feeling particularly useless today. "Not like this."

"Well, what are you going to do about it?"

"The question is more what can I do about it?"

"No idea. You could call your mother back home, I guess. But, I think she'd be irritated to come back for just weird. I mean, he's always a little weird. Maybe she goes to get away from it anyway."

"Annalynn, that isn't helpful."

"You didn't ask me to be a false prophet." She says and stabs her pork chow mein pointedly; indicating the case is closed to her.

"We have to go back to school tomorrow." I grumble after a few minutes of quiet eating.

"Yeah. What do you have as a schedule?"

"Other than Coach Boyles for gym first hour, I don't know. I wasn't able to think after that point—I figure after he's done with me, I won't need to."

"You got the football coach for gym?" Annalynn asks, vague horror in her tone.

"Yeah."

"You know Josh the Rocket is his pet?"

"Nah, why would I know that?" I say sarcastically.

"Maybe you should break your ankle." Annalynn suggests.

"Maybe I should just skip class." I reply.

"You know he'll turn a blind eye to whatever happens to you."

"I know."

I, unfortunately, remember meeting Coach Boyles. He had come to track practice looking for potential players and had picked me out as his new field-goal kicker. Apparently, in the entire history of his tenure no one had ever turned him down. He had later attempted to get my hair cut because it was against school dress-code. And almost failed me in ninth-grade health. The track coach, mild-mannered Joan Price, had taken me aside and told me to watch out for Coach Boyles, as he liked to let his footballers be bully boys.

I'd been doing a good job of not thinking about this, but now the dread has bubbled up again and the rest of dinner is spent in silent contemplation of impending doom.

When I get home the house is dark, and I can't hear the smithy. I poke my head in the kitchen. Nobody.

I backpedal to look into the living room. There is a blanket covered lump on the couch. If it weren't for the gleam of the edge of glasses-frames I wouldn't have realized that the lump was my father.

"Are you all right?" I ask.

"No." He whispers back.

"Mom is coming back, right?" I say, realizing that she may have just left him for good.

"As far as I know."

"Then what's wrong?"

"Stuff."

It's unlike my father to host himself a pity party.

I hesitate.

"Don't you think it's kind of sad that we can't manage to come up with one fun activity between us?" He asks.

"Uhm...."

"I don't understand you. Or your art. You don't understand me or what I do. We live in the same house. Great. Sixteen years of being around and I'm not closer to being competent than I was when you were two months old and uninterested in anything that didn't have mammary glands." He pauses. I wonder if I should make the obvious joke that my mother would have. I don't.

He continues. "Maybe I don't beat you, and maybe I don't tell you what a worthless waste of human meat you are.... But as far as I know it's not about what you don't do. What is it my mother said about my father so many years ago? That he put food on the table and a roof over our heads. I don't even accomplish that. I could become a complete vegetable tomorrow and nothing about the finances here would change. Yes, I don't do anything bad, but I don't add value around here either."

I'm stunned.

And so I wait.

"Why does your mother love me?" He asks.

"I don't really know. She just does. Women, they're like that." I say, completely failing to improve the situation, but I press on. "They just do love us, and not for any reason they can think of. Maybe because we need them."

"But they don't need us." He says, sounding defeated.

I can't disagree. My perspective has been for some time that adult men need women like a fish needs water and adult women need men like a fish needs, as famously stated, a bicycle. "But they like us. We amuse them and make them happy." I say.

"Do I? Do we?" He asks rhetorically. "Wasn't I ruining your mother's life earlier this decade? The fact we don't get along and that I'm a pathetic dad is killing her."

"She can't be killed that easily. And you weren't ruining her life—you came back. You fixed it."

He makes a noise like a bark. "Is that really how you look at it? That I fixed things by coming back?"

"That's how she sees it."

Chapter Twenty-Nine

Josh the Rocket is now almost 300 pounds of seriously ripped muscle.

I'd be lying if I said he didn't inspire fear in my skinny bones.

But, it's been a funny, tense, and awkward morning already and I'm not in the best mood. So in its own way, the fear wakes me up.

"You fucking Spencer yet?" He asks in the locker room.

He isn't big on salutations.

Or preamble.

"Nope." I reply, knowing that he will think I'm lying and he'll pick a fight with me.

He snorts. "You just don't want to cop to it. I mean, that's pretty embarrassing there, Foster, to be getting action from her."

"It's a lot less embarrassing than getting action from a cantaloupe, and watermelons, and honeydews. At least, if I wanted to, I could sleep with a real live girl. You on the other hand, pay homage to your own right hand and rape the fridge crisper drawer."

"What did you say?" He reminds me of Biff from Back to the Future—not quite smart enough to follow the insult, but knows it is one anyway.

"I said, basically, that at least I'm not screwing the fruit bowl. Like you."

Josh shoves me into a locker pretty hard.

"We don't talk about that, Foster."

"You were pretty keen on it in seventh grade. I wonder though, did you do it to make your dick taste better for when you figured out how to give yourself a blow job?"

He grinds me into the locker with one arm and then crams his face so close to mine I can smell his aftershave.

And, it makes me a little dizzy, but in a good way. The same sensation I get from tying myself up swims to the surface and makes me feel lightheaded and floaty, but more so than the ropes ever did on their own. I can tell that Josh can sense the change in me. But I think he thinks he's cutting off my air, and so he unpins me a hair.

"You never talk about this again, or we'll finish this."

"Yes Sir." I say dreamily.

I don't know what he makes of it, but he lets me go completely and hustles out of the locker room. I stay back for a minute to gather up my thoughts.

I know I'm a masochist, and I know that in some situations, pain feels wonderful, but I always thought it was intrinsically hooked into my sex drive. I had actually reasoned to myself that it was my convoluted way of handling something I wasn't ready for, or accepting of, or something along the lines of such psychobabble. I think I've just begun to realise it is a much larger leviathan. Because having Josh standing there with violence on his mind, holding me down, was almost delicious. It wasn't sexy, just good.

I tie my shoe the rest of the way, and stand up. I feel a little emptier without the fear, without the heat it brought into my blood.

We do nothing more than run laps, and Josh avoids me, and also, Boyles isn't there. His assistant coach is absentmindedly watching us, and alternately dozing off. I thank Lady Luck when it's over for one day's grace and scurry off to English class.

Annalynn passes me a note:
Hiding any broken ribs?
No, we just ran laps, no Boyles there. I
scribble back.
Lady Luck likes you.
Agreed.
You going to survive? She writes.
Dunno, not until Boyles gets back.
"Mr. Foster, Ms. Spencer, kindly read your
syllabus." Mr. Hatch intones calmly. Since he can
arbitrarily send us back to normal English with Les,
we wad the note up then and there.

The rest of the day is simply tense. AP classes
are our key to college, and this is the second
semester—time to get serious. We can feel the levity
of the situation and it gives us a somber mood. There
is a lot of material to cover, and not a lot of time. The
morning's events stay with me like a lead ball and
scratch at the edges of mind.

It's rare I feel this way, but I feel like I'm
itching to get out of my own skin and mind by the
time I get home. Fortunately, my mother is still in
New York and my father and Brian are out on their
weekly adventure to the shooting range. They will
probably go have a drink or two afterward. I have the
house to myself. It's nice, and perfect for what I
really feel like doing.

I lock the door behind me, take a deep breath
and let myself mentally leave my scholarly concerns
at the hall closet. I then scurry up the stairs and
strip out of my clothes.

Chapter Thirty

I set the mirror on the floor and strip in front of it, taking time to admire the canvas of skin I posses. From beneath the strategic heap of laundry in my closet I pull a small box and from this I conjure my carefully collected paraphernalia. It has taken me two years to get the final piece, this ball gag, which I lay down next to the o-rings, rope, and assorted steel rings I use on my genitalia. From a sheaf of sketches I pull my favorite, as-of-yet untried, position.

I start with the ball stretchers, and then I tie up my feet, careful to leave enough tail on the ropes that I can wrap them up my legs and bind my knees and still have enough rope for them to become half of the hog-tie itself. And then I tie the elaborate collar whose tails will become the other half of the hog-tie. I pick up the ball gag reverently and stroke it, the keystone to this masterpiece. I open my mouth and imagine my mistress is the one who slips it in expertly and lovingly sweeps my hair out of the way to buckle it behind my head. Or maybe my master. I don't care right much.

I tie my hands using my toes, and then I bring the two o-rings that indicate the mating ends of the half hog-ties together and tie them as tightly as I can. It's the feeling of struggling and not getting free that does it for me. The addition of the ball gag is delicious and I feel like this session could be over too quick, so instead of stroking myself I let my imagination guide me in a series of sensations that become ever-urgent.

When I wrap my hand around myself, coming is almost instantaneous. I'd cry out except for the ball gag and my own modesty.

Spent, I wallow in afterglow and then after some glorious time floating in a warm gooey nothing, the reality of my chilly room invades my head space and I bring my hands up and tug on the strings that should set me free.

They don't loosen. I tug harder, and in different directions and still they don't loosen. Even though the first rule of self bondage is to never let yourself panic, I feel that emotion come crawling up on me, and fairly soon my adrenaline fed fingers have made a much bigger mess of things and the cold has made me start shaking so hard that I couldn't use them to fight against my binds anyway.

I struggle a little longer, and then when I see my own panicked face in the mirror I absolutely explode in fear, rage, and panic. Very shortly, breathing has become difficult around the ball gag. Snot and tears have backed up my nose, and are dripping down my face and chin and congealing into a rank pool with my semen.

I try and let the jag pass, but the only real consolation is that someone will find me sooner or later and I won't die. But the thought of being found out puts me into a new panic which is vastly exacerbated when I hear a car pull up. I pray for it to be at worst my mother, home a day early for some unforeseen reason, as I struggle uselessly again. I'm starting to lose my sight when I realize it actually is my father—home early from shooting and drinks. I hope desperately for him to walk right past my room but he knocks lightly and when I don't respond he lets himself in.

I really do panic then, whatever noise my

throat can make around this gag, it does, and I slide away from him while losing my sight to curtains and I know that I'm sucking very little air and that I'm thrashing stupidly.

The ball gag has a little o-ring attached to the front. Probably for pony play, and he actually grabs this and shakes my head. I roll my eyes in response and try to not look at him.

"Calm down right now." He insists and it is almost enough to get me back to myself. He pulls a blanket off the bed and wraps it around my shoulders. He then unbuckles the gag and lays it down on the floor next to me. His Leatherman comes off his belt and he works loose the knot that was holding me captive. Fairly soon, the o-rings that held the hog-tie are sitting beside the gag and then the rope that was my handcuffs is carefully rolled and there too, and the rope around my feet and legs is removed and finally the rope around my neck.

I'm beginning to warm up, but I'm not nearly together in my head, and it seems he knows this. He places a hand on either of my shoulders and looks me in the face. Suddenly free, I realize just how wretched things could have been, and I burst into tears again, and he stands up and leaves.

I thought him leaving me alone to contemplate things, but he returns shortly with a warm washrag and carefully cleans up my face, and even the ball gag. When he's done with this, he wraps the blanket more tightly around me and pulls me into his lap. His fingers gently rub my scalp and he hums tunelessly to me while just barely rocking back forth.

As my chest loosens, I gulp in air and things become more normal, physically at least. I think my father realizes the need for silence, because he says nothing until he picks me up and plunks me into my bed after encouraging me to put on pajamas. "Emelle, you scared me. We will talk about this, but not now. You'll need to."

"Yes," I agree, "but no, not right now."

He places a hand on my shoulder and kisses the top of my head, and I feel better.

I get up the next day to go to school and find that my box of toys has been neatly repacked and placed back beneath my laundry. The mirror has been re affixed to the wall, and things appear muchly normal. However, there are bruises on my lips and my wrists are raw, so is my neck. My eyes are puffy and my nose is red.

I look terrible.

I rummage for socks anyway, but when I stand back up, I am immediately nauseated, and I drop to the floor and wretch. My father finds me sitting on the floor next to a puddle of bile and propped against my foot board, still shaking.

"You aren't going to school today."

"I didn't think so." I reply.

"What are you doing with socks then, and sitting on the floor?"

"I was thinking otherwise earlier."

He takes the socks from my hands, and puts me in the beanbag. I don't protest his cleaning of the bile, but I try to politely decline to eat breakfast.

"No." He says and places the tray back on my lap. Even though my eyes are shut, I can tell exactly what his expression is. I shake my head a bit.

"You have to."

"No, I don't." I reply.

I hear his feet slip across the floor, and I just drift with the tray in my lap, but he comes back with a camping stool, and sits down right in front of me and sighs.

"Don't make me do this...." He asks.

I don't bother with moving.

His hand comes up to my chin and he rubs his thumb across my bottom lip. I open my mouth in surprise and am suddenly gifted with the knowledge of why he did this as scrambled eggs make it into my mouth. I roll them over my tongue and swallow. I am fed a few more bites before I raise my hand to ask him to pause.

"Dad, why are you doing this?" Yes, he's 'Dad' now, no sperm donor would bother to do this.

I hear a stifled sound and there is a long silence. "Because I love you[15]."

The rest of the day passes in silence.

At dinner, he breaks the silence. "Emelle, I wanted you to know.... I don't condemn bondage, I understand it fairly well. However, self-bondage has some pitfalls. If I hadn't known that you were engaging in it before last night, I would have never checked in on you. You could have gotten very hurt. Even died."

"I know."

He is silent.

"Don't you ask me why I did it, or some such now?" I ask cynically.

"No. Do I need to? Do you need to explain it to

---

15   These three little words have so much power. They move mountains, wage wars, boil the seas and break a lifetime of silence. When said truly they never lose their power.

me?"

"Maybe?" I say. And it is true.

"Emelle, do you need to go to counseling for this? Or was this an accident?"

"What do you mean?"

"Are you using rope to hurt yourself or to do auto-erotic asphyxiation?"

"No!"

"Is domination something you truly need, or does it just excite you?"

I look anywhere but into his eyes. "It's a need." I mumble. "Right now, anyway...."

He nods.

"I've put a different lock on your box. I have the key. I will give it back to you, but we can talk about that later."

And without further word, he steps out and leaves me be.

For such a short conversation I feel understood. Almost hauntingly so.

Chapter Thirty-One

I doze on Friday and then I am cranky the next day when I get up. Fortunately, it's Saturday. I can be cranky. All I really want after breakfast is to go see Annalynn. And so I call her and ask her to come up to the cabin that night with me. When she says yes, I feel a lot less cranky. But it's quite a stretch from now to then.

My father wanders in the back door at about ten-thirty to find me absently sketching at the table.

"Got anything to do today?"

"I'm going to the cabin with Annalynn tonight."

His eyes narrow, as well they should— I didn't ask for permission. "Oh?" He says in a nasal tone.

"I nearly died. I know that. I need to see her, before I deal with that."

"Oh. Right." He sounds surprised instead now. "You can go, if that's it. But." He pauses and raps a pencil on the table. "We need to talk when you get back, before your mother comes home."

I look confused. "Isn't she coming in tonight?"

"I asked her to stay longer. We've made progress. We need to keep that. She's only too happy to oblige."

"Oh... I...." I hadn't really thought about it that way. "We have, I guess."

"You want to come out to the smithy and work the bellows for me?" He asks too casually.

Well, not really. "I could do that."

"You don't look like that's what you want to do."

"It's not. But I don't know what I want to do. For time to move faster."

"It's not going to. Come on, come do the

bellows."

"What are you making?" I ask as I clear away my tea cup.

"Stuff."

I roll my eyes.

"You'll see."

I follow him out to the smithy.

The forge is banked, and the smithy is cold.

"I thought you were working out here?"

"I was. Not everything I do requires the forge." He goes over to his work bench and picks something small up.

No, two something.

He hands me them, slender yet large rings with a careful design in the steel.

"They are Damascus steel mystery bracelets. I had the idea, and I made them, and thought you might like them."

I'm not sure what to do with two bracelets, being a guy.

"One for Annalynn, and one for you." He says when I don't say anything.

"Oh." It dawns on me that in his own way, this is his way of apologizing for having to take the box away. And perhaps approving a different avenue. "Thank you."

"But, I really do need the bellows worked—I've just gotten a request for carriage parts."

"Carriage parts?"

He makes a fair impression of a horse whinnying and clops his hands together a la Monty Python. "Carriage Parts. For a wedding company."

Oh no. "Not the decorative wheels."

My father, who loves making decorative

wheels, smiles. "Decorative wheels."

I escape the carriage wheels for a quick shower and then rush to pick Annalynn up. She seems quiet and reserved for the most part on the ride up and I try to enjoy the soft melody of the radio and the warmth of her presence. It is both comfortable and frustrating, because I want to talk to her and don't know where to begin. Which is awkward for me. I've always been able to just start talking to Annalynn.

When we finally get to the cabin and I've stopped the car, I suddenly lean over, grab her, and hold on for dear life. "I love you. Oh god how much I love you." I say as I rock us both back and forth. "You are so utterly wonderful and I'd miss you so much if...."

"If?" She says, sounding surprised.

"Anything. If anything." I say.

She hugs me back but I can feel her being confused.

I let her go. "Uhm. Shouldn't we go inside?" She asks.

"Sure."

I'm properly abashed and set about busying myself with hot chocolate.

We sip in silence until she rolls her eyes in my direction and then looks down at the table.

"Yes?" I respond.

"You aren't saying anything."

"I was waiting for you to say something."

"And maybe I'm waiting for you to say you love me again."

I look at her. "You aren't saying what I think you are, are you?"

She looks out the window. "Maybe."

Given that, it feels right to walk over and sit down at her feet and lay my head in her lap. I place my hands on her knees and sigh deeply.

She tangles her fingers in my hair. Yum.

"Merryweather?"

"Yes?"

"Would you please sit up? I need to talk to you."

I sit back and stare up at her. It's a new vantage, and I like it. I do go back to my chair though.

"We've been dancing around this since we started coming up here, haven't we?"

"Dancing around what?'

"Sex."

"Well, I don't think so." I think back to all the times I really thought seriously about touching her, and, no, I haven't really been thinking about sex per se. "I think I've more danced around what I really think about you."

"What do you think then?"

"I'm not sure. I've known you forever. Wouldn't it be kind of weird to just suddenly become lovers, and then get up tomorrow.....a la "Say Goodbye"?" I say, referencing an old Dave Mathews' Band song.

Annalynn opens her bag and pulls out a pink plastic box. "When we first started coming up here regularly, your mother absolutely insisted that I take birth control. I explained to her that I wasn't going to be doing anything of the sort, but she said that things could change in an instant, and she didn't want me blindsided." She opens the case. "This is a diaphragm."

"My mother?" The woman is shameless.
"Your mother."
"Uhm. Hmm." I say.
"I'd like to use it tonight."

Chapter Thirty-Two

I believe that I can say this is a fair bit more overwhelming for me than Annalynn. She seems to have been expecting it, and me— I had regulated it to my wilder dreams. Now, it's right in front of me and I feel fear more keenly than anything else. I am recalling sitting on my stool, naked and cold to my bones. All the ease that we had gained around each other in the days following that event escapes me.

That was nothing much, and this is, well... huge.

Well, maybe not, but right now it seems that way.

My thoughts do a sort of frenetically panicked dance. I'm too small; no I'm too big. I'm not what anyone would want to do. Not for a second. I'm not on anyone's "hottie" list. My fingers are almost completely useless as I zip the two sleeping bags together. I can't believe that Annalynn really thinks this is a good idea. She's still in the bathroom putting her diaphragm in when I lay the now single bag out on the pad. I smooth them out and realize my hands are shaking.

I put them together and breathe deeply.

"Do I want to do this?" I whisper to myself.

Yes.

But.

I don't want to screw up a friendship I value more than anything else I have. I don't want to wake up with regrets. Or worse yet, have her wake up with regrets.

On the other hand, she asked me.

I put on pajamas. Because it is hard to be physically uncomfortable in pajamas.

Then I get up and lean against the bathroom door.

"Annalynn— I'm worried." I almost use the word afraid.

"Don't be." She replies through the door, sounding, as usual, rather confident of her own decisions. "This is about 98% effective, and it's not hormonal. If we get really worried, there are some other preventative measures, and anyway, this is my least fertile time of the month according to all the rhythm method research I've done."

"That's not what I meant."

There is silence.

I can hear her sit down on the floor. "Well. What did you mean?"

I settle down more comfortably on my side of the door. "I really, really want to be yours in this way. But it's complicated."

"Is this about us staying friends, or you suddenly developing an ego and having performance anxiety?"

"Both." I could never have been that honest if it weren't for the door. "I'm kind of a loser at school."

"Hey. That loser you are talking about is my best friend."

"You feel their stares more heavily than I do. And you and I both know that it will feel like everyone knows at school on Monday." I say, even thought it isn't very nice.

"Emelle, they already think we are screwing like rabbits. If I had worries about being considered attached to you and being judged for it, they've been dead for a very long time."

"But what about the reality of it?"

"The reality is I've had this conversation with myself already. Weeks ago. A couple of times over."

"And?" I ask.

"I picked this anyway. I decided the next time we went up and the timing was okay by the calendar, I'd ask. I was particularly reassured that you decided to actually say out loud you loved me. But you are sort of raining on my parade here."

"I'm sorry."

"It's okay. Better to settle things beforehand."

"So, you really want to do this?"

There is a very long pause. "Measurements?"

"13 inches long, seven inches in circumference." I say deadpan.

"Yeah, right."

I laugh a little bit. "Okay, that's maybe a little off."

I pause for effect.

"Add a few more inches and you'll get a better idea of the truth."

"No, really. Come on." She says.

I get back to being serious. "About seven and some odd. I don't know how much around. I'm not circumcised."

"Cool."

"Cool?" I ask.

"Not too scary, not too small."

"Oh." I smile.

"Got a better handle on things yet?" She asks.

I think for a second. "We can do this and we can still be friends in the morning?"

"Yep."

"And it's okay if I'm not perfect?"

"Yep."

My fear breaks, and I finally feel excited. "Then I want this too." I say.

For some reason, I sort of expect her to emerge in porn-star glory, but when she comes out she is just my Annalynn. Her darkish, wiry hair and crooked front teeth. She already has some white hair too. But from my perspective on the floor, she has a sort of magnificence.

I stand up and reach out to her. She looks more nervous than she sounded.

I draw her pleasantly close to me and nuzzle her neck and run my hands up her sides.

"Yum."

"Really?" She asks.

I murmur an affirmative.

She wraps an arm around me and kneads my lower back.

"What do we do now?" She asks.

I smile. "Well, some physical things need to happen for this to work. Right?" I stroke her cheek with the back of my fingers.

She smiles and brings her hand up to her mouth again and shakes her head.

I should take the initiative, I know I should, but finding it in me is hard. So I ask instead of doing. "May I kiss you?"

She nods and shuts her eyes. I suppose she expects me to kiss her on the lips, but I can't imagine doing so, and I do what I had in mind, which is to kiss her ear and neck. She smells wonderful. I trail my nose underneath her chin and gently bite the other ear and then draw away. "Thank you."

Her eyes are huge and she grips my hands.

I smile and grip back.

The pause gets almost uncomfortable, until Annalynn places my hand against her stomach. It is warm and surprisingly soft. I run my fingers along it, and then I wonder if I ought to be braver and slip my hands northward or something. I've actually never fondled her, despite thinking about it a hundred times.

I steer us towards the bed instead, and tug gently on her shirt.

She stiffens up.

"Hmmmm?"

"Just give me a second." She whispers. And then she relaxes. "I don't want this to be messy, cold, or over in a flash." She says a bit louder.

I'm confused. It must show.

"You know, all the girls who get pregnant always say how it was over so quickly, it seemed messy, how they didn't feel loved. I always feel bad for them."

"Well," I say, now even more confused. "This was your idea, you know. You don't have to follow through. But, I thought that the chat we just had covered this."

"It was supposed to, I just feel a lot less brave now."

I back pedal and smooth her shirt back down. Then I sit down on the bed.

"Well," I say, attempting to be brave. "I don't think it will be cold. And I'll always love you. In fact, I may have always. I don't see that changing. But I don't know if it will be messy, or quick, or painful. I'd rather it isn't, but I've always been under the impression that it takes some practice."

"Practice?" Annalynn smiles lasciviously.

"Once does not make a master." I reply.

"What does once make then?" She asks as she stretches back on the bed.

"Ravenous, curious beasties?"

"Sounds interesting."

"So, are we doing this?"

"I think so. Yes." She replies.

I bury my nose into her body and suck in her perfume. I am surprised when she tentatively does the same to me, but then suddenly our noses are zooming across each other's skin and we are fighting to be the one not laying still. Fairly soon, noses morph into a strangely satisfying combination of lips, tongues, teeth and nose.

And then, I finally find myself naked, and she is too. I'm crouched at her ankles and I debate if this is it, or if something else needs to be done. I suspect so. I lean forward to kiss her stomach and then trail my nose through her hair until I find the epicenter of her feminine cologne and I am overcome with the urge to do something more than be buried inside her. I come away and tentatively bring up a finger to stroke her.

She wiggles, and sits up a bit. "What about you?"

I cock my head to one side. "What about me?"

"Don't you want to....?"

"I do, but I want you to enjoy things."

"I am enjoying things."

"Uhm, shouldn't you .....uh... first?"

"I don't know." She says. "Should I?"

I think for a second. "Yes. Show me how?"

She takes my hand and then stops. "No. I don't

want that. Come in."

"Really?"

She nods. "Yes, absolutely."

I inch into her. It is insanely good. I could cry tears of joy, I don't think anything else I have done in my life felt quite as good and right as this. She reaches down and strokes my stomach when I pause.

"Emelle?"

"Yes?"

"I love you, too."

Chapter Thirty-Three

I feel subdued when I get home. Happy, but low-key. I sit in the kitchen for about an hour with a cup of tea, watching the snow come down outside. My dad comes in from the smithy with flakes in his hair.

"Brrr." He states.

I can see snow melting on the smithy roof. "Uh-huh." I reply. "Want a cup of tea?"

"Yeah, that would be great." He says.

I stand up and put the water back on and attempt to think of something to say, but he beats me to it.

"Are you feeling better?"

...Uhm.... "I guess."

There is a long pause, in which he looks at me searchingly. The teapot begins to whistle and I just stand at the stove, as if I was confused by the meaning of the sound. He stands up and pours himself a cup when it's clear my mind has wandered.

"Are you and Annalynn okay?" He says, seeming to think that there's a possibility things are going wrong.

"Uhm, we're...."I blush, badly. "Fine."

He takes a step back and looks me over and cracks a small, strange grin.

"Oh!" He smiles more broadly, and stands up on his toes, smooths my hair down and briefly puts his nose against my hairline, as if he thought to kiss me like I was a much younger child.
"Congratulations, I suppose. I certainly wasn't expecting that though."

"I wasn't either." I say honestly. And then I switch gears. "Why aren't you upset?"

"I came around to your mother's way of thinking; realized a few weeks ago that you actually love Annalynn as much as anyone loves anybody."

"And that evaporates your earlier opposition and makes it okay?"

"Yeah, pretty much. Seventeen year old me, and seventeen year old you have very different ways of thinking. You are light-years ahead of where I was."

I boggle for a few moments.

"Look, sit down. I know your mother gave you the typical sex talk years ago, but there're probably a few things you can learn from me." He says and pulls out a chair at the table.

"When I was seventeen, I saw women as specialized machines. Input date and flowers, output blowjob. My understanding was completely focused around that they could provide a newer and better pleasure than what I had been experiencing. I thought that until about the middle of college, in fact."

"I bet you got lots of second dates."

"Not really." He says, missing the sarcasm. "I didn't get second dates until I met your mother. Flowers and date got a giggle, and my suggestion that she provide something for the trouble I'd gone to earned me a peck on the cheek and an invitation to help her clean out an apartment the next day and share a six pack of imported beer. I was so pissed, but I went there anyway. When we finished cleaning that place out, she gave me a hug, and told me that this was worth something more than a peck on the cheek and she let me come home and snuggle with her for the night. It was different. In the morning, she told me that women weren't machines."

I prop my chin up in my hands and look at him from across the table.

"What I had to figure out for myself is that men aren't either. The flowers-date-and-blowjob paradigm stopped working, and I came to realize that once I stepped away from the equation, I had to learn a lot more than I ever wanted to about sex."

I stop him. "I can't believe you thought it was some sort of mechanical equation."

"Well, what is it then?"

"An expression."

"See? Light years ahead of me at your age."

"Okay."

"But, there is probably something that you could benefit from knowing before you get in too deep. Sleeping with Annalynn will make certain parts of your mind like glass when it comes to her. Men share the depth of their emotions with their skin. Once you've opened that up, there are parts of you that she can shatter with the merest touch."

"Seems like it's a double-edged sword for both of us then."

"It is; just be careful."

He drinks his tea for a few moments, savoring it.

"What did you do with the mystery bracelets?"

"I'm going to give it to her on Monday, at school."

"Why then?"

"Dunno, just feels right." I reply.

Chapter Thirty-Four

Thursday night finds my father carefully carving a wax last for a small, delicate ring.

"Who's that going to be for?" I ask.

"MEEEEE!" My mother trills from the kitchen.

"Well actually—" he begins.

She starts growling.

"—Yes." He finishes.

"Oh good." She sticks her head out the kitchen door and into the dining room. "What do we want for dinner?"

"The neighbor's cat." My father replies.

"Right. Let me load up the Remington and make that happen." She mimes the actions to clear and prime a pump action shotgun. "Now seriously."

"Chicken." I offer.

"We have chicken every night." He whines.

"Barbeque pork?" I suggest.

"Hmmmm. I could do that."

She vanishes back into the kitchen. Normally I'd go in and help, but I have a question I'm more comfortable asking my father right this very second.

"Can I take Annalynn to the cabin this weekend again?"

"Addictive, isn't it?" He says without looking up.

I grin sheepishly. "Yeah."

He sets down his tools from one hand and ruffles my hair a bit. "Go, be happy." He grins. "Do we need to run to the pharmacy?"

I am sure I look like a deer in headlights.

He looks worried.

"You've thought about that, right?"

"Annalynn is taking care of it."

He wrinkles up his forehead. "That isn't what I expected."

"Me neither. But it's what she wants."

"Oh. Well then."

We sit quietly, me contemplating the sudden changes in my life, and him, presumably, thinking about the wisdom of letting his teenage son be alone with a girl.

My mother sticks her head back out of the kitchen to look at both of us.

"It got quiet out here." She says, by way of explanation.

We both look at her.

"I'm not used to quiet." She says.

"Maybe it's peaceful?" My dad offers.

She looks at him, and looks at me, squinches up her eyebrows and goes back into the kitchen. Shortly she reappears with barbeque pork.

"Uhm." She says. "Has something happened that I need to know about?"

I look at my Dad, who looks at me. It is the obvious expression of "This is yours Kiddo."

"Our Elephant moved." I say.

"Where?" She asks.

"Out."

"Did it take the Animosity with it?"

"Like so many of our tenants, it left some things to clean up." I say.

"Ted?" My mother asks, looking at him, her eyes engaging in their own variety of parental-couple-in-front-of-offspring speech.

"That's about the measure of it, yes." He sips his tea and looks at her over the rim of the cup. He is waiting for something, and I realize he's hiding behind a coffee mug.

"Well, that's certainly unexpected." She says.

We all chew in silence.

"I am going to clean out the basement." My mother says when our plates are mostly clear.

"Why?" I ask.

"Because." She beckons to my father.

"Wait a second... I'm getting stuck with the dishes." I theatrically whimper.

"Well, kiddo, that's the way the cookie crumbles."

About halfway through the dishes, I have a thought and open the basement door.

"You guys are down there talking about me, aren't you?" I bellow.

"Yes, we are, sweetie." My mother replies.

"Do you think you could at least manage to hide your motives a bit better?"

"Hello, I'm a parent? I'm supposed to be Captain Obvious." She yells back up the stairs.

"Well, I guess so long as we're clear on this." I say and close the door.

Chapter Thirty-Five

Later on Friday, before I pick up Annalynn, my mother bellows from the basement for me.

I crack open the door. "I thought there wasn't any lung-assisted intercom allowed in this place."

She blows a raspberry from one of the storerooms. "I have something for you, get down here."

I shamble down the stairs and poke my head in the storeroom. "What?"

She moves out of the way.

I see a heap of dust and cobwebs on some sort of table.

"Really." I say.

My mother swabs at it ineffectually with a rag and takes something off the top.

It's a very old sewing machine covered in grease and oils.

She looks at me like I'm supposed to understand.

I don't.

"It's your great-great grandfather's machine."

"Oh!" Now, that is interesting. "How did it come to be here, exactly?"

"It's been down here for about 16 years."

"You have something, in this house, that you don't use?" I'm shocked. Miss Utility has something she doesn't use? Surely, there went the center of the universe—my mother has one piece of 'junk'.

"I wasn't supposed to." She says.

"What's that mean?"

"Well, Grampa wanted for you to have it. Not me, but you."

"Why's that?" After all, I knew quite well that

Mom was the apple of her great-grandfather's eye[16].

"Grampa was a tailor. He had a daughter. Back then a woman just wasn't a tailor. My grandmother had two daughters. My aunt, of course, didn't have any children. Grampa told my mother that he gave up—he'd just have to make me the grandson he wanted. He started calling me Paul and taking me hunting. In fact, he even dressed me in little sailor suits and miniature sport coats. And when I got older, he taught me how to sew and tailor. He so very much wanted a grandson. And then I got pregnant, and you'd think he would have told me what a shame I was, but instead, he came into my apartment and told me that I'd better have a boy, or else!"

She pauses to laugh.

"So how does this determine that the sewing machine is mine?"

"I'm getting there." She says. "He thought that you were perfect. He was 96 or something, and he was already planning to teach you to tailor and to hunt and fish and ride a horse." She pauses again and blinks furiously. "He didn't quite make it there."

She continues after a second. "But he made you the most fantastic clothes just like he had for me. As old as he was, he'd sit you next to the treadle in a bassinet and sew these tiny, tiny clothes for you. And while you were staring up at him he told you how he was doing everything. One day while he was visiting with you, he turned to me and said, 'Paul, I want him to have my machine when he's older.' He wasn't sure you'd remember him, but he knew that

16 By Grampa, she means her great-grandfather, as her real grandfather had been killed in the war.

you would use it well, he was convinced of it.

"A couple days later, he was dying and my mother called me and said, all he wants is to see you and his great-grandson. We went to the hospital, and he saw you and smiled, and patted hands and passed away. When we got to cleaning out his apartment, we found the machine like this—ready for long-term storage."

"That seems like a lot of work for a very old man."

"I think he died with a very clear image of what he wanted to leave behind."

"Mom, I'm not very good at sewing. I can make really basic things. A sport coat is more than a little beyond me."

"That's okay. He also left you a book."

"A book?"

"A copy of the one he made for me. It's basically how to do everything. Complete with hand-drawn illustrations. You know, the one I always use."

"He wrote that?"

"Yes. In the last decade of his life, he had this fear that his knowledge would vanish. In his mind, books offered the greatest chance at permanence, so he wrote one, and illustrated it and bound up three copies. All three of which currently belong to me and you."

She hands me a hand-bound leather book.

I open it.

A Guide to Tailoring by Alexander Fairchild.

It looks interesting. I tell my mother as much.

"Well, I thought so too. Help me get this thing into the car; it's probably a mess from sitting down here." She says, patting the machine affectionately.

Chapter Thirty-Six

Annalynn and I are flopped on our stomachs in the living room leafing through college class catalogues.

"Are you sure you want to be an EMT?" I ask.

"Yeah," she says, "I don't think I want to do a four year college with all the stupid pre-requisites. It was a push getting into Running Start anyway. I might go back to college later, when I don't feel so burned out."

I flip through some class offerings at Eastern. "I suppose that's more practical than an art degree."

"It is, but then, I don't have two family businesses to pick from." Annalynn says sagely. "You can afford to do what you want, how you want, and never really worry."

"Well it's a bit more complicated than that." My mother comments from where she is scrutinizing rent checks. She leans over to the catalogue I'm viewing and flips to the business classes. "Take at least a few, Em."

My father wanders in right about then, and looks at the book, flips to industrial arts. "Take some of these too."

"Whatever happened to do your own thing?" I ask.

Annalynn flips to art. "Take a lot of these as well." She winks.

"What about my interests?"

"They don't offer classes on the Kama Sutra." Dad offers.

"Ted!", "Dad!", "Ewww." Mom, myself and Annalynn say in unison.

He pulls a cookie from the jar on the table,

attempts to look innocent and sets a kettle of tea in the kitchen. "Well, it's true." He shouts from the other room.

I return to the catalogue. "I think I'll just take some math and some English."

"And a business course." My mother says with a tone that brooks no argument.

"And a business course." I repeat.

"All he'll do is sleep through the quarter." My dad retorts. "Take something harder."

"Like what?"

"I dunno. I liked taking one course that made me just a little nervous each quarter."

I forget most of the time, that Dad even has a college education. His life fell apart so fast afterward that he never really put anything to use until he got the smithy up and running when I was six. He picks up the book of courses and reads for a few minutes.

"How about this?" He points to an art class about oil painting. "You've never done anything with oils."

"It's still 'art' though." I say. "I'm not sure it would be harder."

He smiles, it's just a bit malicious, and flips around in the book. "Take this too, then."

"Dancing?" I say.

"Cool." Annalynn says.

"Uh. No." I reply.

"They always need more boys." My mother offers.

"On second thought, not cool." Annalynn says.

Memo to self; buy Annalynn something she wants.

"Remember, you've got a month plus to figure

it out still." Mom advises. "They won't let you sign up for classes until about May. It's only March now."

Annalynn and I look at each other. "Track." We say at the same time.

In the hassle to work out kinks with Running Start and keeping up after the accelerated classes' homework, we'd entirely forgotten that track was going to start in less than two weeks.

"We haven't done any pre-season training." Annalynn says.

"Oh god...." I reply, my eyes getting wide. "We are going to be so sore."

"Coach Joan will FRY us if we show up all doughy."

"If we buy new shoes tonight we can get started and not be too far behind everyone else." I say.

Mom checks the clock. "Shoe shopping at eight on Saturday night?"

"Better late than never. The alternative is even less broken in shoes, Paul." Annalynn says.

"Oh." Mom says. "When will you be back?"

I look at Annalynn. She shrugs. "If we go running tonight?"

"Tonight?" I ask.

"Like I was saying, they aren't going to break themselves in...."

"Why don't you guys go stay up at the cabin and go run the obstacle course up there that you set up?" Dad offers.

"Sounds good." Annalynn says. "We can grab something to eat on the way up."

"Start the bath before you go out, and it'll be nice once you get back for a soak." Dad suggests.

My mother gives him a sharp look but says nothing.

"Right. Good idea." I say as I grab my jacket and wallet and help Annalynn into hers. "Shoes, Snacks, Bath, Run."

"Sounds good." Annalynn says to me. "Thanks," she says to my parents and we shove out the door and pile into the car.

Chapter Thirty-Seven

Ducks quacking on the nightstand wake me up.

I wonder briefly what's happening, but Annalynn leans over me to grab her cell phone and I realize it's her new ringtone.

"Wow, that's unusually obnoxious." I mutter.

She flips the phone open. "Hello?"

Murrmrmememmrmrmrur.

"I'm up at the Foster's Cabin with Em."

Murrmmmmmur mur.

"Yeah."

Muuurmmmmmmmr.

"I'll be home in the morning."

Murm Mur.

"You too."

She flips her phone closed and sets it back down.

Maybe it's the time of day, or maybe I'm just feeling callous, but whatever the reason, I finally ask something that's been on my mind for the better part of two months.

"Do your parents actually know where you are most of the time?"

"No." She replies.

"Don't you care that they don't?"

"I'm over it."

"I think it's weird."

"Well, they're burned out or something." She says, her voice taking on a mildly upset tone that she is trying to hide.

"Thank god you're self sufficient then." I reply, since in so many ways she is now.

"I'm really not." She says in a small voice.

"You don't think so?"

"My parents give me a big allowance, and they pay for clothes and school stuff. I don't really have to worry. In return, my job is watching the cats when they are off on cruises. It's not even remotely realistic. All I have to do is show up from time to time. We don't even eat dinner as a family on Thanksgiving or Christmas."

"You eat it with us."

"Yeah. I know. You guys are a lot more like family than my own family is. When my period first started, I talked to your mom, not mine. When I broke my ankle last year, your Dad took me to the clinic."

I think back to when I first met Annalynn. Her parents were so involved and normal. "What happened?" I mutter to the ceiling, halfway knowing, halfway still confused.

"Someone else was willing to take on the work? My mom stopped caring about appearances after her mom died last year. She no longer had to be the perfect daughter, mother and wife, and so she decided she wasn't going to be at all. She's just perfectly selfish. Or something. I don't really know anymore." Annalynn leans against the headboard. "I'm just not sure. They seemed like normal parents, if kind of weak-willed when I was younger. You know I could always push my Dad around." She pauses to look at me, and I nod. "And then she and Dad has this, 'we need to reconnect as adults thing' for a couple of months, and that seemed reasonable. They need to be a couple sometimes. But they really just stopped being parents. And when her mom died, we stopped even being family."

I sit up and put a companionable arm around her. It feels like as I've gotten myself out of the hole with my dad; she's gotten herself into the hole with her parents.

She leans her head on my shoulder and I squeeze her tighter.

She suddenly turns and gives me a searing kiss of earthshaking force. I tentatively return it and she pushes me against the headboard and climbs into my lap. The heady buzz that filled me when I was wrapped in ropes and playing my own imagination starts to leak into my body and I can feel the grind of the headboard against my skull and it's oh so delicious.

I melt, I float, I soar.

Before I know it, Annalynn has a fistful of my hair and has dragged me over her. It doesn't seem like a good idea. For one, I don't think there is any birth control within 15 feet of the bed, and secondly, I'm not sure sex is going to do any good for mental distress caused by errant parents.

"Hey... stop." I say quietly.

"Oh. Sorry." She whispers, and releases my hair.

"That's not what I meant."

"Huh?"

"We're not doing this right this second."

"Uhm, sure we are." She says and reaches to pull me back down.

"No, we're not." I push up and away.

"What do you mean?"

"A sense of belonging and wantedness from me isn't going to fix or change the fact you don't feel that with your parents." I feel awkward and horrible. "I love you, and I don't need to sleep with you to prove anything. And, really, you don't need me to sleep with you to know it either."

Her eyes get glassy. "It has nothing to do with that."

"Yeah. I think it does. I'm not going to do this."

"What the hell? Your girlfriend wants your body and you just say 'no'?" Her voice is getting shrill.

I put my hands on her shoulders. "Annalynn, I love you more than the sun, the moon, the oceans and earth three times over." I say because it's true. "But, that isn't going to help you here. More bread isn't going to help you if you've got scurvy. I'm bread, if you get what I mean."

"What makes you so wise?"

"Nothing really. I just began working things out with Dad though. It's made a big difference in life. You know that."

"Fine, whatever."

I lay back down and throw an arm around her. "Really. I'm only going to have sex with you when it's not to plug emotional holes. Otherwise, it's not safe or sane. It's not a cure-all for all emotional pain. It's just an expression between you and me."

And thanks, Mom, I think, for that huge embarrassing chat about what sex was and wasn't.

Annalynn makes a non-committal sound and scoots away from me.

Ouch.

"I'm sorry."

"Uh huh." She mutters and I get the idea I need to shut up.

So I do.

In the morning, I wake up, and she's already up. Bright sunlight fills the cabin, and I realise that it snowed overnight. I can smell Annalynn's hot chocolate from where I am snug in bed.

"Mmmmm. Is there a cup for me?" I ask, and raise my head a bit.

"No."

She sounds upset and defensive.

"Oh." I say.

I sit all the way up and look at her. Her face is streaked with tear stains, her eyes are glassy and red, and she's pulled her sweater down to cover her hands which means she's been wiping a runny nose most of the morning.

I almost begin to ask what's wrong, but she cuts me off with "You were right, last night. And I don't like you because of that."

Well, that doesn't sound hopeless or anything. I don't say anything.

"Can you just drive me home and give me some time to think about what you said?"

"Yes, I can do that." I say. But I think my soul is beginning to crack in half—what if, in the end, she chooses to go away permanently?

She looks at my face.

"I'm not talking about forever."

This makes it less scary, provided I believe her. I'm still cracking.

"Just, get dressed and drive me back."

I do as she asks and then feel my composure melt some as I drive away from her house.

By the time I park my car, I'm shaking.

I fall with no grace into the hall-tree and sit and shake.

"Really wore yourselves out?" My mom asks.

"Uh. Yeah, but not this morning." I say, scrabbling for words.

My mother takes a better look at me. "You look terrible, what happened?"

"Annalynn told me she didn't like me this morning."

"Didn't like you as a boyfriend? Or?"

"She doesn't like me as a person right now." I clarify.

Mom looks utterly horrified.

She pets my head and walks purposefully into the kitchen.

She reappears with tea. Of course, the universal improve-all.

"Well, it's only temporary?" My mother says.

"It has to be, what will I do if she's wrong, and it's not?"

"Well, we've got to have some faith, I guess, that it will turn out in the end."

"Paul," My dad interjects, stepping into the room. "I suspect that only works for people that have dead angels for a best friend. The rest of us like plans and paths out of the hole."

Just a month before, I might have taken offense that he'd poked one of her core beliefs; that Michael watched over her and helped all the things that should happen to happen. But right now, I'm in his camp. I don't want to be running on blind faith and a philosophy. I want a plan.

"Yes, a plan would be nice."

"Leave her alone for a couple of days." He says. "You can rarely go wrong giving people what they ask for."

"I won't know what to do with myself." I say. It's painfully true.

"Is she still wearing her bracelet?" He asks.

"What has that got to do with anything?" My mother asks.

"Symbols like that mean a lot to her." He says, and when no one interrupts, he continues. "If she didn't feel like a few days of thought would fix things, she'd have taken it off, because she wouldn't be able to accept wearing it without accepting its meaning."

"Which is what?" My mother asks.

"They belong to each other."

He turns back to me. "It's not going to be easy."

"But it's probably going to be okay later." I finish.

"I'm supposed to buy that?" My mother says.

"Makes more sense than angels." My fathers says.

"Says you." My mother replies, darkly.

He looks perplexed. "We should talk later, I think?"

"Yeah, we need to talk later." My mother agrees.

I stare up at them.

"Don't worry." My mom says. "Go take a nap, or just sit and be restful."

They do talk later, and I hear snatches through the ducts.

"Would there be anything left if Annalynn just 'poof' and left?" My mother asks. "I've never worried before about him committing suicide, but now I'm terrified. Love is terrible."

"It is." My father agrees. "But, Annalynn loves him too, she won't tear him apart."

"How do you know?"

"I believe." He sighs. "Would Michael really let you lose your kid?"

"I never thought he was looking out for anyone but me."

"He'd never let it happen. And you swear up down and sideways he is looking out for you."

"Ted." My mother tempers. "I can't tell myself anything concrete—that this is a high school thing, so it's not that important, blah blah, yadda yadda. If my son loses Annalynn, I might lose my son. Faith is an awfully thin wall to lean on in times like this."

"I know." He says. "Just imagine how you'd feel if there was nothing to lean on at all."

Chapter Thirty-Eight

Annalynn and I are not back to how we were until long after State Championships, finals, and a good portion of the summer. Community College starts earlier than Eastern does, and the two week stretch between seems like an eternity. I wonder if the space will be good to us, or if it will stretch us like taffy until we break in the center.

We go to Manito the last warm night of the year, late September. It is a dusky twilight and the stone railing around the Davenport Fountain is still warm from the sun.

"What do you think of college?" I ask, knowing I start the next week.

"It's not really college," she scoffs. "I'm just training to be an EMT."

"When do you get to start doing it for real?" I ask.

"Early winter. Probably January or something."

"I'm going to bum money off you." I say.

"Finally, I won't have to bum it from you." She says, and traces patterns on the stone with the toe of her shoe.

"I can't believe it. You are going to start working in January, and we graduate in June."

"Les-Free, ever after." She offers.

"Happily ever after." I joke.

"Do you think I'm making a mistake going to community college?"

"No." I say very truthfully. "Four years isn't for everybody. I'm not even sure it's for me."

"Really?"

"Yeah, really."

"Neither of my parents have a college

education, you know." She says. "I don't want to perpetuate some dumb cycle."

"Well, you said you were tired of school, and that you just want to be done for now. It's not like you can't change your mind later." I say. "And you're still getting secondary education, it's not like you are skating by on a high school diploma or anything."

"But if being an EMT doesn't work out, that's all I'll have."

"If college doesn't work out, that's all I'll have too. It's not a magic key that opens all doors."

"They treat it like it is in high school."

"They also treated Josh the Rocket like royalty; let's not make too many assumptions here." I argue.

Annalynn sighs.

I don't say anything.

"It seems a lot harder on this side of the fence."

"Future got here a bit faster than expected?" I ask rhetorically; I feel the same way.

"When I was twelve or something like that," Annalynn starts to say as she removes her shoes, "I thought I'm going to grow up and be an EMT and have a cool apartment downtown and you and I were going to still be best friends. Maybe you would even live across the hall. And then," she continues as she pulls off her socks, "when I was sixteen, I started to lose sight of that particular vision. Things got more complicated. Maybe, I thought, you and I would get together, and we'd share the cool apartment downtown and I'd still be an EMT."

"And?" I prompt when she stalls.

"Now I am sleeping with you and—"

"—not for months now." I interject.

"Okay, was sleeping with you, and I'm going to

be an EMT, but what about the rest of it? You know, the liberation and the being on my own and having a spot in the world?"

"Viva la vie Boehm?" I quote one of her favorite movies, *Rent*. "That's not Spokane."

"We could go to Portland or Seattle after I get my certificate. They are like that there, funky and different and liberated and a good place to be young with money."

I look at her.

She looks back at me pointedly.

"But we aren't those things." I finally say. "We can pretend, if you want, this coming summer." I say, to soften the blow. "I'll make myself poet shirts and wear Birkenstocks and everything. And you can have hippie dresses."

She steps into the fountain, as though ignoring me. "The water is kind of warm."

"Uh huh."

She throws a spray at me. It is warm.

"You are evil." I comment, and lose my shoes and socks.

"Just changing the tone of the evening." She says, as I get into the fountain, and then slogs away from me.

I mockingly chase her.

The sun settles lower and lower in the sky as we flick water at each other and attempt to dunk each other. When the light is just a thin orange line surrounded by purple, Annalynn leans against the trunk of the fountain, laughing. I stop to look at her in two ways. Firstly, through artist's eyes; I want to fix the scene in my mind so that I can draw it with chalk someday. Secondly, through my heart.

If I was given a choice about the matter, I'd spend all my hours like this, in this sudden magical moment. The Truth, capital T and all, wells up in my mind. If I knew it before, it wasn't like this sudden knowing that took over my entire being. I want to marry Annalynn.

She notices my sudden stillness. "What?"

I still my lips and tongue from saying a word of what I have just had go through my mind. At our age, it's considered blasphemy anyway.

"You." I say instead. "Come on, before someone calls the cops or ousts us while wielding garden implements."

She laughs, and climbs out of the water and drips on me deliberately.

"Where now?" She asks.

"The cabin, but after we get dry clothes."

"Should we?" She asks. "I mean, would your parents mind?"

"Nope." I say, thinking back to what Dad said the other day while we were washing out jars for Mom. He said the cabin was mine to use now, so long as I saw to keeping up with it. After all, he tempered, they hadn't used it in years.

When we get to the cabin, I notice something in the middle of the table. It's a little brass key, like as for a padlock, on a ribbon. I pick it up and look at it for a bit, before realizing it must be the key to my old toy box. I look around the cabin, and there it sits near the bed, but not conspicuous. It could just as easily be something storing blankets.

Annalynn looks at me staring at the key.

"What's that?" She asks.

"A suggestion from Dad."

"What?"

I put a hand on her wrist and tug gently. I'm feeling brave and invincible from my epiphany.

"Do you remember that box we found at the apartment with all the stolen jewelry?"

"The one in the closet with all the weird sex toys?"

"Yeah. That one." I fiddle with the lock.

"You kept it?" Annalynn says, as though I have pulled a great coup.

"No. Something different, but like it."

I open it, and it's perfectly organized, ropes in tidy order, and the few toys I own hanging on the lid.

Annalynn reaches out and touches the rope.

"You kept this from me?"

"I thought you wouldn't approve."

"But you kept a secret from me." She says. It is not an accusation.

"I thought I had to." I say.

"I can imagine." She said. "Keeping quiet isn't one of your strengths... I'm so surprised that, well, this didn't come out of the, uhm, box, sooner. But..." she lets her words trail off.

"But what?"

"I knew you liked pain, a bit. You are a masochist, aren't you?"

"Yes." I blurt, shocked. "How did you know?"

"I got rough a couple of times, and you always got dreamy when I did."

"Oh." I smile a bit goofily.

"Can we play with this stuff?"

I think about it. "Maybe. But we should, you know, talk first."

I pull a few of the simplest things out, and

begin to explain them.

Later I drowse against the headboard, Annalynn resting her head comfortably on my stomach. I feel free, really and truly free.

"We are liberated." I say.

"You think so?"

"Maybe being liberated is nothing more than sometimes getting to be exactly who you are, and for a few minutes, not pretending anything."

"What about being exactly who you are all the time?"

"Well, maybe that's honest, but it's more out-of-control than liberated, I think."

"So, when liberated, you are a masochist?"

"I'm not a masochist in every situation. It's just who I am in this one, and getting to be the person I am in this exact situation is liberation."

"And who am I in this liberating situation?" She asks, coyly.

"My lover?"

She rolls and looks at me, confused.

"Isn't that exactly who you were in that situation, no pretending, no holding back?"

She nods. "So liberation is sometimes letting yourself be something to someone else, because being that person is your most honest state in that situation?"

"I guess so."

She thinks.

"I love you dearly, you know." I say.

"Yes. I do." She looks at me. "It feels like an ocean, you know. It's overwhelming at times."

"What?"

"Being loved by you, it's like swimming in the middle of the ocean, or staring down a tidal wave. There's just so much of it."

"It feels like that inside of me, sometimes." I agree. "I could, and sometimes do, get lost in it."

"I just don't feel like that. It makes me wonder if I'm the lesser of us."

"You aren't." I say.

"But I don't feel it like you do."

"Do you have to?"

"I don't know."

"It will come sometime, when you least expect it." I say.

"You sound so confident."

I think more hopeful. But I don't say that. Instead, "You'll like it when it does." I say.

"Oh?"

"It's one of the best feelings in the world. It should feel limiting, but really, it makes me feel infinite and boundless."

She smiles.

"You are beautiful." I say.

"So are you."

Chapter Thirty-Nine

The big difference that I can note between college and high-school is that less happens. I start working afternoons in the smithy because there is virtually no turnover in my mother's units, and she doesn't need me. Otherwise, it's the same thing: I go to class, I come home, I do homework, and I work.

"I kind of thought college would be more exciting." I say one day while weeding the garden.

"Me too." My Dad says as he works on a sketch of a part.

"Really? I always thought you had sort of a party-hardy time at college."

"I only showed up to the ones where basically the whole town was invited. I wasn't exactly the life of them. Or really, invited."

I look up from the raspberry tangle, my cheeks shoved full.

My father meets my eyes. "Oh, for god's sake, you just snatched that out of the dirt, don't put it in your mouth."

I swallow. "For better or worse, I can actually say what precisely the dirt in here consists of, and therefore, much about the contamination or lack thereof in the fruit I just ate. We make our own compost, remember?"

He looks at the compost barrel. "That thing smells like a cesspool."

"Garbage in, great results out." I smack my lips.

"That is so gross." He shudders.

"Anyway." I say as I put the rest of the

raspberries in a bucket. "I've been there three weeks. I'm not sure it's all that different. Not perhaps the experience I was thinking about."

"Are you disappointed?"

I look up at him again. "I don't know yet. I suspect I am."

"Why?"

"I thought I might meet someone like me."

I hear a very big sigh. He puts down everything. "You know, I always wanted to say something...."

"About?"

"The way your mother reared you. She wanted to raise a good kid, but she wanted to you to be the sort of person she wants the world to have. I'm not sure that was healthy. Because you aren't like your peers...in ways that probably make a big difference."

"Well, is it a good difference?"

"I don't know; it certainly causes distance. And a lot of it." He pauses. "You were the epitome of gender neutral. People would see you in the park and they wouldn't say, "oh, what a cute little boy", or "what a cute little girl." They would start to say "what a cute little," and then they'd squint their eyes and pause before finishing with "kid."

I think this is amusing.

"It didn't help that your mother never, ever dressed you in anything indicative, and she referred to you as 'the sprogling."

"The sprogling?"

"Your aunt Sprite came up with it when you were three and half hours old. She marched into the hospital room and announced that you were possibly the ugliest sprogling she'd ever seen."

"That's not a very nice thing to say to your sister."

"It was kind of true, according to your mother. I thought you were perfectly normal for a baby, even cute perhaps." He says, with a whiff of holier-than-thou in his voice. "But you were the gender-neutral baby, and then a gender neutral kid, and now.... You're kind of a weird boy."

I do not like this. "Excuse me?"

"What are you doing right now?"

"Weeding the garden?"

"And you like weeding the garden?"

"Well, not a lot, but I get to eat stuff later." I explain.

"Most people consider this a chore. They don't come out on their own volition."

"Yes, I know that." I say. "How has this got to do specifically with me being a weird boy?" I leave the emphasis on the last word.

"Gardening is traditionally the work of women or old men."

"That's nice." I say and angrily smash a weed.

"I'm not saying it's bad, it's just that most of your male peers don't get you. You do track, but that is basically the co-ed sport of nerds, which is by the way, the most gender neutral social standing to acquire. You are heavily addicted to science fiction and fantasy, but again, that's an aspect of nerddom." He holds up a hand when I begin to protest. "Nerddom is fine, certainly I was one of the prominent members of it in high school. But it wins no favors. Competencies, yes. But not favors."

"So being competent at gardening, two languages, running in ovals and art makes me too unlike my peers for comfort?" My nostrils flare.

He completely gives up the pretense of sketching. "Basically, yes. I don't think you would have been so odd in the eighties, because it was more acceptable to have hobbies. But now, either you're the outdoorsy type, or you stay at home and play video games. Or, you can be a music geek, I guess."

"Art is a hobby, gardening is something I do because it needs to get done. It's kind of like the laundry. Art is not such an odd hobby, is it?" I say, and then realize that my art class is populated with girls and self-declared homosexuals. I get a vague sinking feeling.

"It didn't used to be, that's for sure." He sighs loudly twice before continuing. "I'm not saying this to be mean. It's just, you aren't like your peers and that's okay. But at the same time, it gives you limits. Especially around here. Spokane has a lot invested in conformity still."

He closes the sketchbook. "You're actually a lot like your mother. She's so competent at so many things, and sometimes you have to make yourself remember that she's female as well as being a person. Because she comes across so strongly as just a person. As she gets further away from very obvious motherhood, which is this very quintessential feminine thing, the sense of person is even more powerful."

"That's very sweet of you, Ted." My mother says as she sticks her head out the back door. "But I sort of think that since you hug me every single day that you'd have noticed that I'm very, very woman-shaped and therefore, most decidedly female." She smiles.

He turns around and sighs. "Not quite what I was trying to explain."

She comes outside all the way.

"Is this the old argument of my 'hippie-granola pseudo-feminist' parenting screwing up our kid?" She says, a little wearily.

"Hippie-granola pseudo feminist?" I ask.

"Well, I called it well-rounded child-rearing."

I glare at Dad. "You called it hippie-granola pseudo-feminist parenting?"

"No, Sprite did."[17] My mother says. "At the time I was pregnant, there was a lot of literature about letting your baby grow up to create their own personal identity, free of pre-determined gender roles and societal pigeonholes. There was this big push towards letting your children have options to work with both sides of the spectrum. You know, put your boy child in ballet, and your girls in wrestling and let them see what they liked. I thought it seemed very reasonable."

"And I thought she was a little overboard." My father offers.

"And Sprite thought that it was a pile of, quote, horseshit." My mother offers.

Having grown up in an era of gay pride, gender sensitivity, and theoretically, complete political correctness, I'm a little confused as to Sprite's opinion. "Why?"

"We grew up in a family of almost all women. The men were dead or simply... not there. All the girls had to be competent all-around because of that. Sprite had a word for when we had to mow the lawn

---

17 Why do I get the impression Sprite didn't like children?

or wash the cars. She called it 'man-chores.' And while she learned all of them, she and so many of the other women in my family, couldn't wait to hand over the man-chores at the first opportunity. Which meant the men didn't have to be anything more than men once they arrived."

It makes sense. "Okay" I say.

"So," she continues. "I was essentially raising you like a girl in my family; being able to do everything. But when I paired it with all the pick-your-own-adventure parenting stuff, it turned out you were really kind of domestic."

"Which," my Dad interrupts, "was about the time I decided things were going overboard. I didn't mind if you knew how to cook and garden, but I wanted you to be more little-boyish than you were. Like, you never wanted a puppy."

"The first time I saw a real puppy I was almost nine." I don't mention that it was sick and puked on my feet. "It didn't seem that great." I say, instead of offering details.

Both my parents shrug.

"But," says my father, "That's why you don't find too many people like yourself. There aren't a lot of domestic men to begin with, and I think a lot of them are stopped from being that way before they really get to develop that aspect of themselves. I still wonder if you'd be happier or better off if we had encouraged you to be more masculine." He finishes.

I look to my mother.

"I think you turned out fine. You're one of the good people of the world. It needs more of us."

Dad shoots me the I-told-you-so look.

"But do you think I should have been made to

be more boyish?"

She thinks. "No. I think that our boys have been left behind in the recent times, the way the girls of my generation were left behind. I think the way I raised you lets you be the sort of person that boys should be allowed to be if that's who they are. Although your Dad is right, you are very domestic. Which is odd, but not bad." She opens the door. "I like you, and I suppose that means things turned out okay." She goes back inside.

I look back at my father.

"I still wonder, Em. But then, I'm not a secure person, and the sort of person you are perhaps points out my failings a bit poignantly. Or so said one of the therapists I saw."

"Which part did they say?"

"The part about you pointing out my failings. I knew I was insecure walking in. Never have been secure."

"Why not?"

"My father always thought I was too much of a brooding girl."

"So you were one of those stunted domestic men?"

"I recall liking to bake with my mom, yes."

I get the impression that this might be a tender spot, and I let it go.

He, however, doesn't. "I was encouraged to be more boyish. I wasn't allowed to read science-fiction and fantasy. Too soft, he said. I wasn't allowed to bake at all after I turned ten. My car had to be washed and waxed every weekend. I wasn't allowed to wear red or purple. And I wasn't even allowed to think about taking art or French in school. It was a very divided environment. I hero-worshipped my older sister, too, which I guess was a big part of the problem."

"Were you happy?"

"Not really."

"Did you have more friends?"

"I guess not. Just Brian and a couple more of the guys."

"And you read science fiction anyway."

"Yeah."

"Well. I'm happy enough, if a little disappointed. I could probably use more friends, but you get what you get."

"You think so?" He asks.

"If I felt I needed more, I'd go after it more aggressively."

Chapter Forty

As time crawls towards my eighteenth birthday, I spend some time doing a frank appraisal of my manliness. It is genuinely lacking. Unfortunately, I do a frank appraisal of what manliness is for mainstream culture, and I don't find myself particularly happy at the prospect of being the burping, farting jock, or the work-hard play-hard square-cut type. The metrosexual guy-in-girl-jeans type also seems like a step in the wrong direction, as well as reliably uncomfortable.[18] Perhaps it's just laziness, but it seems like a lot of effort and posing, when I could be spending my energy better elsewhere.

"Biologically speaking," Annalynn tells me, "The real definition of manliness is the ability to attract a fair mate with whom to produce lots of fat and happy babies. The means by which you do that are completely justified by the ends."

"So pretty much once I've reproduced, my manliness is assured?"

"Biologically speaking, yes."

"Can we get to work on that then?" I joke.

"Fortunately in this day and age, we aren't limited to the whims and ways of our biology."

"Bummer."

"But you get points for trying."

"Yay-hooray." I state sarcastically. "Points. Points do not mean scoring."

Annalynn does a remarkable job of not squirting her coke through her nose, but I can tell it

---

18 My father surmises that they hide their 'junk' in inter-dimensional space. My mother just thinks he's being gross when he says so, but I have to admit, I'm not sure where else it would go.

takes some effort.

"That's charming." I say of her various facial contortions.

"Screw you."

"Exactly! When?"

"Don't be an ass."

I give her puppy-dog eyes.

"UUUUGH."

"You know you love me." I say.

"I seem to have forgotten that fact. What are you getting me for my birthday?"

"Thigh-high rainbow striped socks with individual toes and black latex panties."

"That's totally awesome!" She says.

"I was just kidding. Do you really want that?"

"Sure!"

"I just got myself into a deep, dark hole, didn't I?"

"Yeah, pretty much." She grins. "What do you want for your birthday?"

"You, in thigh-high—"

"Stop."

"Okay." I say, slightly abashed.

"We need to record these conversations for your dad. 'See Mr. Foster, nothing to worry about, he's got plenty of testosterone.'"

"We won't be doing anything of the sort!"

"Are you sure I haven't already?"

"Not entirely." I admit.

"No, I'm really not."

"Good!"

"So what do you seriously want for your birthday." She asks again.

"I don't know. How about a nice dinner?"

"Your mom always makes you a nice dinner." Annalynn counters.

"That's true." I muse for a moment. "I need art supplies."

"I can't pick them out. You know that, and if you go with me and I just pay, I feel like an ATM."

"Well, why don't you surprise me?"

"What kind of surprise?"

"A nice one. Not involving rainbow-striped socks and naughty underwear." I clarify.

"Awwwww." She jokes.

"So, how is school going for you?" I say, changing the subject to something slightly more important.

"Good! I'm doing my practical stuff at Deaconess and they'll probably pick me up part time after the new year."

"Whoa. That's really fast."

"Yeah, I'm surprised that I'm going to be done with high school six months early. Technically we are still part of the student body, but that's it for me."

"Our lives are sort of splitting in January then." I worry. "I'm staying in school, and you are off to the big world."

"Yeah. But not that much. I'm still living with my parents and I'll still being seeing a lot of you. It's only part time."

I'm not sure she understands my point of view, so I let it drop.

"So... what about you, how's college?" She asks after a moment.

"Boring, really. At least right now."

"Boring?"

"Yeah, it's three hours a day of lectures. The

course work is lighter, but harder than high school when you do get it. Also, running start students have a second-class citizen status on campus. Like we're faking or something."

"That sucks."

"Yeah. The college students that are high school graduates are loath to talk to us, and I don't know the other running start students. It seems really cliquish. I was hoping, you know..."

"No, what were you hoping for?"

"Find some more friends, fill out my life a little."

Annalynn looks wistful for a second. I know she's always wanted more friends, but that never seemed like it was in the works for either of us.

"I would go after them, but I'm not sure I've met anyone I want to be friends with, either." I say.

"Why so?"

"Too many stories starting with, 'I was too drunk last night.'" I explain. "We aren't peers in anything other then age, and it shows."

She frowns and sighs. "Yeah, getting drunk shouldn't be a hobby."

"Well it seems like the 'doing stupid things' is the hobby, and the alcohol consumption is a necessary preparation."

Annalynn laughs softly. "Nope, doesn't make sense."

"I didn't think so either. Most of the artists in my class seem to do drugs too."

"That's sad."

"I think they do it because they were the only fish in a small pond, and then they get to college and realize that they aren't the only talented artist.

Maybe they turn to it for relief, and then feel like they are inspired by it. Actually, all their drug-induced creativity starts looking the same to me." I say, because I've been thinking about it. "They brag too, 'I did three ounces last night, and look what I came out with.'"

Annalynn is listening.

"Okay, to be really honest… it's depressing." I hang my head into my hands. "I wanted to find a few people, my own age, maybe my own gender to be around. Sometimes I think it's a bit much to ask you to be my girlfriend and best friend. I thought college would be a place where there would be less cliquishness and less posing and less arbitrary social rules. It's not feeling that way."

Annalynn wrinkles up her face. "Maybe it will be more like that when you are graduated and really a college student as opposed to an add-on."

"If they are too good for me right now, why should I wait?"

"You have a good point, but there will be an influx of new freshman. They might not have the same 'tude."

"Yeah, but next year I won't be in freshman classes so much."

Annalynn cups my chin in her hand and brings me to eye-level. "You don't sound like yourself."

"Like I said, it's a bit depressing."

"Why does it bother you now, when it didn't in school?"

I think about it. "Not sure. Because you aren't there, I guess."

Annalynn drops my chin and looks at the

table. "Maybe you've got a point."

"I've been eating lunch with Sean from the track team, at least. But we aren't.... great friends material."

She nods. "No, probably not."

Chapter Forty-One

It turns out to be a long winter, without much to break the monotony of school and smithy. My mother's units are calm, nearly too calm, but the economy has been down, and so rentals have been stable. The weather, too, is a long monotonous note of grey; sometimes spitting enough snow to streak the dirt, but never enough to cover the world in clean white, or enough to ski in.

"It's kind of dismal." My father says to me one day.

The weather is particularly grey and dreary, and there is a 'plink-plink-plink' of a dripping somethingorother keeping a steady beat on the porch roof. Inside, the sound of my mother's sewing machine drones.

"You think?" I say, sarcastically.

"Reminds me too much of Portland. Which was, on the whole, a dreary, dismal place to spend winters."

"I thought you missed Portland." I say.

"If I missed it that much, I wouldn't have stayed here for 23 years. I miss the fact that in the spring and fall Portland was vibrant: the city was always buzzing and there was so much to do and see and appreciate. There were also a lot of craftspeople, like me. And the community was nice."

"But?"

"I like snow, I like the fact that you can park downtown on Friday night. I like the fact that things aren't too expensive and that life is a little slower and bit more sensible around here. It's a good place to live and stay. Portland is a good place to play."

I think about Annalynn's suggestion. "Yeah.

But it would be nice for a year or two, don't you think?"

"In your early twenties—absolutely." He says, reinforcing her point of view. "But now that I'm older, not so much. And besides, it still has some bad memories."

I look over at him. Part of me wants to ask, and part of me doesn't. So I do my best to let it be his floor.

"Emelle, my mom and I are estranged—have been since before Dad died. Margaret is dead, and I moved the smithing business up here. What's the point in Portland when it just reminds me of all that?"

"I guess there isn't one." I say, even though I want to ask who Margaret is, and why he's estranged from his mother.

"Margaret would have enjoyed being your aunt, if she hadn't committed suicide." He says, suddenly, after a stretch of silence. "She was twenty-two, and wanted to go to college so badly. And my father wouldn't let her. I was twelve at the time. I found her, after she died." He looks at me, his eyes owlish and startlingly clear. "It haunts me. I worshiped her. She was the best sort of sister, but also kind of like a mom, too. She liked children and thought I was the best thing in the world. Or at least, that's how I remember it."

A picture begins to sketch itself in my mind. "She was the bulwark against your parents?"

"What do you mean?"

"She protected you against the fact that all they saw were their children's inadequacies—so much as they measured them. She treated you like a kid, not a failed adult."

"I suppose that's about it." He looks small
when he lets his shoulders sag. "I know my parents
are from not only the old world, but also something
of an old order of thinking. But I can't help but think
that they shut their minds against change, and that
it killed my sister and stunted me."

"Old world?"

"They were from Germany. My father was born
in '32. My mother was born in '40. The both made it
through the winter after Hitler fell. I'm not sure how,
they never talked about that. My mother came over
with her father in '50, and my father had already
come over in '47. I think he might have been a war-
orphan or maybe a POW. That I don't know either.
They met when she was 14, and he was 22. The
story goes that she thought he was quite handsome,
and she promised she'd get him, and spent the next
two years trying to impress him with her domestic
skills. It was awkward for him, but he danced with
her at a wedding of a mutual friend when she was
16, to be nice. Two years later she somehow finagled
a marriage. Five years later there was my sister, and
ten years after that, me."

He pauses to sip his tea, and then continues.
"They had grown up, though, with a terribly bigoted
view of the world. White people were better than
everyone, and Germans were the best of the white
people. They had extremely rigid ideas about gender
roles and the place of children. My father once
described beating my mother as necessary for my
mother's psyche. If he didn't put her properly in her
place, she'd not feel entirely like the woman of the
house."

I gape a bit. The idea of violence being necessary for mental health reasons completely defies logic.

"I was born in 1973. I thought it was a crock."

"It is a crock."

"Glad you agree."

"I never knew you were a first generation American." I say, to steer the conversation away from violence.

"You didn't?"

"No." I reaffirm.

"You thought I spoke German as a lark?"

"No, I thought you had German grandparents."

"Well, I do. Did. Never met any but my mother's father." He says.

"Why did you teach me German—it seems to have so many bad memories?"

"It's my native tongue. And I only knew German Lullabies at the time. It's odd, but I do miss hearing it."

"You and Mom speak 'auf deutsch' all the time." I point out.

"Yes, but she's not a native speaker; and so it sounds just a touch funny to me. You don't." He states bluntly.

I took German in high school, all three years as a way to better my technical understanding of the language and improve my literacy, since I'd only ever spoken it. But I haven't a spoken a word of it at home for years. I know that before the Great Animosity truly drove a wall between us we would have conversations in it, but after that, only very rarely.

"I didn't know you particularly missed it." I

say, slipping back to German, though it feels awkward outside a classroom.

"You modulate your voice like Margaret did. It's very peaceful." He smiles.

My mother pokes her head in. "Why German all of a sudden?" My father is right, she has a touch of an American accent.

"No reason really." We say at the same time.

"The menfolk are plotting against me, I know it."

We both grin wickedly.

"Eeeeep!" She runs back to her sewing room in an exaggerated way.

I make a note to speak to my father in his own language more often.

Chapter Forty-Two

The weather suddenly dumps buckets of sleet on us for three days, and then freezes hard. Ambulance sirens wail past our house nearly hourly, and one of the Spokane-Cheney buses slides right off the road and falls on its side. People call for Eastern to shut down operations, but they point out that no one was hurt in the bus accident and continue to remain open.

I try not to worry as I ride the bus in the mornings, but Annalynn tells me that most of the people they've scraped off the road have been college students.

"They're in older cars; that seems to be the trouble." She says on her lunch break.

I push some more of the pastrami sub I brought her towards her plate.

"I'm almost stuffed, Em."

"But you'll probably work extra hours today. You need to eat enough that you aren't starving by the end of your shift."

She nods. "I know. You're right." She takes a few more bites.

"Ride the bus, it's safer than a car right now."

"Will do." I nod.

"I have to go now. We don't have enough people to handle the mess." She gives me a quick kiss and shoves the leftover sandwich in her locker. "I'll eat more later. Thank you for bringing it."

I grab my coat and stand up. "Okay. I'll try to swing by after school."

The bus is late getting to Jefferson Lot, where it picks up the students brave enough to deal with the horrible ice. Our sluggish cruise down the highway ebbs to speeds of 20 miles per hour, as several accidents have backed up the road into Cheney. By the time I get off the bus at the pub, I have less than a minute to get to class. I can't show up even a second after because if I'm late, I won't be allowed to take today's test.

No big deal, I tell myself. I am the cross country champion from my school. I can do this with ease, and quite possibly with finesse. I literally fly down the stairs and bolt out the doors just to realize I have not committed the landscape nearly well enough to memory —right in front of me is an iron handrail. It isn't a hurdle, but I make a very valiant (read stupid) attempt to clear it anyway.

I probably would have been okay but I launch from black ice which sends my left leg directly into the frigid iron, and on the other side there are steps upon which I land with my other leg, which gives way so that I land face-first in the packed sleet.

No finesse points, not any. Not an "e" for effort either. I involuntarily scream and attract the attention of a passing student who whips out her cell phone and calls 911. And then leaves, presumably for class.

I pass out, or at least enter the hazy of world of too much pain for my brain to process.

Something slides under my head and I get the impression of people being around. Someone has injected me with stuff because I feel warm and I'm floating, neither of which I should feel, lying on packed sleet and ice over concrete.

"Okay, let's move him."

"Oh, let's not." I croak.

"Emelle, we have to move you."

Annalynn!

"Anna?" I say.

"You are my third ambulance ride this morning, you idiot." She replies.

"See, destiny." I reply, it makes sense in the daze. "Third time's a charm."

I'm rolled onto a stretcher, I think, and placed in a humming vehicle. Annalynn takes off a glove and pats my hand gently.

"You guys ruined my best jeans." I comment.

"You ruined your only left leg and the jeans were already coated in blood. I'm calling your mother now."

She takes a cell phone out of her coat and rings my parents.

I hum on the ride into Spokane.

Both my father and mother launch themselves at me when I come through the emergency doors at Deaconness.

My mother is saying things to Annalynn, but finishes with "...and you scrape your best friend up off the concrete. That sucks."

"No no no, it's destiny." I chirp. Pain drugs are good, and I think they just gave me some more.

"Shut up sweetie, you sound like a moron," Mom says.

"I removed all doubt ages ago, Mom, I don't see a reason to worry about it now." I reply.

"Thank you, Annalynn. We'll call you when we know something." My mother says before turning her attention to me.

"What did you do to yourself, anyway?"

I try to describe the events without making myself out to be a complete idiot, but my mother sees through it.

"You knew it was icy, why did you do this?"

"They've been salting campus... I hit the one patch of ice still remaining." I protest.

"Still—clearing a handrail?"

"Cross country champion. It didn't look that big."

My mother sighs and rolls her eyes.

"You aren't anymore."

I look down at my knee packed in ice. "It's okay. It wasn't my life or anything."

My mother pats me on the head. "Try to get some rest; they're going to have you talk to a surgeon in a bit."

I sleep for a bit, and then the next thing I know is that an orthopedic surgeon who introduced himself as 'Scott' is talking to me about the fact that my knee isn't too damaged and if I wear a leg brace of some sort for the next eon, I won't need knee reconstruction surgery. However, my bone isn't so much going to be set but is going to need surgery for screws. I've also broken an ankle and cracked two ribs.

I have no idea how I managed this.

I tell him so.

"Track kids always come in with the freakiest injuries when they come in at all." He says.

"If you say so."

"Oh, I do. I'm never sure how they've managed to get hurt so badly, or hurt so little. The damage never seems to jive entirely with events that supposedly caused it."

He makes some notes on a piece of paper.

"We're going to have you in for surgery this

afternoon. So you're going to rest up until then."

He hands me a waiver.

I do my best to sign it.

"You can just do your initials."

"Oh." I say, as I fumble the pen. My initials look sloppy, but they are much more manageable than my full name.

When I come to again, I have no jeans and no shirt.

Ooooh. I have my own underwear. Good.

And stupid hospital booties.

I have stuff sticking out of my left leg and my right ankle is in a cast.

I feel gross.

My mother shuffles into my vision.

"Hi, Sweetie. How are you doing?"

"I have my own underwear. My favorite jeans are missing and I don't know where my t-shirt got to. The nurses must all be thieves, and where is my coat?"

"In other words, Puppe, he's peachy and on lots of happy drugs." My father notes.

"I just wanted to make sure." My mother replies.

I conk out again after they put me in the car. I think I sleep for days. I have no idea what is going on. I am pain medication and it is lovely and I feel like lots and lots of sleep. Annalynn comes by one night and sleeps beside me, whether my parents know and care is beyond my concern. I happily pat her hair, and I don't know when she leaves but she has left a get-well card. It has clowns on it and I like it.

My father brings me a blacksmith puzzle one

day after work, his hands still covered in the dark grime of the forge and the metal itself.

"Emelle?" He says after letting me futz with it for a while.

"Yes?"

"You really need to think a bit harder about what you are doing."

"Why's that?"

"What you did the other day was frightening. If you cared more, you wouldn't have taken that risk."

"Don't be so serious. I was late for class and made a dumb split second decision, it's hardly a life theory."

"I wonder if you'd let yourself make these sorts of dumb split second decisions if you had a bit more respect for yourself."

I place the puzzle in my lap. "Dad, I want to live long enough to see all of Annalynn's hair go white and have puppies outrun me. I'm clumsy, not stupid."

"Are you really going to marry Annalynn?"

"Yes." I say with relish.

"You count the time, don't you, until you feel like you can propose?"

"I was hoping to ask her in three Christmases." I say. "We can have a nine-month engagement, and it would take away all of the stress of trying to pick out a Christmas present."

"Were you going to share this with your Mom?"

I look at him. "Doesn't she already know?"

"She only seems telepathic," he laughs.

We pause to chuckle.

"Does Annalynn know?" He asks.

"Nope."

"Shouldn't she?"

"And ruin the surprise? I don't think so." I reply.

"How's your leg feel?"

"Uh." I move it a bit. "Not great."

"You have to go back to school in two weeks. Your mom talked to your professors."

"Oh. I was just beginning to wonder about that."

"Yes, she got you some medical leave. You aren't the first student that's needed it this quarter because of the ice storm. Lots of broken bones, lots of car wrecks." He nods to himself. "Your mom wanted to know if you wanted anything special for lunch."

"Hmmmm." I think, but it's still pretty foggy inside my head. "No. Whatever is fine."

"Okay. I'll bring it up in a bit."

Actually, Annalynn brings up the tray. She's still in her uniform. "I wanted to see how you were doing."

"The meds are good. The leg, not so much." I say.

She slips the tray onto the bed and then sits down heavily on my beanbag.

"I'm so tired." She says.

"Long shifts?" I mumble.

"Yes, really long. The pay is fabulous though."

"You can nap." I say, patting the bed next to me.

She shakes her head. "Your parents are home. That'd be awkward."

"Didn't you sleep here the other night?"

"Night?" She giggles. "No, I watched you one

afternoon and evening when they went on errands and watched a movie."

"It was dark though."

"Yes, it was, it was a really dark day, but it wasn't night."

"You slept, you didn't watch me."

"I did fall asleep, that's true. I tried really hard not to. But you looked so comfortable, and I thought I'd lie down for a minute with you... and then it was four hours later, and I heard the front door open." She smiles.

She stands up.

"I'm going to borrow some dry stuff."

"Okay." I say, and poke at lunch. She wanders into my closet and digs up a dry shirt and some old jeans.

"I don't like the uniform, it gets too cold when it gets wet."

I look at it. "Polyester?"

"Yep."

"Buy some long underwear, it should help." I suggest.

She sits back down on the beanbag chair.

"It's cute when you wear my clothes." I say.

She grins again, and pulls the blanket over her lap and leans back.

"Careful, you'll fall asleep."

"I might. Sitting feels so good."

When my mother comes up to grab the tray from me, Annalynn is sleeping soundly, and I'm beginning to drift off.

"Awwwwwwwwww." My mother says softly.

"Mmmmmhmmm." I reply.

"No, I meant both of you." And she silently

takes the tray and draws the blanket up over Annalynn's shoulders.

Chapter Forty-Three

My father makes me a very nice cane with an iron pineapple topper before I return to school. I appreciate it, but the fact I need one bothers me.

"You know," my mother says at dinner, a few days after I've returned to school. "I don't think you should be quite as tired as you are."

I agree. I took a two and half hour nap when I got home, and I still feel like I got run over by a cement truck. "I'll get better soon." I protest.

"We should swing you by a doc if it doesn't get better in a week." She replies, her voice is all business.

"It's a compound fracture," I protest. "It probably takes a lot of energy to heal it up."

"I've broken my arm, five, er, six, times in my life, and I never looked like I need bellboys to drag around the bags under my eyes." My father says.

More like an entire Union Pacific, but I don't say that. "I'll be fine, it's just the combination of a bad break and this pain."

"Pain?"

I look at my Dad. "My leg hurts. I did bad things to it. Remember?"

"Isn't it getting better?"

I think about it. "It feels like everything is sore, it's not piercing pain anymore."

"Well, did you mess up your back?"

"Maybe." I hadn't considered the possibility, but I may have.

"Let's take you to the chiropractor, and get that ruled out, then."

The chiropractor examines x-rays of my back.

"Nope. He could stand some maintenance, but there's nothing big here that I'm seeing."

My mother looks perplexed.

I'm dozing in the chair.

"Are you losing hair?" The doctor asks.

"No."

"Thirsty?"

"No."

"Just tired?"

"And I hurt." The pain has spread from my leg up to my torso, a vague sense of soreness that goes away only briefly in the morning or after naps.

He writes down a name on a pad. "I'd like you to see this doctor, if you haven't seen an internist already."

My mother takes the paper. "Why this doctor specifically?"

"He's worked with me for about ten years, and I've never heard a bad word about him. I'm always impressed by his abilities. I'd like him to rule out any conventional problems."

My mother looks at the paper again. "What do you think could be wrong?"

The chiropractor looks at her. "I really can't venture a guess."

Not reassuring.

All of my free time is being spent napping or chugging Tylenol like it's candy. I hurt and I'm tired. Dr. Scott has ruled out infection and poor healing, and the doctor the Chiropractor recommended has been equally stumped.

"There is one possibility I'd like to look into if this hasn't cleared up in a few more months. This could be Chronic Fatigue Syndrome, or fibromyalgia." He says after reading the returned test results form my first visit.

"Aren't those old lady diseases?" I ask.

"They tend to be associated with that demographic, but like most things, they can strike anywhere. I'm going to assume that your accident this winter triggered it early."

"Well, what tests need to happen?"

"There are no definitive tests. But, what I'd like to do is have you come back in a few months. If you are still like this, with the exhaustion, the pain, and the poor, if frequent, sleep, then I think it's a more worthwhile consideration. In the meantime, I'd like to see you remove junk from your diet, and be as healthy as you can be. While these tests are normal, it can't hurt to make that particular change."

I nod at the same time my mother does.

When we get in the car to go home, I turn to her. "Do you think I have either of those things?"

"Sadly, yes." She says as she maneuvers out of the parking spot. "Your great grandmother had it, and there's some evidence other members of the family do or did as well. I think it's really pretty likely." She looks grim.

I scrunch down in the seat, feeling grumpy.

"Do you want to get anything to eat or do anything while we've got the car out and warmed up?" My mom asks, trying to be practical and generous at the same time.

"I dunno." I say.

"Do you want to do anything when we get home?" she asks.

"Nap." I say.

"Anything other than nap?"

"Veg." I say, as honestly as I can.

"Thank god I don't need your help with any of the rental units right now," she says. "We'd be drowning."

"I can help with them." I protest.

"Not much. Just going to school and coming home on the bus wears you—" She stops herself.

"What?" I say when she doesn't finish the thought at all.

"I was thinking I have an open unit in Cheney, it rents for almost nothing a month, and I haven't found the right person to take it. Maybe you should use that as a crash pad for the bad days. Or at least a place to pause so you aren't doing the boomerang on the bus everyday. The bus stops almost at the front door."

I look back at her. "That isn't a bad idea."

"No, and you don't have to live there, just take a break. We can keep some simple stuff in the fridge, and I've got some furniture you can use. Also, it'll make a nice home-base out there for you next year."

"Why wouldn't I live at home?"

"You'll be a real college student, you know. You should have a little place like the other kids."

I don't think about it. "Mmm." I say instead.

"Your dad and I can do it."

"Why does this sound like a plot to unload your old furniture and get new, more than a favor to me?" I tease.

"Oh gosh, was I that transparent?" She says, playing along.

"Like a window."

"Nuts."

Two months later I have a diagnosis of fibromyalgia and what my father has dubbed 'The Pad.' It's made no small difference. I'm mostly functional as a human being.

"You know." My father brings up one day as we clean up the smithy before dinner. "Prom is coming up."

"Uh huh."

"Are you going to take Annalynn?"

I wasn't planning on asking her or anything. "She'll tell me if she wants to go."

"Of course she wants to go."

Ugh. That's all I can think. "I don't know."

He looks perturbed.

"Mom has fabric lurking around that's Annalynn's color, doesn't she?"

"Maybe."

"She's probably had some dress dreamt up in her head for the better part of three years."

"Five. I've seen the drawing."

"Will she cry if I don't take Annalynn to the Prom?"

"Of course not." My father says. "But she was hopeful."

"I can ask." I say.

I sweep for a bit.

"Em?"

"Yes?"

"I've been meaning to ask you about Annalynn's parents."

Oh no. "What about them," I say cautiously.

"It seems Robert and I used to talk some, and I saw her mother a bit, and I know you guys are teenagers and parents aren't in the picture as much, but I don't think I've seen either of them for almost a year. It's odd." He says, equally cautious.

"You wouldn't believe me on this, but I don't think I've seen them in almost six months."

"What?" He says, turning to look at me.

"I haven't been inside their house for probably three months."

"Do you think something... bad... is going on?"

"Nothing overt. Like, I don't think she's being abused or anything. But, I think things have gone downhill since her grandmother died. Really downhill."

"Define 'downhill'?"

"I think her mom is in some other world mentally all the time now. Her dad is lost without his wife. He doesn't know what to do with himself without being ordered around. Annalynn hasn't had real parents for awhile. They hand her money and don't even count the bills."

"Is someone drunk or something?" He asks.

"I don't think so." I say. "Just on a permanent vacation from parenthood."

"They seemed really reasonable and normal when you guys were first friends." He seems confused.

"I think it's been an accelerating process of losing sight of their daughter. A couple of years ago," I muse aloud "they were just buying into the idea that you need to reconnect as a couple. So they went on a retreat and a cruise. It seemed normal. And that they were more focused on each other later seemed logical. Get away from the mom and dad roles and replug into being a spouse." I shrug. "But it's almost like her mom saw it as an opening to becoming more selfish. Then *her* mom died, and it seemed normal that she'd need to focus on herself for awhile, not Annalynn. But she never stopped that emotional selfishness."

"Sounds like you've talked, or thought, about this."

"I have, actually, a lot lately."

"But Robert too?"

"He seriously is lost without his wife. He's a real sheep."

Dad cringes. "I can't believe I didn't notice this stuff going on sooner. I had this feeling that things weren't quite right, but I didn't really think that much about it."

The conversation carries on over dinner.

"I'd noticed something." My mother says. "But what can I do? We can't be her parents too, even though I'd happily make that happen. We can watch and try to be careful, but if her parents are checked out, they're checked out and there's jack-all to be done about it."

"She's her parent's roommate, Paul. Surely we can do something, it's not right." My dad protests.

"She's eighteen, there's nothing we can do."

My dad glares, his mad-at-the-world face. "Fine." He turns to me. "Let her know that we're here —all of us, if she needs something."

"She knows."

"Then remind her."

"Okay."

Chapter Forty-Four

A trail of thread.

Three dropped pins stuck to a pair of scissors.

Scraps of peach and teal colored silk.

My mother is sometimes one gigantic pig. I get down on my hands and knees and start scooping it all up before it makes its way out the door on the bottom of my shoe or clinging to an embarrassing spot on my pants.

"And," I narrate to myself in the best impression of Tim Gunn[19] I can manage, "Fashion Week in New York City has been a great success; Paul Foster really delivered with her newest line of silk cocktail dresses."

I change voices. "I agree Tim, I think Paul Foster is really giving women what they want. Fit and a fabulous fabric. I really think we're going to be wowed by her collection in Melbourne this year."

My mother sticks her head around the corner. "I don't think you can present at multiple fashion weeks."

"I don't know. It just sounds good."

"Well, come in and take a look."

It is a peach and teal cocktail dress, actually.

"What do you think?" She asks nervously.

"It's not Princess Leia's slave costume."

"It's not 1980 either." My mother retorts.

"Oh, but it could be, if just for the sake of that." I whine humorously. "What's it for?"

"Oh, I don't know. I just felt like making something like it."

---

19 I've never watched Project Runway reruns with my mother. Never! Of course not! And I certainly didn't eat popcorn while doing so. Perish the thought.

"Hmmm." I consider it some more. "Where would you wear it?"

"Maybe out to dinner?"

"It's a little mother of the bride." I finally admit.

Instead of being insulted, she nods. "I thought maybe it was. But what do you think of the color?"

"Eh." I admit.

"I thought it was better for me when I bought it. But now I think it's more Annalynn's color, don't you?"

Oh boy..... "What are you saying, Mom."

"Well, I can't use the fabric for me. I just can't.... waste it. Maybe it would look good on her."

"Dunno. You should ask her."

My mother brings out her sketchbook. "Or I could just surprise her, maybe." She flips it open. "Do you think she'd like any of these?"

I look at the sketches of evening gowns.

"Annalynn doesn't need an evening gown. She maybe needs a cocktail dress. Maybe. Big maybe."

My mother pouts.

"She might want an evening gown, though." I say.

She pouts less. "Well, maybe you could ask her to Prom. Then she'd need one."

I give my mother the hairy eyeball.

"Uh. No." Annalynn says. "Prom is, uhm, for popular kids. I'd rather train for a polar bear swim."

"Oh, it's not that bad." I say.

"Do you really want to go?" She asks, and then bites a gory wound into her sandwich.

"My mother bought fabric for a prom dress. By accident, according to her."

"I can't let your mother down." Annalynn says, looking suddenly guilty. "Oh my god, I'd feel like the bad person of the year."

"But you don't want to go." I say.

"No, not at all."

"Let's not, then. And say we did. Literally."

"Sounds good. Do I get smashing good dinner in the bargain?"

"Yeah, where do you want to go?"

"The Davenport."

I mime removing a kidney.

"Hey, it's a lot cheaper than your mother's pouting."

"That's true."

Chapter Forty-Five

I'm comfortably sprawled across the bed in the "pad" one evening when I am just energetic enough to finish my homework and art assignments, but not energetic enough to hop on the bus and go home. I'm learning, albeit slowly, what does and does not push me over the edge into the realm of walking zombie.

I think about dragging myself up and into the kitchen to snag something to eat and maybe spend some time surfing the net, but honestly, laying down really feels amazing.

I wake from my dozing when I hear a key in the door.

I prop my head up, anticipating my mother, coming out to check on me.

It's Annalynn.

"Mmmm?" I rumble happily.

"Hey, your Mom said you were out here. I wanted to see you." She sets down a bag from the grocery store. "Brought some easy nibbles."

"Mmm. Thanks."

"Are you having a flare up?" She asks.

"No. I'm at the edge of pushing myself too hard, but I'll be okay if I just rest."

"It's only eight-thirty."

"Hey, that's life." I say as she undoes her coat and hangs it up on a peg.

"Do you want to sit up and have some tea or anything?"

I tap the lamp next to me to shed some extra light in the room. "Sure." I roll over and struggle up into a sitting position.

She turns on the automatic kettle in the kitchen and sheds some more outerwear. She's wearing silk long underwear underneath her uniform. I can tell because her uniform is short-sleeved and the underwear is long-sleeved. I smile, glad that something I said was worthwhile on her new job.

She nudges me awake for tea.

"Either you are really relaxed, or really tired."

I smile. "Both." I take a sip. Ah, oolong. "Thanks. This is good."

"I like it after work."

"So what's up?" I ask.

"Parents are gone again. I'm just not interested in being all alone again. The cats are Mom's, and I'm this big afterthought in their world. Food is available, and life is fine for them. They don't need me."

I brush her hair out of her face and pull her forehead close so I can kiss it. "I love you even if the cats are a bit hesitant."

"Thanks."

"What else is up?"

"I like my job. When I'm not scraping you off the ground."

I smile.

"You look pretty tired." Annalynn observes, and it seems a bit petulant.

"It's been a long day for me."

"Me too, but I don't look like I'm halfway sleeping."

"I'm sorry." I apologize. "If I had known you were coming in, I'd have taken a nap early in the afternoon."

Annalynn looks concerned.

"I find I have to plan life a bit more nowadays."

"Oh."

I put my teacup down and pat the bed. "Why don't you join me? We can sleep and go for breakfast in the morning. I promise to be more lively."

Annalynn rolls her eyes.

I'm taken aback. It's not like her.

She picks up the empty tea cups. "I though you'd be a bit more...perky."

"Is there something you want, particularly?"

"Yes. I'd like my boyfriend to be lively enough for a screw once in awhile." She vents.

The only thing I can think about is sleeping, but it's true that since I smashed myself up, nothing has been going on. This was okay while she was working too many hours, but the winter workload has lightened up significantly in the last few weeks. Thusly, things should have gotten back to normal. The problem is, she's only work-tired, and I'm tired-tired. The last thing I want to do on any given day is put up the kind of energy that goes into a good horizontal boogie.
I groan.

"You don't even have to put that much effort into it. You can lay there, or something." She says, and flares her nostrils.

I'm in no mood for it, and I know that tomorrow I'll pay if I do so anyway. On the other hand, I do have sympathy for her and what is likely a genuine problem. On a mutant third hand, I doubt that perfunctory, lousy sex is going to be of anything more than token value. It might even have subtractive qualities.

"Okay. Fine." I say. "If that's what you want."

Later when she's finally done, curled up and

sleeping comfortably, I sneak out of bed and sit down on the bathroom floor. I feel gross just thinking about what's happened. I assumed that laying there would not be so bad, but it's made me feel absolutely disgusting inside. All I really thought about was how much I wanted it to be over or stop happening altogether. I could also feel the painful exhaustion settling into my muscles.

Now, I just feel dizzy and nauseated, even though I'm just sitting on the floor.

Throwing up vastly improves things. Throwing up twice makes me feel almost completely normal, if a bit wobbly. I stand up, flush the toilet, brush my teeth and wash my face. This is better.

When I crawl back into bed, Annalynn loops an arm around me. I gently remove it. "Not right this second, please."

She pulls it back to her body. "Is everything okay?"

"I wish we hadn't done that. I feel sick." I say.

"What?!"

"My body isn't with us on this one. I'm sorry." I say, skirting the issue.

"You don't want me?"

"It's not like that. I love you to pieces. You know that. I just need so much sleep, and everything takes too much out of me right now. I don't want sex. It's not a commentary on whether I want you or not."

"It feels like it."

"I know. I don't want it to."

"It's not really pleasant to have it get shut off either."

"I'm sorry. I really am. But I'm not up for this right now. I just can't, and I shouldn't try." I turn towards her. "They say if I'm careful I'll be a lot closer to normal in a few more weeks. Give me some time. I'm not ignoring you or what you want or need."

"Sure feels like it." She grouches.

I roll onto my side and run my hand through her hair. I can feel her relax a little.

"I'm sorry." I say.

I can almost hear her thinking.

"Okay."

I rub her exposed shoulder and kiss it lightly.

Chapter Forty-Six

"What did they do?" My mother asks, as she stares at the disaster that has been made out of a small home she'd been renting in Cheney. Technically, it was my responsibility, but from the outside it looked fine, and no issues had been reported. There had been no reason to come inside.

Now, I'm wishing I had come up with a reason to peek in. My mother and I usually do. But, the rent had never been late, they had seemed like great renters.

"Do you think we ought to take it back to framework?" My father asks.

"Is it that bad?" I ask.

We hear a yowl from the basement. I bolt towards the door.

"Oh my god." My mother says as a Siamese-y kitten comes flying out from the dank down-below. "There hasn't been heat on for a week. Did it have food and water?"

I flip on the basement light.

"It did. The bowls are empty now." I say, sickened.

My mother turns on the faucet in the kitchen. The kitten drinks gratefully. "Look, take this little...." she flips it over, "guy home."

"I don't want a cat."

"You do now."

"He'll poop everywhere."

My mother sticks her head down the stairs. "I don't think so. He's got a very full litter box down there."

She pulls a few twenties from her wallet. "Get some supplies and come back after you've got him settled into the bathroom."

I dutifully buy some cat food, litter box and bedding. When I get back to my car, he's conked on the backseat.

"Must be nice to be warm again, eh?" I say and rub his throat.

He starts up like a gas-powered chainsaw.

Awwwwwwwww.

"You're cute." I can't help it, he is. Big green[20] crossed eyes and soft creamy fur is pretty irresistible.

He curls up comfortably in the bathroom sink after I settle him into my apartment.

"Well, if it suits you." I say.

When I return my mother is still assessing the holes in the walls, the mold in the bathroom, and the unique problem the kitchen represents. The appliances are gone. The cabinets have no doors. The sink has broken handles.

"This is just depressing."

"Why is that?" I ask.

"This is the first house I ever bought. I spent two months making this my dream kitchen. Then I got pregnant with you, and I had to rent it. And it's always been good to me. I've always just had great luck with this house. And now look at it."

It's rare that my mother is sentimental.

My father drapes his arm around her shoulder and draws her in next to him. "It's okay, think of this as Micheal's way of telling us that a remodel is long overdue."

My mother doesn't look convinced.

---

20 Definitely not a pedigreed pet, but quite the looker.

"I don't think we need to tear it back to its bones." He says. "We just need to patch a lot of walls, and paint. And overhaul the kitchen and bathroom. It's a big job, but not as big as what we did to the old bookstore."

My mother nods.

We pile back into the car, run to the hardware store, and get supplies.

"So, what are you going to call the cat?" My father asks.

"Little Big Claws." I say sarcastically.

"No, really."

"Don't know. It will come to me, I hope."

"This from a guy who dubbed his car 'Horseless.' I'm worried."

"I can call the cat 'finless,' then, to fit with the theme."

Finny turns out to be a mostly healthy older kitten. He's good company.

"Mew." He says while walking between Annalynn and I, post coitus, one evening.

"I really like him." Annalynn says as he curls up beside her ribs and rumbles to life.

I like the interplay of textures between his kitten-y fuzz and her soft, pale skin.

"He never stops purring." She marvels. "It's the perfect white noise machine."

I pet his side a bit. "I feel a lot better, having his company."

"I've noticed." She says, and raises her eyebrows suggestively while grinning.

I reach out and grab her and pull her, and incidentally Finny, right up next to me. Surprisingly, he purrs even louder.

"It's almost like a family. Except our kid is hairy." Annalynn giggles.

I peer down at him. Little green slits peep from between her breasts.

"I like it." I say and kiss her nose.

Things get frisky.

"At this rate, we'll have the hairless version of a kid soon." Annalynn teases.

"Yes, but we use protection... this is all just practice production. Not the real thing." I affirm.

"I have to get up and go to work." Annalynn says, and pushes out of bed. "Come on, I'll take you home to your parents."

Finny seems to either not mind or not notice my irregular hours, but I miss his presence when I'm gone. I look down at him, he yawns.

"ohmygodcute," slips out of my mouth.

"He'll be cute when you get back too. It's not like you leave him alone that much anyway."

She's right. He spends plenty of time with me, and comes into town on the weekends.

Still, it's cold, so I leave him a cave of covers when I get up.

"You know, I feel more like a college student now, with the cat and the apartment." I say.

"Really?"

"Yeah."

"I don't feel like a high school student or an adult." She says.

"You don't?"

"No. I feel like I'm living in limbo land."

"Maybe that's because you aren't living on your own?"

"I don't want to. It's bad enough coming home when the house is empty—I think my own apartment would be depressing."

I look up at her. "Are you asking to move in with me sometime?"

"Maybe. I'm not sure."

Chapter Forty-Seven

Annalynn and I proudly pretend to go to Prom. Stashed in the trunk of my car, however, are swimsuits and towels and two inflatable inner-tubes as well as some waterproof flashlights. We'd decided on the reality of our excursion when the weather went from crisp spring to blistering summer one weekend.

And anyway, Fish Lake gets warm early in the year.

Mom gleefully snaps pictures of us, and we stand and pose in our finery, counting the minutes until we can yank all of it off and run into the tepid lake waters.

Our next stop is not a restaurant, but a photographer that had agreed to take three pictures for us this evening. Then, we can escape and spend an idle evening on the lake.

"Your hair will get ruined, you know." I say, as the photographer sets up for another shot.

"Hahahhaha. With this much goop. I don't think it can move. Besides, I think it's impervious to water until I shampoo it."

I gently touch a strand. She isn't kidding.

We pose again, and the photographer snaps a picture.

"You can pick them up two weeks from now." He says, and then waves us out of the studio.

When we get to the lake, there is a flurry of activity in my car. I had not understood just how much underwear a girl wears underneath a prom dress, but when Annalynn starts yanking off a girdle of all things, I mentally count the layers.

"How can you move in all that?"

"Miracle." She replies, yanking off a stocking.

I hand her a swimsuit top.

"Thanks."

Anyone looking at the back seat would think we were doing the traditional thing of losing our virginity on prom night. That, or skinny dipping.

Nice idea, but I don't want fish nibblin' the bits.

Annalynn grabs an inner-tube and so do I, then we set off down the sandy path to the dock and run into the water.

"Oh! That's colder than I thought!" I say when I come up from dunking my head.

Annalynn sputters. "No kidding."

I pop on my flashlight.

"Local legend speaks of a mysterious light in Fish Lake."

Annalynn pops her on too. "Lights."

"Lights." I agree and kick off away from the dock while narrating. "These lights appear in early to late June, always in pairs. While they are not dangerous to swimmers, they are a visible reminder of students brutally murdered on prom night by the local Loch Ness Monster."

"Awwww. You almost had a good story there. Then you brought in a totally crap element. No one believes in the Loch Ness Monster. And those who do say it's an herbivore."

Annalynn would know these things.

"Okay. Fine. You come up with a story."

"In 1946, a cheerful year after the war, Ward Sanders and his girlfriend Meg Clark left for an evening with friends at their Senior Prom." Annalynn begins, and then starts talking into her flashlight as though it was reporter's mic. "Pictures show that Meg was dressed in a silk gown and a corsage of roses and bluebells. Ward was wearing a new wool suit. Friends claimed he was going to ask Meg, his best girl, to marry him at dinner. Though no one is certain that she said yes, it was presumed that she did, as they left the prom early, telling friends they were going out to Fish Lake for some post-prom fun. Meg left her jewelry with her best friend, saying she didn't want to lose it at the lake."

Annalynn pauses.

"Only Meg returned. She had driven Ward's car home in the early hours. Her dress was bedraggled, soaking wet, torn and dirty. She claimed that she and Ward had been attacked at the lake by a mysterious assailant. He had shoved car keys in her hand, and begged her to drive for help. However, when she stepped into the car, it would not start until their attacker had dragged Ward into the Lake."

Annalynn smiles. "Teams of people headed out to the lake in hopes of finding Ward safe and alive, but ultimately only the jacket of his new suit was recovered. Shortly after the memorial service, Meg started talking about how she felt a pressing need to return to the lake, to remember Ward. Some months later, she was found drowned on the shore, wearing her prom dress."

Her smile gets bigger, and I start getting the willies.

"Some people claim it is a story of mental disturbance, a young girl depressed by the loss of . her fiancé. And some people claim otherwise. In 1998, a young couple from Eastern Washington University decided to go skinny dipping in early

June, and saw, from a distance, two frolicking lights. They swam out to them, thinking that they were the flashlights of fellow skinny dippers. However, what they described next, was anything but fun."

Annalynn takes on a sort of airy, panicked voice. "We swam out toward the middle of the lake, calling out to the people with the lights. Suddenly, we felt cold, slimy ropes around our ankles. We screamed, and I was dragged under. Suddenly, I bobbed the surface when my friend smacked the rope with his flashlight. But then, it grabbed again for us both and dragged us under. If it hadn't been for the sudden appearance of headlights, we would have been doomed. The ropes stopped attacking us, and we were able to get out of the lake. On the shore, there was an old car that had been restored, or just kept very well. I think it was a thirties model Chevrolet. There was a girl in a ripped up prom dress driving it, and crying. We tried to figure out what was wrong, but she just waved us away, saying we couldn't help her. It's only when we reported her to the police that we realized we'd been dealing with a ghost."

Annalynn finishes, and smiles wickedly.

She's dragged us out to the middle of the lake, where an old buoy is taking on water, and the rope it is attached to has grown slimy and drifts just below the surface.

I let loose an involuntary, and very quiet "eep."

Annalynn grins. "Now that's a good story."

The rope moves.

"Story or no, I'm going back to the shore." I say, and start paddling back. It's slow, because I'm not willing to get off the inner-tube to really swim.

She joins me, and we get back to the dock.

"So," I say, as we get dressed. "How was that for a fake prom?"

"Amazing. I'd say that scores a ten out of ten."

"Really?"

"Lake, scary story, skimpy clothes vs. too hot, too many clothes and too much standing around looking pretty?"

I nod in agreement. "Let go get some food."

Chapter Forty-Eight

In the fall, Annalynn is still unsure about living with me, though clothes, movies, posters and her favorite chair have migrated to my apartment. My parents have steadily nudged me out as the weather gets cooler and cooler. I would have thought it would have felt a little cold and lonely, but it's been a gradual adjustment, and I appreciate it.

Also, I've met my neighbors.

The people in number one are two Japanese students that don't appear to speak any English. They give me their rent in cash, in fact.

Then there's Alexis.

Who is sitting in Annalynn's chair, sobbing her eyes out into Finny's fur. Most cats wouldn't tolerate this. Finny, however, is purring like a maniac.

Alexis is the perennially dumped, perennially short on cash, living on food stamps and the kindness of strangers. My mother's stance on her is so long as she pays half or more of the rent each month, she can stay there. I think my mother genuinely likes Alexis, and that's why she puts up with it, because usually she's kind of a cut-throat business woman.

I personally think Alexis is likely addicted to something.

Right now, other than sobbing into the ribs of my cat, there are signs of mental disturbance going on; she's wearing thigh high stockings, plaid boxer bottoms, and a lace camisole. She's covered this with a thin nylon robe that has fake fur at the collar and cuffs.

"I don't have any power." She snuffles, when finally, she sets Finny down.

"I know." This is why an extension cord is snaking down the hall, with a heater at the other end of it. "It'll get turned back on tomorrow."

"But it's still cold!"

"I know." It's an unusually chill late September. One little roll around heater isn't great, but it was what I had.

"And Mike won't come home."

Ah, Mike. As I was saying, the perennially dumped. He was a loser, but she doesn't seem to know she was better off without him.

She sobs again, this time into her robe. And then finally looks up. I'm doodling at my easel.

"I'm so sorry." She always says this once she's overstayed her welcome.

"It's okay." I always say this, and then I walk her back to her apartment with a couple of pieces of fruit and some granola bars. She looks anorexic, and maybe she is. Or maybe, as Annalynn thinks, she's chasing the dragon too much to eat.

I shut her door, and go back to my apartment. But, really, I want to be out. Her dismay is sort of palpable. I slide into my running stuff. Even though I'm not in track condition, I enjoy going out when I have the energy.

Tonight, it's chill, and though I can't see my breath now, I know in a week or so, I will.

I notice Annalynn's car when I get back, which is odd, because normally she'd need to have left sometime ago to be there on time, and anyway, I wasn't expecting her. My door is unlocked when I come up the stairs, and when I let myself in, I realize she's sitting at the table with no lights on.

I can make out an oversized white pen in front

of her.

"Emelle?"

It is a pregnancy test. That's the only reason she'd miss an hour of work.

"Emelle?"

"Are you pregnant?"

"Yeah... this is the third one that agrees...and they are all different brands."

I sit down at the table.

There are no words for what I'm thinking.

"We are keeping it?" She asks, as though I will instantly veto such a thing.

"If you want it, then absolutely." I say.

"Well, don't you want it too?" Annalynn asks.

I shut my eyes. I don't know if I'm qualified to answer such a thing. I think of Annalynn's baby pictures, all precious and toothless grins and perfect skin. I think of my own, all chaotic and busy. I think of my mother talking about me when I was too little to remember, and I think of the girl that went into labor in class and how horrible it seemed. Her husband was unreachable and she seemed overcome by terror. I try to imagine holding something that was mine and Annalynn's. I think of holding Annalynn in my arms and how wonderful she feels. Annalynn would give me perfect children. If there was a better person to be the mother of my baby, I can't think of her.

"Yes, I do."

"I have to go to work." She says, obviously relieved and also shocked to silence by the news.

"I'll drive you." I say.

"Why?"

"I need to talk to my parents."

"Oh no...."

"Oh, yeah. And no time like the present, right?"

She doesn't say anything more. I think she's holding back.

Chapter Forty-Nine

I walk in the door and wander into the kitchen and help myself to the contents of the fridge. My mother appears from her office about fifteen minutes later.

I look up at her.

She looks down at me.

"Annalynn had some news—" I start to say just as my mother says, "Annalynn's mother called this afternoon."

"You go first," my mother suggests.

"Annalynn had news, but I guess you already know." I say.

"Don't be mad at her...her mother told her not to come into the house, and that woman called me to have at it too. Awful. I just finished the paperwork to add her to our company health insurance. She'll be okay in that regard. You know we'll be supporting you."

"What?"

"She apparently thought her mother would be excited, but she wasn't at all. Apparently she was told not to come into the house, and that she could send you for her things if you were so bold. No daughter of hers was stupid enough to get 'knocked up.' I don't know what got into the woman, really."

"Why aren't you yelling at me?" I'm stunned stupid by this.

"It wasn't a matter of if, just a matter of when." My mother replies cryptically. "Besides, doing the same thing to both of you as her mother did to her doesn't help anyone. And you are going to be doing this properly, yes?"

"What do you mean?" I'm still gobsmacked.

My mother pulls something from her apron pocket. "Annalynn wore this to prom, remember? She's always loved it. I don't mind giving it to her." My mother opens her hand to me and there is her ruby ring in her palm.

"You can't....Dad made that for you!"

"And he can make me something else."

I let it fall into my hand, and then I stare down at it, the light blinking here and there from the perfectly cut facets. It's beautiful.

"Mom, I can't fathom it all."

"What do you mean?"

"I can propose, that's true, and she'll say yes. But, health insurance for the baby is just a little tiny piece of everything that needs to go right. I need a real job, and a larger apartment. And a really reliable car. And...oh a thousand other things that I don't know about."

"You can have the unit in front....the Japanese people told me yesterday that they're moving. The little room is perfect for a baby nursery. And you already work for me; even if you are working for your mom it really is a real job. Annalynn has been already registered. She'll be covered in three days at most. So will the baby. The car needs some work... I know, we can work it out." She says.

We talk some more, about what I don't really care and then I drive over to Annalynn's with some boxes. I let myself in and walk up to her room silently to begin packing her more important things. Clothes, shoes, some of her other things; as much as I can shove in the car safely.

Her mother walks in, takes one look at me and walks out.

I don't understand how this woman—who was willing to let her daughter go up with me to the cabin for year after year, who let Annalynn stay almost every weekend with me —can take the high ground, but she is.

I drive back to Cheney and haul it all up the stairs, my knees protesting every step, and then I drive back into Spokane to get Annalynn from work. She starts crying in the car, and so I drive us up to Manito instead of going right home. Once there, I reach across and loop my arms around her.

"It's okay," I whisper.

"No, no it's not. My mother told me I'm going to hell." She replies.

"You aren't." I reassure her.

"But she said it!"

I suspect that she means that she doesn't agree but that her mother said it is the point. "She did." I repeat.

"She said you were going to hell too."

"I'm not."

"I know. Hearing it bothers me."

I walk us both up to Duncan gardens. The flowers are freshly planted for the fall; all golds and reds to match the trees. I sit us both down on the smooth and grand marble of the memorial fountain and wait for the cascading water to calm Annalynn down.

It does, in time, as it has always done to me.

"Annalynn, if I have to go to hell, and you have to go to hell, I'd rather we go together."

"Scared to go it alone?"

"Are you?"

"What do you mean?"

I un-suavely fish around in my jacket pocket for the ring.

"Life is not a singular adventure. I'd like you to marry me."

"This is just because I'm pregnant."

"No, it isn't."

She looks down. "Isn't that your mother's ring."

"She wanted you to have it."

"Did she talk you into this?"

"No."

"I don't believe you."

I'm perplexed. "Uhm, why not?"

"It's just because of the baby. You wouldn't be doing this right now if it wasn't a consideration."

"No, I wouldn't be, but that doesn't mean I wasn't thinking about proposing to you anyway, planned for a slightly more auspicious time." I really, really want to bonk her on the head, and make her see straight.

"I'll think on it."

She refused to snuggle with me that night, making a distinct effort to stay on 'her' side of the bed.

'Our' bed, damn it.

I give up trying to disarm her at about four in the morning, two hours after crawling in. She shoves me out of bed when my alarm goes off instead of pulling me back to snuggle with her.

I stick the ring on a spoon and leave a tray with breakfast on it for her.

I come home and it's been untouched.

I don't know what to do, so I start moving

things next door[21], and wait for her to come home.

She arrives at her usual time, and is surprised to find me up and waiting for her. "I moved us next door."

"Us?"

"Yes, you and me. We are moving to the bigger unit to accommodate our child." I say grouchily.

She takes the keys I offer her.

I had rather carefully set up the bed, her favorite sheets, the satin ones, and I had set out massage oils and the ring on a tray. The oils almost always got an enthusiastic response from her in the past. She just shakes her head and puts the tray on the floor.

"Don't be all noble to me, Emelle."

Again, she sticks to her side of the bed and it is hopeless trying to snuggle her.

I can't sleep, so I get up and go and clean the old unit until I can't smell anything but ammonia. Then I come back to bed. Annalynn is crying in her sleep and I feel completely hopeless.

"I don't know what's wrong." I say to the air.

The next few nights, she doesn't even sleep beside me, but in the giant leather beanbag in the living room. I don't sleep at all at night. I nap fruitlessly during the day. I chew the ends of my fingers until they bleed.

I wait for her to fall asleep the next night and then carry her off to our bed, but no sooner am I comfortably stretched out beside her then she wakes up and her anger blooms.

---

21 My neighbors literally vanished. There was no sign of recent habitation, despite the fact I'd seen them taking groceries in less than three days ago. Some renters are like that. You wonder if they were there at all.

"Why are you doing this?"

"What do you mean? I love you, I want you here beside me, I don't even know what I did to make you so angry."

"You are so stupid. You think that marrying me will make this all good and happy, don't you?"

"Well, not entirely."

"You are willing to tie yourself down because you don't really think about things. This is a bad idea."

"What is a bad idea?"

"All of this. I should get rid of it. Then you'd go back to your studies and I could get back to work and it would all be normal and you wouldn't be chasing me around asking me to marry you."

"Anna....no. I don't want you to get rid of it. You were the one scared that I did when you first found out, remember?" I pause. "Come here, let me hug you while we are talking?"

"No." She says. "You and your stupid sensual self got me into this trouble and this mess."

"Are you listening to yourself?" I ask, incredulous.

"Oh shut up." She says, and jerks on a sweater over her flannel pajamas.

I hear the front door slam and I'm left wondering what is going on, and what I ought to do.

Chapter Fifty

Annalynn returns to sleeping in bed with me, but there might as well be the whole Pacific Ocean between us.

I don't understand her anger. I'm not sure how she accepts living here, perhaps because she has nowhere else to be. Her things are here, and I stock the fridge with her favorite food. It goes unnoted. She goes to work, she comes back.

I feel broken, and my fibromyalgia flares horribly.

I have enough energy for class, and that's a stretch.

I come home to ultrasound pictures one afternoon. They are high quality, and a sticky is pasted to them. "Look at our pretty baby girl!" I realize it is exactly one month since my failed proposal.

'Our' baby girl. Yes, 'our' baby. But not 'our' home, or 'our' bed, 'our' life or 'our' family.

I go to bed.

When she gets home, she's humming.

I get up and wander in to the kitchen where she is.

And fairly suddenly a wave of anger comes spilling through. "I wanted to go, you know. I don't want to be forced into the position of an absent father. I wanted to hold your hand when they did the prenatal visits... 'our' baby isn't really my baby at all if I'm reduced to looking at pictures."

Annalynn looks at me.

"It's not 'our' baby, Annalynn. It's yours right now. It won't be ours until it's our home, our bed, our life and our family. Until then, it's my pathetic life and my home and my bed and my unending grace towards your pathetic life and your baby that I desperately want to be mine, too."

Finny mews nervously and wraps around my legs when I raise my voice. I pick him up and stagger back to bed.

Annalynn screams. I bolt back out of bed and rush into the kitchen.

"You aren't supposed to be doing this!" She screeches at me. "Why aren't you mad at me like my mother is? Why are you so okay? I'm ruining your life and you still want me to be part of it, are you stupid?" She pauses. "I'm ruining my own life...why are you picking me back up, why am I living here?"

"I love you."

"No you don't. You just think you do, you want to! You are being noble and righteous and you shouldn't be. You stupid, stupid man."

"I loved you before you told me you were pregnant. You didn't doubt me then. Why do you now?"

"Aren't you listening to me? I fucked up. I got pregnant. I just lost my job because I can't be an EMT with a baby inside me, not at three months, I'm a huge burden. How could I possibly burden you with me? You are all noble, and I'm not worthy of it."

I take pause at this. "You lost your job, when?"

"Today."

"Annalynn. Will you please listen to me for a second?"

"Must I?"

"Yes."

She stares intently at me.

"You aren't a burden. You've never been and

never will be a burden to me. You're my best friend. I don't have direction or purpose without you. Every fiber of me loves every fiber of you. You aren't ruining my life, you are enriching it. If you weren't so hellbent on being insane, I would soak up you living here like a cat soaks up the sun coming through the window. I think the baby should have married parents, but that isn't *why* I asked, all it changed was the *when* I asked. I'm not being noble, I'm being me, a little ahead of schedule. And nobody on the face of this planet is more worthy than the mother of my children."

She says nothing.

"Please, be happy with me." I plead.

I go back to bed when she just sits awkwardly at the table and doesn't look at me.

Much, much later, Annalynn crawls into bed and snuggles up beside me. A rush of relief courses through me. I wrap arms around her and curl up tighter.

"Merryweather?"

"I love you." I reply.

"I love you too." She says. "I didn't realize by attempting to not ruin your life I was ruining it anyway."

"You aren't yourself."

"I'm not." She admits.

"Will you be anytime soon?"

"I don't know."

Silence.

"I need to be touched." I say.

"Hmmm?"

"I need to be touched. I need to feel your hands

on me, not me holding you." I clarify.

"Why?"

"So that I can feel you too. So that it can be okay to love and want you and have faith that it will all settle and so I can believe we can be happy again."

Chapter Fifty-One

Annalynn's tummy fascinates me. I rub it in the morning, and she giggles madly while I do so. I listen to it, and imagine that I can hear both heartbeats.... I kiss it twice, once for her as always, and now, once for my daughter.

"Do you think she'll be pretty? Like her mother?"

"I think she'll be cute, like her Dad." Annalynn replies.

"I hope not, he isn't pretty. And I want a pretty little girl."

"What about smart?"

"Pretty girls marry rich men and put their parents up in the style to which I would like to become accustomed."

"Emelle!"

"What?"

"Sigh, and sigh again. You are hopeless."

"Yes, I want her to be smart and pretty, just like you."

"There we go.... That's what you tell people when they ask."

"Yep."

Annalynn's breasts, heretofore not the subject of my dreams, are also fascinating me. They are, for lack of better terminology, pneumatic these days. Since we are still in bed, albeit awake, I gently bring my hand up from its lazy circles around her growing stomach to cup one breast.

"You know......" Annalynn begins and then stops. "What are you doing?"

"Admiring your impressive rack."

"You are so male sometimes."

Finny hops on the bed and purrs at us both; temporarily interrupting life.

"Hey, my hormones are perfectly normal, thank-you-very-much." I say, when I finish petting him.

"Mine are normal! Pregnancy is a normal female state of affairs." Annalynn retorts.

I am not paying attention, I bring both my hands up and push her breasts together underneath her nightshirt and admire the limited view. "This needs to go," I say of said nightshirt.

"What?!"

"In case you hadn't noticed, I've missed you. All of you."

She blushes, but obliges me and pulls off her pajama shirt.

Annalynn, my relay partner and cross-country team member, reliably as curvy as a broom handle for years, now has curves in all sorts of places. She's a rather lush picture of motherhood.

"I love you," I say. "I love my new baby girl, too."

I pause.

She stares.

"I'd like to love you for the rest of my life, wake up beside you and know that I am yours, and you are mine, fully. I want you to be my wife, as well as the mother of my children. When are you going to marry me?"

I offer her the ring.

She takes it and rolls it between her fingers.

"Thursday." She replies.

Chapter Fifty-Two

Annalynn and I peep our eyes up over the divider that separates our booth from the booth next to us. There at the far wall, my parents sit at a table, unaware that Annalynn and I are at the restaurant celebrating our engagement.

My mother smiles at my father and swirls her wine around in the glass a bit.

"Their timing is amazing." Annalynn whispers.

"No kidding."

We drop into Ninja mode, and watch them from our table.

"Do you know that we've known each other for 20 years, today? My mom says.

My dad grins. "Uh huh."

"It doesn't seem that long."

"Really? It always feels to me like you've always been there." He leans across the narrow table and gives her a gentle kiss.

"Awwww." Annalynn whispers.

Ugh. Parents and mushy stuff.

He scoots a little box across the table to her.

"Happy Anniversary, Paul."

We can't see it, but I have an idea of what it is.

"It's a new wedding ring, since you gave yours to Annalynn." He explains as she opens the box.

"It's beautiful, Ted."

"Allow me?" He says as she starts to put it on.

She gives him her hands and the ring, and he slides it onto her finger.

My mother holds it up when she is finished, and wiggles her fingers to make the stone sparkle.

"It's beautiful." My mother says, as does Annalynn.

"I wish I had better eyesight," I grump.

Annalynn sticks her tongue out at me.

"I can put that to good use elsewhere." I give her a cheesy but winning grin.

"Shush. You are ruining a perfect tear-jerker of a romantic moment."

"I am not. It's just my parents staring dewy-eyed at each other."

"I hope you still feel that way about me in twenty years." Annalynn admonishes.

"Yes, but without the middle stuff, eh?" I suggest.

"Yes, without the middle stuff."

I become more serious. "I've been crazy about you for eight years. I don't think it's stopping anytime soon."

"That's good." She sets down her napkin— we were almost done when my parents sat down. "Let's go tell them."

"But it's their anniversary." I protest.

"Trust me, good news is always good to know." She drags me away from the table and over to theirs.

"Mom, Dad." Annalynn starts. They look up. "I'm marrying your son next Thursday."

They both burst into huge grins. "That's wonderful!"

"I'll get to be your family for real." Annalynn nods solemnly.

"Oh Annalynn." My mother sighs. "You've always been our family."

"But it's official now," My dad says.

My mother and I are not entirely on their wavelength. However, my mother rises to the occasion first. "Welcome to the family." She air-kisses Annalynn. "I'm going to make you a very pretty dress."

"I'll lend you my sister's pearls." My father offers.

"I think my grandmother has a veil. And she has been very happily married for a long time." I say, getting the gist of things.

"May I have a blue petticoat, Paul?"

"Absolutely."

My dad shifts to the side. "Come join us?"

We sit down.

Annalynn giggles shrilly.

"What?" My mother asks.

"Oh, the baby is kicking. She just started last week." Annalynn grabs my hand and sticks it on her stomach. Obligingly, the baby kicks into my palm. I grin.

"Me, too?" My father asks.

Annalynn places his palm next to mine, and he too grins.

"Would you like to, Paul?"

"No. Not right now." My mother smiles. "There's not enough tummy to go around right now. And anyway, I know what it feels like."

True to her word, my mother makes Annalynn a beautiful dress with a blue petticoat.

My grandmother lends her the veil.

My father lends his sister's pearls, and a nice suit, for me.

My grandfather, however, is the one with the big gift. He rents a ballroom at the Davenport Hotel for us and two rooms for getting ready.

Sprite flies into town.

She charges into my room where I am sitting, holding the nosegay I ordered for Annalynn. "So. You're marrying Annalynn."

"Yep." I'm a little too nervous to be cheerful.

"Let me make things clear. You are not going to behave like your father did. Ever. Or you will regret being alive." Sprite brandishes her words like a sword. "You just produced a Sprogling. You WILL be responsible. You WILL love your wife. Forever."

"Actually, Annalynn is producing the Sprogling." I clarify. "I wouldn't have done half as good a job as she has."

"Yes, but it's your fault."

I'm a little shocked.

Her entire demeanor changes. "Glad I've gotten that out of the way. Congratulations, sweetie."

I don't think Sprite has entirely gotten over her man-hating tendencies, or her outdated opinion of my father.

"Now. I have to go threaten Annalynn."

Let me restate that. I don't think Sprite is entirely sane.

"I don't think Annalynn needs torturing, Sprite." My mother argues.

"Not torture. Just a little chat to explain that my nephew will be happy the rest of his life, or she won't be."

"Is that necessary?" My mother asks.

"Of course it is." Sprite pats my mother on her head, and it's obvious that my mother is the little sister. Sprite bounces out the door, and then sticks her head back in. "It worked wonders with the Sperm Donor."

Ahhh. Family.

My mother looks at my dad. "Did she really?"

"Yes. She called me on the phone the morning of the wedding."

"I cannot believe my sister."

"I can." My father and I say in unison.

"She's horrible." My mother says.

"You should go stop her."

My mother looks surprised. "Oh, but then I'd have to do it myself."

Like I was saying.... Ahhhh, family.

I take a few seconds to wonder if Annalynn knows what she's gotten herself into.

Probably.

Chapter Fifty-Three

"Mr. Foster, would you like to hold your baby girl?"

"Yeh—" The midwife begins to hold her out to me, and I suddenly realize that every clumsy circumstance in my life prior to this was merely practice, culminating in the event of dropping my own child on her precious head. "No!"

My grandmothers' eyes, earlier wide and smiling, narrow to disapproving slits.

"I think he just needs to be shown how." She insists and takes my baby from the nurse. Holding my daughter in a seemingly precarious hold that leaves one arm free, she rearranges my arms and then slips my daughter into the resulting cradle.

"There." Grim gives me the aren't-you-ashamed-you-didn't-figure-this-out look.

She's so small and very unreal. She is not pretty, or anything anyone says politely about newborn children. But she is mine, and she is wrapped in a green blanket.

I like her, and so I sit down in the rocking chair beside a sleeping Annalynn. With the new best-beloved in my lap. I hear my mother maneuver her mother out the front door for a 'quick cup of coffee'.

I make a mental note to send her an enormous box of chocolates.

My father steps in, strangely imposing for a skinny man with scraggly hair and overly large glasses. Annalynn shifts in his shadow.

"Would you like to hold her, Dad?" I say, and offer the baby.

He reaches out his arms and curls her up in an inescapable embrace.

"Why don't you get some sleep?"

"I'm not sleepy."

"After hours of labor, you aren't tired?"

"Yes, but, no, not really. Annalynn did the work."

He sits down on the ottoman.

"I made you something." He says.

"For me or for the baby?"

"For you." He hands me back my daughter and digs around his coat.

He pulls out a long flat box.

It is a puzzle. With the number of important milestones in my life that have been dutifully honored by the creation and delivery of such, I am not surprised. This one is different though. Instead of a brass ring, it has a brass heart.

"Thank you, Dad, it's lovely."

"Uh hum." He says approvingly, and reaches out his arms and wiggles his fingers at his granddaughter.

I hand her back over to him.

They look serene together; his long fingers creating a bony shell of protection around her body and her pulse bringing life to hands otherwise lifeless in appearance.

"I wish I had gotten to do this with you." My father whispers.

"You were here the whole time, Dad." I say, confused.

"Infant you," he clarifies "I didn't hold you when you were little tiny. I was too angry, and too frightened. I wish I had, it wouldn't have taken so long to feel connected. My love for you was bondless for a long time, it had no connection."

He lays her down on her back on top of his legs with his hands behind her head and gazes down. "Do you think she'll love me?"

"Yes! Why wouldn't she?"

"I wasn't a very good father, and I really don't know the slightest about being a grandfather." He replies. "There are plenty of parenting books out there to help you make it up, but there isn't an *Idiot's Guide to Grandparenting.*"

I sigh. "You've been both a good example and a terrible reminder, but I think you've been a better example more often. Besides, being a grandfather is different than being a Dad. You know plenty about how to make things that can spoil a kid rotten."

"Not for a girl."

"Girls like armor and swords just as much as boys."

"Better," Annalynn adds sleepily.

"And she'll need puzzles." I add.

"Yes," he agrees. "I didn't realize.... She couldn't possibly get through life without me."

I decide later, while watching three generations of my family sleep, that my daughter has brought me to a new understanding of male-female relations. First I had a hierarchy in which I was reverent of my mother and thought my father to be the same. Then I had equality and love with Annalynn, and understood my parents as a working pair. Now I am the revered, and understand my parents as parents.

I settle my sleeping daughter in her bassinet and make a quick sketch of her in a pretty maroon color. I'll turn it into a birth announcement, I think.

My mother is the most awake after me, and

she slips out to watch me sketching.

"Isn't she beautiful?"

"No, but she will be." I say.

"You know.... That's what I thought about you, too. I don't really like babies the way my mom does." She says as she peers over the edge of the bassinet.

"I don't know if I like babies." I reply.

"Your father does."

"He does?"

"Yes. He's odd that way."

There is a pause.

"What are you going to name her?"

"Nora." I say.

"Nora." She repeats down to the sleeping baby. "Nora what?"

"Nora Theodore Foster." I reply, and write it in calligraphy on the birth certificate that is there for that purpose.

"Theodore? Does your father know?"

"No, but he will."

"Very well. Is there anything else we can do?"

I think for a minute. "No, I don't think so. Probably go home and get some rest and help out when we next get overwhelmed. Maybe try and tell Annalynn's parents happy things about the baby?"

My mother looks sadly at me and wrinkles her forehead. She had spoken to Ms. Spencer when Annalynn had first gone into labor last night and was told that she was a heathen slut with no morals that had corrupted a good catholic girl via her "spawn."

There is a faint knock on the door. My mother goes to answer it.

"Mr. Spencer?" She says, surprised but quiet.

"I came to see the baby." He says, low and secretive.

I pick Nora up and take her out to the kitchen.

Mr. Spencer is older than my parents, and he looks worn beyond that still. Years of being second fiddle to his wife's whims might have done that. I'm not sure. But, he sees me with Nora and his face crinkles up in a smile that makes him look younger.

"Healthy?" He asks.

"Very." I say.

"Boy or girl?"

"Girl."

He peers in past the blanket. "Oh, she'll be a pretty one. What are you calling her?"

"Nora." I say.

He smiles. "Pretty name for a pretty baby girl."

"Thank you." I feel a little awkward.

"I'm sorry Marie wouldn't come." He says as though he's deeply saddened, and he might be.

"It's okay." I say, at a loss for words.

"Well, not so much, I don't think." He replies, "She ought to stop her religious blithering and be a good mother and wife, and manage to be a decent grandmother too. Not so much to ask that she be a good person instead of a judgmental Christian." His face becomes stormy and his voice angry.

My father has roused from his dozing and comes out to the small party in the kitchen. "Hello, Robert." He says, obviously surprised by the sudden presence of Annalynn's father.

"Hi, Ted. Congratulations on your granddaughter." Robert says, suddenly congenial.

"Same to you. She's very nice." He smiles at Nora again as if he can't keep his eyes off her. "Can I hold her some more?" He asks me.

I pass the sleeping baby to him and she doesn't even stir.

Suddenly Mr. Spencer digs into his pockets. "Emelle, I know you aren't catholic, but we are, and I hope you don't mind if we give her a traditional gift of a first rosary." He hands me a slim box, and I open it for everyone to see. It's quite lovely, pearls with a little gold cross. "And then I thought, since Marie might never change her mind, that she ought to have this too."

He hands me another small box and I find inside it a square locket with their wedding portrait in miniature and also one of Annalynn as a baby in her christening gown.

"Thank you very much." I say on Nora's behalf. I suspect I know how much it has cost him to give up the locket that has lived on his keychain for twenty-five years. He nods at the baby and then turns a bit towards the door. "Well, I've been out long enough. I'd best get home. I'll try and come see Annalynn soon, when she's feeling up for visitors." He says and scurries out in a guilty manner as though he was out committing adultery, not visiting his new granddaughter.

"That poor man..." my mother sighs when he goes out of the building. "Do you suppose Marie will ever come out of it?" She asks my father.

He looks at her. "No. I don't really. That poor woman is racked by something deeper in her soul than we can understand. First years of eating disorders, and then her mother died and she became fanatically religious? She's punishing herself for some irreconcilable sin that we can't even imagine the pain of. She'll never feel she's paid enough for it, and so she'll just go on punishing herself, becoming more unreasonable in hope of atonement."

He shakes his head. "Why don't we talk about happier things?"

So we retire to the living room and they sit down in the over-sized chair together and share holding Nora.

"What is she named?" He finally asks.

"Nora Theodore."

"Really?" He lights up when he looks at me.

"Yes. We had decided on Theodore as a middle name weeks ago, and Annalynn wanted me to name the baby anyway."

He coos at his namesake. Then nudges my mother.

"We aren't having another one." She says.

"But it's so cute!"

"She. Not it."

"She's really cute." He agrees. "Why not?"

"We have this one to spoil and play with. And we already got our chance." She says, and when he opens his mouth to argue she kisses him on the nose and comes up with a new reason, "It would take me forever to get pregnant anyway."

He flutters his eyes at her.

"Oh stop it. We have this nice one here at our disposal. We don't need one of our own."

He puffs up his cheeks and neighs. "But...." He whines comically.

"I can't top that anyway. That there is a perfect specimen of brand-spanking new baby. Can't top it. Sorry."

"Oh all right." He fusses and then turns back

to cooing at Nora.

Chapter Fifty-Four

I'm awake, unusual for me, at about three in the morning. I can't sleep and I'm not really motivated to do much. I sit down at the upholstered armchair that sits in front of my sewing machine and look at the little stack of sleeper pieces I'd cut out a few days ago. I stitch one up and fold it up, and start in on the next one.

I hear the fussing begin and launch from my chair to pick up Nora up from her bassinet so she can't wake Annalynn.

She quiets quickly, she's neither hungry nor damp. I suspect she was merely wanting to be where I was. Annalynn says she's unusually aware of people. I settle the bassinet on the floor next to the treadle of the machine and let the gentle clunking lull her back into sleep as I make another one of the tiny sleepers.

I finish two before her morning feeding, which for the first time goes off without a hitch. Well, apparently 'Dad' has recently received a vote of confidence, because she hasn't tolerated me well at all during feedings before. A quick change and burping sends her back to sleep, and me back to the sewing machine.

I finish the last sleeper on the stack, pick Nora up from her bassinet and rest her comfortably against my torso. It doesn't seem like two weeks since her birth. It seems like an eon and an era. She has already lost the weird red blob look and has some vague human attributes. Dark hair is emerging from her scalp and I'm kind of hoping for some indication of whom she might look like soon, since I have a weird suspicion that she might have inherited my father's and my nose, and really, that's just not fair for a girl.

The phone rings.

"Hello." I say into the handset, wondering who on god's green earth might be calling at 8:30 in the morning.

"Mr. Foster? It's Professor Shoenberg. I need you to come down to my office, I'm sorry about the short notice."

"Uhm, when?"

"Right now would be great."

Er.

"Okay."

I throw on yesterday's clothes, pull my hair back and run out the door, putting Nora in Annalynn's arms after roughly awakening them both.

I'm nervous. I'm fairly certain that Shoenberg just saw my final project for his watercolor class and is incredibly angry. I'd be angry if my student turned in a dime-store style comic book as a final project too. I'm sure he's going to tell me that I won't be passing, that I'll be doing the project over next quarter. I have no defense, it was the only thing to come to mind, and it was slapdash. I'll be embarrassed to repeat a quarter and a class, but I definitely deserve it.

I step into his office at a few minutes after nine. I'm slicked in a thin layer of nervous sweat that does nothing to improve my rough appearance.

"Professor?"

He looks a little taken aback at my appearance. "You didn't have to run. Could you please sit down? I would like to speak to you about something important. The other fellow isn't back from getting coffee yet, so we'll wait."

My eyes bug out. Other guy? Who all did I accidentally offend with my ill-considered project? Oh god, oh god, oh god......

The other fellow steps in, and he looks important. I'm doomed. I'm about to not only lose my degree, but also get expelled. I gulp and look entirely like a deer in the headlights.

"Mr. Foster, this is Drew Halfmore. He and I have discussed your project in significant detail and he'd like to speak with you regarding it."

Sweat bursts down the back of my neck and pours like a river between my shoulder blades. "Okay." I squeak.

"I know this may seem a little surprising—"

"Not really." I choke. "I knew it was pretty bad."

Both of them look at me with the same confused expression.

"What do you mean, pretty bad?" Halfmore asks.

"As watercolor projects go. It wasn't, uhm.... representative, really." I say.

They both laugh.

"What?" I ask, feeling small.

"It was wonderful, Mr. Foster. That's why I'm here. I represent a major comic book company and we feel Dangerous Dick could be an excellent addition to our current franchises." Halfmore says.

Major comic book company and I have on yesterday's clothes, I don't remember the last time I showered, and I'm certain there is a spit-up stain somewhere on my shirt. I'm mortified. And silent.

"I know it's a little surprising, but you could say something." Halfmore says good-naturedly.

"Uh." I blink. I'm never going to live this down, my art professor must be seriously embarrassed by my appearance. "I'm a new Dad. The baby is a girl. She's two weeks old." I babble to him. "Is this a joke?" I ask, since suddenly the current situation sounds incredibly unlikely.

"Well, that certainly explains some things. Congratulations! And no, this isn't a joke."

Epilogue

Ted and Paul stood outside the comic book store, and stared at Dangerous Dick in the window.

"It's remarkable, isn't it?" Paul said.

"Our son wrote that."

"I know. Who would believe this all?"

"I know that if I hadn't lived it, I wouldn't have believed it. You and I got over the Big Uncommitment, and then Emelle and I got over the Great Animosity. Everything fell into place after that. It's stranger than fiction." Ted agreed.

"A fortunate reminder that Murphy isn't always right."

"Yes. And Peter's Law is still functioning." Ted said.

"Peter's Law?"

"Basically says that you can fix anything that has gone wrong."

"You aren't the sort of person I'd ever have pegged as believing that." Paul offered.

Ted looked at Paul, and then at the ground. "I didn't, not until recently."

"Oh?"

"It took you, Emelle, Annalynn and Nora to convince me."

Paul raised her eyebrows. "All of us?"

"And in the process I answered the question of life, the universe and everything, didn't I tell you?"

"And what's that?"

"Different for everyone." Ted pauses. "But it's not a joke."

"Nope, life is no joke."

Paul went inside and bought a copy of Dangerous Dick, Episode 1.

"It's an extraordinary thing, isn't it?"

"Well," Ted said, considering the comic. "I thought it was a little campy myself."

"No. Life." Paul clarified.

"Oh. That. Only so much as the people in it." Ted answered.

"Well. We are, you know."

"Not me. Remember, I'm ordinary, just like my name."

"Ordinary in the world of extraordinary is extraordinary. Didn't Emelle ever tell you that?"

"No." Ted said.

"We're all extraordinary, therefore, so is life." Paul concluded.

"I want an autographed copy." Ted said.

"Then let's go get one."

Acknowledgments

My thanks, as always, goes first to my mother whom despite much impetus to do so has not yet killed me. Or grounded me for life. Secondly, to the rest of my family, whom also, despite much impetus to do so, have not yet killed me. My thanks must also go to the many friends who have inspired me to hurl this work into the universe and pray. Without them this would be a dusty manuscript on a shelf. But in particular, Mike and Nick went above and beyond the call of friendship to help realize this as a published book, and so they get my especial gratitude.

Note Regarding the Dedication

I told Nathan in 1998 or 1999 that I would write a book, and I would dedicate it to him when it was published. I'm sure at the time it seemed a frivolous promise from one teenager to another, something to be forgotten after a time, or sometimes dusted off for humorous retellings. It was, however, never frivolous to me nor him. And so, when the opportunity presented itself, so then the promise was kept.

CPSIA information can be obtained at www.ICGtesting.com
Printed in the USA
LVOW101351110612

285529LV00001BA/208/P